DATE DUE

DEMCO 38-296

The Useless Servants

Rolando Hinojosa

Arte Público Press
Houston
Texas
1993

: from the National Endowment
llace-Reader's Digest Fund and

Arte Público Press
University of Houston
Houston, Texas 77204-2090

Cover design by Mark Piñón

Hinojosa, Rolando
    The useless servants / by Rolando Hinojosa
        p.   cm.
    ISBN 1-55885-068-6 : $17.95
    1. Korean War, 1950-1953—Participation, Mexican American—Fiction.
2. Mexican Americans—History—Fiction. I. Title.
PS3558.I545U83   1993
813'.54—dc20   93–12812

                                                              CIP

Other Works by Rolando Hinojosa

KLAIL CITY DEATH TRIP SERIES

Estampas del valle y otras obras
Klail City y sus alrededores
Korean Love Songs
Mi querido Rafa
Rites and Witnesses
Dear Rafe
The Valley
Klail City
Claros varones de Belken
Partners in Crime
Becky and Her Friends
Los amigos de Becky

Contents

The Useless Servants

Prologue

Behold! human beings living in a sort of underground den, which has a mouth open towards the light and reaching across the den; they have been here from their childhood, and have their legs and necks chained, and can only see before them; for the chains are arranged as to prevent them from turning their heads. At a distance above and behind them the light of a fire is blazing and between the fire and the prisoners there is a raised way; and you will see, if you look, a low wall built along the way, like the screen which marionette players have before them, over which they show the puppets.

I see, he said.

And do you see, I said, men passing along the wall, carrying vessels which appear over the wall; also figures of men and animals, made of wood and stone and various materials; and some of the prisoners, as you would expect, are talking, and some of them are silent?

This is a strange image, he said, and they are strange prisoners.

Like ourselves, I replied, and they see only their own shadows, or the shadows of one another, which the fire throws on the opposite wall of the cave.

True, he said: how could they see anything but the shadows if they were never allowed to move their heads?

And of the objects which are being carried in like manner they would see only their shadows?

Yes, he said.

And if they were able to talk with one another, would they not suppose that they were naming what was actually before them?

The Republic of Plato,
Book Seven
Jowett translation

Part I

Part 1

Form, Riflemen, Form!

When the war started on June 25, we of the 219th were out in the field. A Sunday, but in training; and, from what we've seen (and saw), few outfits trained as hard as we did. Too, most of us had been together since the summer of 1949 in the Kwansai District.

We knew what we were doing, manning the 105s: laying the guns, re-laying them, putting on and then removing the blocks and sights, registering the guns on some target or other, leveling the bubble, working with our forward observers, etc. A team, then. Of course, we also had the Old Guys with us, and this is what saved most of us on July 5.

It's been a week since then, and ten days or so since we drove to Itazuke A.F.B., but I'm telling this all wrong. It should begin more like what follows to keep things straight:

When the war started, all of us, enlisted and Os (Officers) thought it was the Russians, what with the Siberian Peninsula above us, and with China now Communist to the north and west; so, it had to be the Russians.

When the word first came, though, we covered the guns, hitched and se-cured them to our vehicles, the two-and-a-half ton trucks, our prime movers. Charlie and I took charge of the breech blocks and Joey and a new guy named Stang got the sights. (We only had two batteries in our battalion instead of three; everybody operated under strength here).

Once in the trucks, all the guys were excited and jabbering, but the Old Guys sat there, keeping to themselves. All three of our Old Guys had served in China in the 1930s, although they had fought in Europe during WWII. So, the three Old Guys—Hatalski, Dumas, and Frazier—sat there, smoking and talking in low tones.

All three had come to Japan in Feb., 1949, direct from Tienstien, China, and they formed the cadre which trained us.

By the time we drove to camp, things had settled down. A guy got the word from Armed Forces Radio Service despite the static electricity of the SCR-300 radio: North Koreans vs. South Koreans, not Russians. A neighbor's quarrel, someone said. At this, Hat broke in and said, "It's war, and get used to the word starting now."

The Nor Kor! All I knew about Korea was what Wendell Cohen kept saying when he was here with us: "It's a horrible place; it stinks of shit, and you feel like vomiting all the time. Don't screw up or they'll transfer you there, Rafe," and so on and so on. Ellie Cohen wasn't wild about Japan's Kwansai District either, so who's to say, I thought back then. But, as it turned out, he was right about the smell.

Things moved fast that June 25 Sunday after we got back to camp, and here I have to shift again. This list will help me put this down in some order:

June 25: the war starts

June 26-29: more training, but in camp.

June 30: to Itazuke A.F.B.

July 2: Not enough aircraft to fly us to Korea; driven to seacoast.

July 3: In Korea. Land in Pusan; wait for other troops to join us from other parts of Japan. Issued some equipment.

July 4: By train to Taejon then to Osan; boarded So Korean army trucks and headed northwest. Driven to a site between the towns of Osan and Suwon.

July 5: In place by dawn; our guns on ridge. Our infantry placed some 2000 yards to our front and set up a roadblock.

July 5: Fighting begins that morning; ended by 1600. We made our way east to where we started.

June 26-30. We were restricted to camp. The Old Guys went about their business, and we trained again. This was done to settle us down, I think.

Except for Capt Bracken who seems to live in Tokyo for the little we see of him, our Officers (the Os), know their stuff.

Lt Billy Waller is the Exec; Lt Edwards is our Lt; Lt Merritt and a new one, Lt Brodkey, just transferred here in the Spring. They're the forward observers. Lt Fleming is a 2nd John, but he knows his stuff about artillery. The enlisted guys who serve as forward observers are new to the unit; transferred here from Camp McGill (Hayama).

Lt Merritt was not chosen for this detail nor was Capt Bracken.

Drew 120 rounds of carbine ammunition and 2-days of C-rations. Were promised hot chow in Itazuke and when we were to land in Korea also.

June 30. Itazuke A.F.B. is south of us and not far from the Korean Peninsula. It was raining in the Kwansai and it was raining at the air base when we got there. I got up at 0300 and wrote notes and cleaned the equipment again until 0700. Orders to pull out: 1) Sometime, 2) Anytime, 3) Army time. The Old Guys took us aside and said our battery was the only one chosen from our battalion.

"You guys got pride, and that will keep you alive. Don't abandon the guns. Continue the mission. You'll be scared, but stick to the work, stick to the guns."

With this, we got on the trucks and rode off toward Itazuke. It rained the entire way there. All of us very nervous and tired.

July 1: Hatalski lined us up at Itazuke; Dumas and Frazier checked the guns: okay.

Big transport plane waiting for us. Joined a gun crew already there and waited for the other units. Joey, Frazier and I walked over to the other arty outfit and spotted their 105s; in poor shape.

Frazier: "A piss poor outfit is always trouble." After that, I went inside the truck and made notes. Joey climbed in from the rain and said he'd checked the blocks and sights just one more time. Everything Jake. Then the whistle blew, and we fell out.

Hot chow. Still raining; not hard, but steady. Jap workmen helped us load. Assembled again. Five to six-hundred of us. (We only know our guys). Good sized troop. Told that some guys will have to go by naval small craft across the Yellow Sea; there aren't enough transport planes for all of us.

Spotted some recoilless rifles and a couple of 2.6 rocket launchers (bazookas). Because of rain, M-1 and carbine barrels pointed down, but all of us, enlisted and Os were soaked.

Brought to attention and out walked the force's CO, Lt Col Smith (we're Task Force Smith). Some old-looking Gen with him. The Gen says a few words to us and finished by saying "God Bless You." Col Smith saluted, and some of the guys boarded the C-54; the rest of us were loaded onto trucks and driven to the coast.

A hard rain followed, and the wind blew the rain on a slant.

Most of the guys got seasick on the way to Pusan by naval craft. Landed in Pusan. The train taking us to the base camp was waiting and puffing and blowing at the station. A military band greeted us and the civilians waved and waited in the rain. (Told that guys on transport plane had to turn back: fog, rain, etc. They flew in this morning).

Everyone pretty tired now.

Hot chow again. Rain did not stop. An Old Guy (Infantry) came by saying it's the Monsoon season. Cold for June, we said. Old Guy laughed and said it'd be up to a hundred degrees when the rain stopped.

After chow, lights went on and we checked the guns and counted the ammo crates: Issued over 1000 HE, high explosive shells; and six HEAT (anti tanks).

As John Dumas said: "It depends on what kind of tanks."

July 2-4. Getting to know the other arty battery. Look slow, dull-witted. Much whining. Their Old Guys are good and tough; Os look good, too. Our

Col (Drake) is a Light Col as is Col Smith.

A quiet one; confident. Dumas served with Col Drake in China and Belgium. Knows his guns, according to Dumas. An Old Pro, he called him.

The rest of the troops also came in via Navy craft; they too got seasick. This is a makeshift outfit.

To the sack and to leave tonight or early tomorrow. They'll tell us where, when they wake us. Before hitting the sack, we—Charlie, Joey, Stang and Al Skinner, and our Old Guys from the Kwansai District—went outside; raining off and on.

"Take care. You'll be scared; but that's okay. Listen carefully out there. No rush. You know your job, and you'll do it. Don't miss tomorrow's ride." (This last always get a laugh.)

July 4-5. Train took us to Taejon. No stops. Not sleepy at all. Rode west and trucks waiting at train station. Drove to a main road between the towns called Suwon and Osan. (Closer to Osan.) Infantry placed on main road between the town. We on a ridge some 2000 yards behind Infantry.

Lt Edwards spotted the town through his binocs. We watched the Infantry digging in and setting up a roadblock. (Infantry and us using old Jap maps). We waited in place for an hour-and-a-half.

Raining; sun was up early but did not break out, not with the Monsoon rain. (Traded two packs of Camels for four pair of socks with Stang; can never have too many socks in the Army.)

Chilly. Ate cold pork and beans and registered the guns on hills up front and all along winding road. All set and waited for the word.

At 0700, a column of tanks, eight appeared and headed for our ridge. An hour later, 0800, Lt Brodkey, the Forward ob who was close to our Infantry, came over the phone: "Fire Mission!" And we went to work.

Loaded the tubes. Breech blocks clicked home. Sights were set. The bubble was leveled, Frazier's arm went up at 0815 or so, and the number two howitzer fired away. We then fired our first round, and the others followed suit. Almost like practice fire.

Fired HE which works v. troops but worthless v. those tanks. The eight tanks were easy marks since they brought no Infantry with them, but shells proved ineffective. Our Infantry down there brought no mines (was not issued any?), and since we had no air support, the tanks rumbled on.

We waited. Five minutes went by and more tanks appeared; thirty this time, and still without Infantry support. Sitting ducks, but we were without armor piercing shells that could stop those tanks. Phones were working and the wires had not yet been chewed up by tanks; Infantry was ordered to wait for the thirty tanks to close to within 700 yards. Infantry waited. At 700 yards, the recoilless rifles went against the tanks. We ran up to see the fight: no effect from the recoilless rifles. Then the 2.6 bazookas went to work, but they got beans since tank armor proved too much for the 2.6. No effect, no effect.

Tanks drove past our Infantry. Paid no attention to it. Tanks headed for us on ridge again. Col Drake told us to fire HEAT, and this worked on one tank. Damaged one track. Tank damaged, not destroyed. With one track blown, tank pulled off the road. Still no North Korean Infantry at that time.

Tanks kept coming. By-passing our Infantry and heading for us. And then, more tanks. We kept up the fire. Pieces laid and relaid since the range kept changing. Then we relaid right on the tanks. Fired. We fired at ranges of 300 and 150 yards. No effect. Shells bounced off. But tanks knew we were firing, so they buttoned up. Driving blind, since they still had no Infantry to help them along. Immobilized another tank, and it too went to one side of the road. Again tank damaged, but not destroyed.

Our anti-tank shells gone. But this is still okay since Nor Koreans had brought no Infantry to help them. Buttoned up, they had no clear idea where we were.

Our Col (Drake) led some men down the hill to destroy the hit tanks. Col wounded on way down ridge (calf wound). One of our guys killed right off, but tank crew got theirs too.

Tanks then chewed up phone wire and we had no communication with our Infantry. Radios old and wet. We had no idea what was going on down there.

And then? Three more tanks, but now their Infantry showed up. Long columns of Infantry. Lt Edwards checked maps and reckoned columns to be six miles long. Troops marching on both sides of the road.

From the ridge, tanks would have been easy marks, but we had no anti-tank shells; those six shells had been it. Suddenly, some of our guys up here bolted—the Os and the Old Guys ordered them to stop. But up they got and ran like hell.

Our Os and the Old Guys yelled themselves hoarse and said "fuck it" and they started working the guns with us. Col Drake, wounded and all, got up and tried to rally the other men; some came back.

Old Guys and Os pulling the lanyards while we loaded, sighted, and gave the signal. The North Korean Infantry scattered and took cover, but did not follow the tanks.

At this point, some of our Infantry fired on the North Korean Infantry. Col Smith ordered mortar fire and M-gun fire, too; the North Koreans started getting hit right then and right there. More action then: North Korean arty opened up; we just sat it out: no radios and no targets.

One gun crew was killed by direct tank fire. The gun was destroyed and this left five men dead along with one O.

What happened was this: Col Smith had let the North Korean Infantry go by his troops and then caught them with a M-gun and mortar crossfire. The North Koreans suffered casualties here.

But it was the tanks. They didn't stop coming and passed right below us. Finally, some of our guys came back; they'd seen the tanks most likely. Our Os went out and talked them into coming back.

We started firing again and disabled another tank; hit the tracks, as usual, since we couldn't do a thing against that armor plating. And then one of the tanks stopped, traversed the tube (an 85mm cannon, according to Col Drake) and pounded, smashed and set on fire some of our vehicles parked off the road. Col Drake still hobbling along and full of fight.

Rain poured on and the tanks kept coming. A runner was sent to fetch the forward ob (Lt Brodkey) and his crew. We had no idea what was going on. Right then, much of our Infantry down there took off. Left their positions, flat out. To the wooded area, to the rice paddies, crazy running, abandoning their crew-served weapons: M-guns, mortars, recoilless rifles, bazookas ... they just snapped, took off.

Col Smith still had some Infantry with him and began climbing the ridge when Hat and Frazier grabbed a couple of us to show Col Smith where we were. Looking back, I saw Col Drake leaning against a tree dressing his wound. As we were going down hill, Lt Edwards reported that five of our guns were still in working order, so Charlie and Joey got some help and lifted the blocks and sights and left the ridge.

We were assembled and walked the three miles in good marching order outside Osan, where the rest of our vehicles were parked under guard, all undamaged.

Osan was in North Korean hands by now, so our group drove toward Ansong—and who do we see? Our overrun Infantry sloshing through the rice paddies and smelling like shit, 'cause that's what the K's use for fertilizer. Most of our Infantry lost their boots in the paddies, some were shirtless, others had on nothing but their shorts: no uniforms, no helmets, nothing.

Weapons? We counted eight rifles and later saw a few men with two-three clips of ammo. The rest? They dropped their pieces right there when they ran.

We were in our trucks when the Infantry hollered at us. We picked up a hundred in that bunch acc to the Old Guys. Col Drake hung in there, bleeding now and then on account of the fragment in his leg.

A few minutes later, we came across the Co C guys, sixty-five total; picked them up too and then Lt Brodkey nudged me; looking up at the ridge through his binocs, he said, "The North Koreans are up there, Corporal."

"Yessir, one gun was blown up, but we brought back our blocks and sights from the other five."

We, the arty guys, lost five Os and 20 EM, all killed. Infantry suffered most casualties, and I learned a new word: straggler.

The firing stopped around 1600 hours. That was seven hours worth of fighting and so our convoy headed east to Pusan.

July 10. During fight, I caught two pieces of thin wire above my left eye. Medic discovered them, and a doc pulled them out. Till then, my eyes were not puffed up like now.

Charlie asked the Old Guys if guys who cut and ran would be court-martialed. No, is what they said. They may turn out to be okay later on.

Changes: We're now the United Nations troops; the North Koreans are called North Korean People's Army, NKPA or NK and our brand new allies, the Army of the Republic of Korea, are referred to as ROK.

Lt Waller came by and said we of the 219th Field will be attached to the 24th Division some time this week.

A Troop Cometh

July 10. 0840 hours as I write this. Eye okay, a bit puffy; looks like I was stung by wasps. Told medic and doc I didn't feel the wire go into the eyebrow. Asked how it happened, told them NK tank blasted the howitzer to my right, some twenty yards away.

"HE" they both said. (High Explosive gets in your eyes, you're blind for life).

I was left behind at the Aid Station because of the eye, but I'm okay. Left this afternoon by train to meet guys at Taejon. Much confusion at station. Korean railroad engineers pull out fast; sometimes take with them the equipment they brought in. Scared stiff. (ROK uses old Jap materiel at times. Old Guys reminded me: just like NK may now be using the equipment we abandoned in the Osan fight.)

Squared away at depot. Hitched a ride and found my way to the unit. Was told that 34th Inf Regt of 24th Div fought a delaying action on July 5-8—while we were reorganizing after Suwon/Osan fight. Was then told Col Smith fighting inside Taejon. No way to check this.

We got new Engineers and a company of light tanks, M-24s. (Old Guys say we need Shermans. Old Guys say it's a great tank, works in mud, dust, name it. The equiv of an old US Army rifle called the 1903 Springfield, which Old Guys swear by. Never let you down, they say). M-24s said to carry a 75mm tube. Not seen one in action.

Anxious to see NK tanks now that we're getting increased air support, and now that we've got enough armor piercing shells.

Damned supply gave me some loose, unboxed cans of C-rations; wound up with four cans of lima beans and ham and two of that bad tasting beef stew. Spotted some cans of pound cake and two of Grandmother's cookies, so I just helped myself.

Hook Frazier wired some ham and lima beans to the jeep's block and ran jeep up and down for five minutes: hot chow. Nothing can be worse than ham and lima beans. Nothing, except that beef stew.

Lt Edwards assigned me to my old howitzer again. Gun in great shape.

July 11. 0600. Report is 21st Inf Regt of 24th Div (maybe of 34th Div?) falling back to Chuchiwon. (We're just north of Chuchiwon; set up a three-quarter mile front on our ridge).

Some of our arty on delaying action screwed up royally: fired on own GIs. Don't know the number of casualties.

Inf fought hard. Lost a ridge, took it back. Told that six GIs found with hands tied behind their backs and shot in the head. Our Inf found them when they retook the ridge after a hard fight.

Third Bn slammed by two divisions of NK which then rushed through and set up roadblocks. Dumas said NK Divisions are smaller than ours, which number 16,000 plus. (A runner stopped by; confirmed murder of GIs by NK.)

We, part of old Task Force Smith, have been reorganized under a new CO (Lt Col Wells.) Took new rear positions; orderly withdrawal at 1400 hours. This is a delaying action: stay, fight, advance, retreat, stay, fight, etc. (Buying time is the order.) Crossed the river Kum around 1645. Some 300 to 500 of us set up a roadblock. All arty got across river Kum, no guns lost. Col Wells' tactics delayed NKPA for three days. (Were in action for one-and-a-half days of this fight.)

The River Kum is wide and fairly deep in spots; shallow in others, with sand bars too. River runs (in SW Korea) and winds above Taejon. We're to make a stand at the Kum. Don't know how long we are to hold here.

Feel very tired.

July 12. Up early. Checked guns, blocks and sights. Okay. Ate something. To new latrine. Some shelling behind us; shorts, I thought. After shorts, expected longs and then we'd be in a bracket and me in the latrine, but no such thing. A latrine orderly said he saw me with our arty near Osan. A latrine assignment is not a safe job; arty shells and mortars can drop anywhere.

July 13. Forward troops deployed. Can see them from up here. We're on a reserve roadblocking position under Col Wells. Reserve roadblock sounds safe but it isn't, since our entire division consists of less than 12,000 men, and this includes everybody: clerks, cooks, service troops, etc.

The 63rd Field Artillery is also here and facing rear of forward troops and ready for support. Hat knows four Old Guys and some of the Os with 63rd Field. Dumas said we were losing too many Old Guys and Os this early in the war (June 25-July 13).

Resting here in reserve roadblock but standing close to guns.

Mail truck (a weapons carrier) going out today; wrote two letters home.

July 14. Up very early: rain again. Ground fog. Can't see 100 yards in front. Fogs up awful in bottoms too. After morning chow, spotted low-flying liaison planes passing over NK lines and then watched NK propeller fighters drive it off. NKPA fighters are called Yaks. (Frazier explained that whenever we see liaison planes suddenly shoot upwards, it's because of heavy ground fire coming at them; tough job, says Frazier.) Those pilots have to fly low for the observer with them to make accurate reports on enemy troop strength, position, etc. (I've seen two Army reports where the enemy is referred to as the en, Army shorthand.)

At noon, there was some sporadic arty fire ahead of us. Raining hard during fire. Runner came by HQ, and on his way back, he said some NKPA units crossed the River Kum. Also: reconfirmed murder of GIs by NK.

Old Guys kept us busy. No time for rest, even though we were back here. And then, just like that, hard firing. The 63rd Field came under attack; the NK had by-passed our Inf and went after that artillery unit ahead of us. NK fired mortars first, as always. We were standing by the guns during hard fighting ahead of us when a lone South Korean agent came running in.

The 63rd Field is no more. Hit hard by NK. Some fought well and marched away with their blocks and sights. Their Inf guard fought well but were overrun; no idea of how many casualties.

After S Korean agent's report, the outfit was rescued by ROK horse cavalry; of all things. Many of our guys killed. Other GIs did not fight well and our First Bn was sent to rescue and retake position. It was too dark, and retaking was impossible.

Hours later: our planes night-bombed lost position. We ordered to pull back briefly and then went up (forward) to yesterday's position.

Two regiments. (The 19th Inf and the 34th Inf) were holding crossing places on River Kum. Fighting went on behind them because NK infiltrated; this is supposed to be part of NK that hit 63rd Field, according to the line crossers. Both regiments were under strength, as always. Just buying time.

We joined five additional batteries and gave Regts direct support. (No fighting by our unit to speak of, but men dying ahead of us.)

Much firing during the afternoon. No sleep for us for twenty-two hours straight. Punchy with smell of cordite.

Old Guys and Os: Okay to be nervous, just do the job.

July 15. Daylight. Not hungry. Up most of the night. Charlie, Joey and I to latrine and then right back to guns. Strange silence. Worked binocs, spotted Signal Corps guys repairing lines. Found a can of warm beer in my bag under some paperbacks.

Shared beer with Hat. Stood by guns. Hit the sack from ten to twelve noon. Got up, smoked a Camel. Runners in and out all day, but not a word to us.

Lts Waller and Edwards talking to Lt Brodkey on phone. Just checking.

Frazier took a shave and supervised loading of shell crates (armor piercing and HE). To sleep early.

July 16. Daylight here at 0400. Woke up with no idea what was going on or where I was, but could hear heavy firing by us and NK. No air support for our troops on the river. Very strange.

No rain by late afternoon, skies a blinding blue and the sun came out blistering hot. Those 100 degree days the Inf Old Guy talked about back at Pusan. Hot and humid. Much, much fighting, but we weren't in it. No firing by our battery at all.

To the sack and rousted at 2100: full alert. NK broke through and came right at us; one HQ company wiped out. Many, many Old Guys killed and many more Os killed too.

Our ridge overrun twice. Damned NK infiltrators came at us, overran us, and we fired M-ls and carbines as they ran by us. Our Inf guard fought well; half-an-hour later, forty of our additional Inf guys retook our ridge and drove NK off. We went back to guns but couldn't fire: too many GIs mixed in with NK in hand-to-hand fighting.

Some light flares were set off and we watched the fight; and then, a second NK group came at us. Ran right by us one more time, and again we fired M-ls and carbines at them, just like a wagon train.

A lull, and our Inf came right back and again drove NK out, away from the ridge. Once the ridge was secured, the order was given out: Move the guns, save the equipment. Move it!

We stopped to fire our M-ls, but were ordered to stop.

Orders: See to the guns! Hat, Dumas and Frazier firing for us and standing up and lobbing grenades while we dismantled the guns.

Off came the blocks and sights. Took a five-minute rest and then Lt Waller pointed the way.

What about the other guns?

Carry what you got.

We left half the guns and no time to thermite the barrels.

No running. Some of our Inf showed up along with cooks, clerks and service troops, all carrying rifles and carbines.

Time was now 2200, and it was still light. Heard fighting behind us and to the right. A team of Engineers passed through our unit with two nine-man Inf squads on their way to thermite the guns we left on ridge.

Firing to the right continued and then we came under direct fire. Lt Edwards hit by concussion; helmet knocked off; got up and was then shot in the throat. Dumas picked him up. Joey and I were carrying sights; Charlie and Stang in charge of blocks. Skinner firing wildly until Hat put him to work on carrying the blocks. Some Inf also helped us carry the stuff.

Quiet for a while and then more firing. Less heavy. We marched down hill and held our marching pace; no running, no yelling.

And then: mortars! We dropped to the ground and waited. Then NK stopped firing, and we went on. March halted and we caught our breath. Firing again, but this time to our left.

Up the ridge, flashes of thermited barrels up on the hill. Looked at my watch: 2300 and not too dark yet. Waller ordered another halt to count the men. Three Inf Os with us, all wounded; one hit in head and hand; other two all bandaged up but marching. Got to new friendly ridge and hill. Hell to climb, tired and hot, but made it up.

Sat down and ate three cans of pound cake and washed them down with water.

Guards posted. Engineers who thermited the 105s passed by us under Inf escort on way to their unit.

Started writing on/about midnight. Can't sleep. Miracle any of us alive. Hat tells me to sack out, but first to check the equipment (I do this automatically, like saying one's prayers.)

Then: quiet again. Some rifle went off in the distance; heard some more small arms fire. And then, quiet again. The hell with it.

Souls Among Lions

July 17. Spent the day setting up howitzers, unloading and stacking ammo crates: high explosive (HE), anti-tank (HEAT), white phosphorous shells, plus VT (variable time fuses), etc. Rested up and read some.

The report on Lt Edwards is that he is among those evacuated to Tokyo General Hosp.

Talk about going home (Japan) for Christmas is crazy acc to Old Guys.

"Just get it out of your head," Frazier here. "This is a war and we're in it."

Was told during work that we still have troops north of the River Kum. (Runners bring word to HQ, but we also get news from them. A tough job being a runner. I thank God I wasn't picked for that job. I'd crack for sure.)

Runners say fighting still going on here and there, north and west of River Kum. Also, that at least two of our Bird Colonels are among troops captured by NKPA.

Heard some cannon and small arms fire to our right and left most of the morning.

"Has to do with the defense of the rear guard holding on north of the Kum. The rear guard is set up along the meanders of the river." This acc. to Lt Billy Waller. Meanders are the same as bends of the river, he said; bends I know because of the Rio Grande.

The youngest-looking runner I've seen to date came and went straight to HQ. Told us during coffee break that many of our troops giving in, giving up the fight and running. He left a few minutes later in a direction different from the one he came.

Soon after, Frazier and Dumas took us aside. In five minutes they explained why we hadn't run at Osan fighting: pride.

Pride in the outfit, in ourselves? That's part of it. Mostly pride in each other and so on.

I don't know about this. I know why I didn't run. Joey, Charlie and I were all born in Klail City, Tx. We enlisted together, and how would it look if I ran? Everybody back home would know of it. I'd die here first before I'd face that.

Joey asked John Dumas, how can we have pride in the unit if we don't belong to anybody. Good question. Dumas said it's too early in the war for us to belong to a division, since we came here as orphans (part of Task Force Smith). But we'll join something, he said; so, for now, we belong to a small unit, the battery. As soon as the war settles down and fighting picks up, we'll prob be assigned to a division.

Frazier cut in to say that it always boils down to the smallest unit anyway: the soldier. From there to the squad, platoon, etc. In our case, the gun crew, the battery and each other.

A pep talk.

Hat then came up and said Lt Edwards is out of the war for now; may lose his voice, but too soon to tell.

After midday chow, we loaded up again and were driven outside city of Taejon. Due to move inside the city in one-and-a-half hrs.

Got there and waited. Learned that the 24th Division's 34th Inf Regt is inside Taejon and making a fight of it. We can't fire inside the city because of US troops there. So we waited; tried the C-ration lima beans and ham again. Ugh. Milled around; our Inf guards set up; got sleepy and turning in now at 2000, with sounds of firing going on inside Taejon.

July 18. Early this morning we again hitched guns to trucks, loaded the shell crates, got squared away and were driven to the outskirts of Taejon. Then, almost as soon as we got there, we were ordered to get going again: further east this time. Away from the city.

Communications bad all around; radios don't work most of the time, and you need a Guglielmo Marconi to get them to operate.

Still much fighting inside Taejon. Runners and South Korean agents say fighting disorganized; house to house; street to street. City fighting.

Another runner showed up: NK dressing up in white robes, which is what Korean farmers wear. Runner got shot at by snipers, but he made it to give HQ order to go east again. Runner hitched ride with us; his name, Petey Sturmer (Donora, Pa). Running is the worst job, I swear.

July 19. On way eastward yesterday, rear element of our convoy was ambushed. NK let our unit go through and I guess they thought we'd leave our guys behind. Tough luck, NK. Were driven to a knoll and fought NK off. Our 105s fired at 200-yard ranges.

Blasted away for seventy minutes straight.

Continued east as a unit, stopped at designated point, the first Y on the road east and set up a roadblock. We're to serve as cover for Gen Dean (24th Div, Commanding) when he and his troops make it out of Taejon.

Runners coming in from all directions now. One said the 34th Inf Regt has a new CO. A Col (maybe a Light Col) named Pappy Warrington. He's with Dean inside Taejon. Hat served with Col Warrington in Europe. An Inf Major then. Good man, acc to Hat.

The radios stink! Nothing works, and the hills don't help. Much, much firing inside Taejon. Disorganized groups passed through our roadblock (mostly service troops at first, but all armed).

July 20. Taejon is no more. Gen Dean among the missing. Col Warrington walking with his men out of Taejon. Looked too old to be fighting, but there he was, passing through our roadblock: walking. No rides for him. That hasn't changed, says Hat.

We marked targets on hills just east and west of us; pre-selected sites just in case we have to fire there. Roadblock re-strengthened with additional arty battery; if more troops on the way to safety, NK sure to follow.

Liaison plane reported more US troops headed our way. Turned out to be 24th's divisional artillery (Divarty) and we waited for them to pass through us from Taejon. Our roadblock opened the way and held the door open for retreat. (It's called a retrograde movement, but it all amounts to the same thing: we give up ground, real estate, for time.)

Air Force flew over the troops as cover part of the way; my gun crew relieved at 1900, ate some canned peaches, smoked, read and worked on journal.

July 21. Making a stand at roadblock; we're still east of Taejon. More 24th Div guys passed through most of the day—to reorganize somewhere is my guess. The Div lost much equipment. Plus: no less than 2400 GIs missing in action inside Taejon. Many Os dead and many Old Guys dead too. These last important to hold us together.

All kinds of reports: high, very high, heroism, and many low lifes running away, abandoning their units.

Old Guys say heroism and cowardice (panic) are part of war; trouble is that individual heroism is just that: individual. Army doesn't operate individually, say Old Guys. But: heroes are important, make no mistake.

Sometimes, it takes just one guy, alone and gutsy, to turn a platoon around, to stop the enemy and put them on the run. What the Army wants, what any army wants, is for you to hold your ground; this is important since you don't have to fight for it again. Second, taking a position is another big act; and, if it is held until relieved, that is heroism of a high order. It's usually a matter of setting an example for the other guys. We then talked about retreating and stopping to fight, and making it out of roadblocks, etc. In those situations, and we've all seen it happen over and over, one guy sets the example and the fighting improves.

Of course, if the example is a bad one, then it works the other way around.

This results in bugging out, and the God above this Korean sky has seen that happen many times this month.

The talk went on like that for a while. Our Old Guys lost more friends in Taejon. These guys are regulars, like Hat who lied about his age—he was fifteen when he enlisted in 1930. And here he is with twenty yrs in in 1950.

Fighting in and out of Taejon is sporadic. Told to expect probing by NK patrols but that Inf guard will handle them; stand by the guns, stand by the guns, etc.

Soon after, we fired guns off and on for three hours with help of a light liaison plane spotting for us. Gave protective and cover fire for remnants of 24th Div dribbling in from Taejon.

That, said Frazier, has been a major league battle.

As troops straggled by in small groups, Charlie rushed out of the road-block and handed a pack of cigarettes to one of the guys of the 24th.

Others followed suit until ordered to return to the guns.

These guys have had the war for now; you can see it by the way they walk and bunch together.

July 22. Up early, 0430. Scheduled to leave this village, Yongdong, at 0930. To be replaced by two new divisions just in from Japan. The 24th Div gave up much real estate but it delayed NK, and we needed the time. A delaying action.

Replaced at roadblock around 0630 and got to work loading and making ready to move. Ate, packed up the small gear and all set to go when the word came: unload. We're staying in Yongdong.

Right away, Lt Brodkey left our ridge, went up a knoll and set his forward observers. Signal Corps guys relaid the wire and made phone contact again.

The 24th Div happy to leave the area; some of their guys are still going through the roadblock.

We're being assigned to the First Cav, which is really an Inf Div. The First is just in from Japan.

The 24th Div is being reorganized and being given new guys as replacements. Bulk of division moved out by noon, and our Old Guys then went to see their buddies from First Cav. Their Old Guys are cadre, just like ours.

As for the 24th, those guys are due for a rest; maybe even Tokyo, but most likely Pusan.

Charlie, Joey and I, along with Stang and Skinner and the rest of the crews helped the relieving division set up. (What we wanted was a look). Looking at them, and they looking at us, we must look like bums to these guys. We'll see how they do. We'll help, but they're the ones who must hold Yongdong if that's the order.

(One of their medics spotted my eye, felt the bone ridge and the eyebrow, and then pulled out two bits of black thread. Stitches rotting off, but no danger of infection, he said.)

Hot chow. First Cav unit has three kitchen trucks! Standing in chow line and spotted some sixty to eighty GIs from 24th Div that just straggled in. This must be the last bunch out of Taejon, perhaps the rear guard. Not wounded; exhausted and looking like death. These have to be guys that fought thirty-hours straight.

One fell in with us in the chow line and asked if we were part of the unit leaving with the 24th. Told him we held the roadblock. Asked us one more time if we're part of the unit leaving with them, the 24th. We said no, and he said: "Lucky you, you get to stay behind."

We laughed and so did he. First Cav guys didn't find it so funny. They'll learn to laugh, though.

Worked on journal and was hitting the sack when bam! bam! bam! It was on again and out we went to the guns. But our unit was pulled back and away from the developing fight.

July 22, second part. The First Cav held Yongdong briefly, then gave way. Couldn't hold it. Faced a superior force, was the report. With Yongdong lost, we rode south again in the night and dawn. Ride hot and humid. Inside the truck, I helped Lt Brodkey with stashing phone and wire; he rode with us. Quiet, college guy.

The war is almost a month old, and it's a far cry from Task Force Smith days; more men and equipment coming in, including a new division, the 25th. We're to set up next to them acc to Lt Waller.

Stopped and unloaded at 0700. Ate some, went to latrine and then set to work. Old Japanese maps call this site Sanju; it's an area or a region, not a town or a place.

After assembly, Lt Waller told us that the loss of Yongdong is most serious. We are between two rivers, the Kum and a bigger (longer? deeper?) river called the Naktong. No idea what Naktong means in Korean; no idea what anything means in Korean.

After this, the usual: Brodkey and his observers go out, the Inf guard is set up, we stack the crates and leave them half open in case of rapid fire, we stand by guns, etc. I read for two hours straight and was then assigned to binocs. Tired after all the riding and work.

July 23. No fighting for our unit yesterday after loss of Yongdong. Had some time to look around the area today; Ellie Cohen was right: this place smells bad. Rank, as Lt Brodkey puts it. Glad I'm not a full-time infantryman. I'd be throwing up 24 hours a day.

Korean farmers are said to use human fertilizer on their rice paddies. Big, blue flies swarm around and cover whatever they land on. I hadn't noticed how bad the stink was; Charlie said that he remembers the stinking guys in the trucks after the Osan fight.

Chow line was set up, but the stink got to me. I ate a can of pears and some beans.

We have the River Naktong to our backs; walked up to a higher ridge with some of the guys to try to see it; couldn't. It's some 15 mi behind us, I'd say.

Unit change: runner came in and later on we were told that our unit is now a part of First Cav, which is part of Eighth Army.

Joey: "Yeah, I thought the neighborhood had changed."

Village/town nearest to us is called Kumchon; we're here because we lost Yongdong.

July 24-25. Reorganization. This gave us a chance to rest, screw off, do laundry, shave; waited for shower truck to roll by and it did so; couldn't find soap and so we used sand to rub off grease and grime. Turned the number three gun over to Ordnance and got a refurbished one in return. Scrounged for pound cake; traded my lima beans and ham for cake; the guy threw in some cigarettes as part of the trade.

July 26. I was told that lines not stable or stabilizing. NK has the initiative, Os say. An hour of heavy fighting near Hadong Pass, but we weren't in it. Don't know, but my guess is that GIs set up roadblock; hill and mountain passes good for that.

Reminded by Old Guys and Os that we have only two places to go: south to the Sea and east to Pusan; so we're to hold here as long as we can.

Boiling hot by noon. Where's the rain? Hot up here on hill; you can forget the valleys and the rice paddies; like BBQ grills down there and with that stinking smell as a bonus. Like a house made of shit.

Much truck movement. Inf trucked here, trucked there. Little walking, but how long can anyone walk in a hundred degrees? Well, the Old Guys say: the NK Inf does it. True enough.

Some Air Force about. A big help for Inf at times, but you still need Inf and arty to hold the land.

Talked about strafing. Frazier showed us how one can beat strafing if troops are not pinned down; and that's the secret. What usually happens, why strafing is effective, is because 1) troops are pinned down by ground fire and then the planes come in, or 2) people are caught and don't know what to do, so they run, panic, and that does it for some.

Here's what Frazier says—and he's lived through it in Europe. If on a road or field, and not pinned down by ground fire, spot the plane and move sideways. Run like a scared rabbit, of course, but do it to the right or left of the aircraft. Planes travel at high speeds, and they have to go straight; they can't make sudden turns. Pretty gutsy, but it works, acc to Frazier. Will keep this for future reference. Like everything else around here: don't panic.

Dull day but on guard duty and couldn't read. Dumas came up and said, "Remember this, guys. When lines stabilize, you're going to have to be more careful when you stand by the guns. Snipers will start showing up and try to pick us off." He then grinned and said, "Just one more thing to worry about."

Worst things here are the hills and the heat; and Korea is one hilly, hot, smelly country.

Used binocs a while and saw some US Army units below us on the road and pulling back. We're holding fast here. Saw the Air Force bombing hills, ridges and roads. Joey said they were carrier planes, Navy planes. We in no danger here; like watching a movie.

July 27. Spent day loading, unloading and moving. Tired.

July 28. Moved south; our backs still to the River Naktong. NK on offensive, or maybe hard probing. We'd stayed on hill to cover three converging dirt roads, and so we were the last unit to pull out under guard.

July 29. Received the fighting reports regarding Taejon: many individual acts of heroism, but reports also tell of others who did not perform. Once again, a good-sized number of guys quit; dropped their weapons, canteens, ammo, etc. Patrols and Battle Police units brought stragglers in wearing nothing but their shorts; no uniforms, no rifles, most without helmets.

Worse: they threw away their canteens and then drank from the rice paddies. No idea if they'll die from that, but that's what they get for abandoning their canteens and equipment.

Acc to runners, some Os too exhausted to go on. Os doing too much. There was just too much fighting, too much to do, and then to see guys dropping everything and running away . . .

The word is that NK Os and Noncoms won't hesitate to drop one of their own if he acts cowardly. Don't know this for a fact, though. I wonder if our Os would ever shoot someone who deserts or runs?

Later in the afternoon heard some mortar fire, but we were not engaged. Standing by guns when four runners came in: were told that some units pulling back but still engaging NK. Retreating is part of the plan, but keeping NK in sight. Gives NK something to think about.

A runner named Garstkiewicz said some Inf units not engaged nor firing their weapons when they're supposed to. This creates trouble since orderly retreat by unit saves lives. If Inf not engaged, NK has a free ride.

Nothing stirring around here; wrote letter to Aunt Mati, but no idea if/when mail truck is due.

July 31. Sad day for many in our unit, but first things first. Ate early and by 0730 we registered the hills and came up with pre-selected sites. Hat: if NK comes by, we'll have them cold.

Attack came, and we started the fire at 1300; fired most of the afternoon. A long fire; we'd been assigned to the rear guard since First Cav was moving in force to the east bank of River Naktong while we were to train guns on the west bank when we crossed and reorganized.

During intense fire by both sides, one of our batteries, all the guns, caught five direct hits; there were no survivors. None. We were told this by a runner and a South Korean agent with him. The battery couldn't have been more than fifty yards away from us. That sector was then held by the arty's surviving Inf guard. Soon after, a company of Inf was double-timed there in case NK tried to punch its way in now that all the arty was gone from that sector.

We ended fire at 1800 and Lt Brodkey, along with three guys from the listening posts, were left in place overnight while we made preparations for a night ride, just in case. Guns not hitched, but trucks were moved up facing the road to be ready if order came.

Quiet night, but night patrols out; not a breeze or the hope of one; the heat and the humidity take everything out of you.

August 2. Main body of First Cav across bridge, and we covering remaining First Cav units assigned as rear guard.

Refugees. As soon as we get off a ridge to move somewhere, we bump into refugees on the road. Happens all the time and is part of war, say Os and Old Guys. They're a bother, and Battle Police has a hard time with them. And so, Battle Police's job is to clear and rid the roads of refugees so we can get through.

Refugees not to blame; who wants to stay here with the NK on your back?

But this is the point: We're on rear guard and, in our sector, there is only one bridge open and reliable, but we couldn't cross because of refugees. Air Force was holding back the larger NK units and no danger there. Hundreds of refugees (maybe 2-3000). Like a town full of people. Much crying, screaming, yelling, and Battle Police pulling and pushing, shoving, cursing to get us across.

It's an old bridge, too, and mobbed with refugees. Entire families carrying what they own on their backs.

Finally the bridge was cleared. Battle Police made room for us. We turned guns westward and drove east, and we got out of there, fast. As soon as we crossed the bridge, we began to reorganize on the beach. The refugees rushed to the bridge, as everyone knew they would.

We reorganized and watched the Battle Pol holding the bridge and pushing back the refugees. We stood on the hoods of the vehicles and watched all this. We could see the columns of refugees (in the hundreds, maybe thousands: people, carts, oxen, etc.) running to the bridge which was already full with other refugees, but the bridge had to be destroyed to deny access to NK, etc. This was the last operable bridge in our sector of the long Naktong.

The Battle Pol fought for control of the bridge, since not all units of Cav guys had crossed yet (our Inf guard). They were the last unit and they went by picking up GI stragglers and guarding several NK prisoners wearing their easy-to-spot mustard-yellow uniforms. Finally, the First Cav guys and our Inf guard make it across, but the bridge was still full of refugees with more on the way, and the Battle Pol telling them to go back, back.

The order to destroy the bridge was given, relayed, and passed on three times.

"Get those people off the bridge."

The Gen (don't have his name yet) gave the order himself. And then, the bridge was destroyed. Blown up. Hundreds died on it: kids, families, animals.

Joey and I turned our backs to avoid seeing the bodies. The bridge was blown up in all kinds of pieces. A roar, a geyser of water and who knows what else went up in the air. All the time, our vehicles revving the motors, but we could still hear the screaming and the crying. The Engineers had set the charges and were waiting for all units to get across.

This was worse than any hand-to-hand fighting we had had in Chuchiwon. The Os and the Old Guys ordered us off the hoods and told us to mount up, mount up. Move it! We then drove to this site cleared for us by the Engineers.

After late chow, we moved in with First Cav sector. Below us and along the Naktong, the unlucky 21st Inf Reg of 24th Div was dug in. To the south of us: the 25th Div. Asked Frazier if the 21st Inf Regt was on reserve. Said he doubted any units on reserve, the way we've been moving lately. Army will use every unit available to hold the line, to hold the NK on west bank of the Naktong.

Gun crews assembled and told: no more retreating. No place to go.

The US Army and its ROK friends are to hold. We hold or we're run out of Korea. (For once Brother Leo's Greek lessons at St. Boniface came through: Possession for all time.) Joey laughed when I quoted Thucydides and then said he always knew our Catholic education was worth something.

Don't know which First Cav unit posted in front of us, but told that ROK divisions are now to north, east and south of our position; don't know how many troops, though.

August 3. Bridge day plus one. Chaplains and doctors made the rounds; spoke to groups of us, explaining actions and destruction of bridge. (And the refugees? No mention.) Joey and I walked away; told Lt Waller we had to go to latrine. Skinner already there, and he said he felt like shit; said the Old Guys had a better version of the why of the destruction of the bridge: "It's war, that's all. War."

Skinner said Hat told him we had to talk it out somehow, get rid of it, something. That shit like this happens all the time. NK dressed as farmers, dressed as GIs, shooting our guys in the head, clubbing and bayoneting them to death, burning them, all that was war. And no, it wasn't right to kill civilians, but that's what war came to. That's all that it is. As for the people on the bridge, that too was war. Skinner said he wasn't religious, and that he didn't know how anyone could believe in a God, etc.

Joey said, "It's not about God at all; it's about us, people."

And, as for the refugees, that was war and nothing less. Skinner cried some, and then we all sat down and looked at the mess in the latrine without looking at it, without looking at anything is my guess. Two cigarettes later we walked back to the area, and the Old Guys came up with some busy work, but that didn't help.

Would I have given the order? That's a question I didn't have to face then and won't, but the Old Guys say we'll face other decisions, and then the war will be brought even closer.

Dumas: "What if NK pressed on and killed all of us? Then what?"

Too many questions, but what made them palatable was the tone of Dumas's questions. He understands; he knows he's got young guys like me here, young guys who had no idea what war was like, what the enemy could do, and what we would do ...

After late chow, which most skipped anyway since it was eat-your-own C-rations, Billy Waller ordered us to sit, light up. He said he'd never give the order to murder NK, but then he said, "All right, would you throw a grenade at a truck full of wounded NK? All I can say to you is you'd damned better, because I fail to see the difference between a truck of wounded NK and a trench full of massacred GIs.

"What bothers you is that you saw it; that you saw civilians get killed.

That it was our side that did it. Well, I'm sorry that you saw it. But I'm sure as hell that the General who gave the order will remember this for a long time. It may even cost him his career. But think of this: he gave the order because he had to. And don't, for God's sake, don't dig in too deep; you'll then start thinking of the Engineers and the Battle Police, and so on down the line to the dead civilians.

"We're not animals, we're human, and that's why we feel the way we do. The war's young, and if you survive, if you live through this—and there's no guarantee, is there?—you'll see worse. Bank on it.

"Maybe now you'll know each other better, know yourselves better."

That wasn't a pep talk, but it sure as hell beat what the chaplains were saying, explaining away.

The Os last word, "General Walker says no more retreating. We have no place to go. This spot is it."

The phone rang right after that, and we began registering every inch of ground, hill, ridge in our sector. NK goes into those places, they die. Lt Brodkey's voice came over business-like during registering: Mark, mark, mark.

To the sack early, and then Frazier woke us up at 0300. He brought a case of beer and each one of us got a GI razor; gift from the First Cav, because we looked like tramps.

The Army is a smart piece of business at times: the talks were handled in small groups, and none of the usual "Let's assemble the troops and talk to them." For all the talk, there's nothing the Army can do about what one thinks; and one does think, and remember.

As Joey said at the newly-dug latrine, "By the waters of the Naktong, Rafe, and if we should ever forget Klail, let the right hands that pull the lanyards wither."

Five Weeks into the War

Notes of August 3-4. The 24th Div is in worse shape than imagined. To add to this, another division, the 25th, is in doubt about its "offensive capabilities." This is the word, according to the the Os and the Old Guys.

We're in a solid defensive position here, though. All the talks by the Os and the Old Guys (and some are pep talks) amount to the same thing: This is it. This is it. We're holding. We're holding, men, etc.

And I believe it. You've *got* to believe or go crazy. I wish I had a map, though. Wish I knew what Korea looks like; where we are.

Our defensive position: we've been told our artillery battery is in the middle of eight divisions—three American and five ROK—and that we are west of the town of Yongsan. Two ROK divisions are to the N and E of us (mountains and sea there), and one is to the south. It's the only ROK Div in this sector. The US 24th and 25th Divs are also south of us.

The talk is that the Port of Pusan is receiving troops and equipment daily. This, then, explains our strength: eight divisions and one Regimental Combat Team (an RCT) the 5th. This Regt is on the northern tip of the defenses.

We now have a continuous battle line; this means that boundaries are identified along the lines of us (here) and them (there). Os and Old Guys are familiar with this type of fighting; European-style fighting, they call it.

Lt Brodkey has two new Pvts with him in the Forward Observer holes. They joined him last night, but I've not met them as yet. I can see them through the binocs from up here. (They don't live in the holes; they usually sit on some hillside manning the phones.)

Dumas told us of line crossers. These are S Korean agents who gather information and pass it on to our G-2, the Intel guys. Line crossers are civilians, and I guess on Army payroll.

At times, the Forward Obs are hard to see because of the lush Korean greenery. They too use binocs and phones—phones that work, because there are no tanks to chew up that wire. All three of the Obs smoke and, once in a while, I can spot a puff of smoke. Asked Old Guys if smoking up there was dangerous. Dumas said no, but if I start thinking that everything is dangerous, I'll be in a straitjacket in a week. (I just have to learn not to worry about everything around here.)

So, the battle lines are settled. If we're prepping for a hold, then the NK is prepping for an attack; comes down to that.

Much firepower on our side. Transportation is a big part of that. Our battery can be moved anywhere at anytime. We merely hitch the 105mm to the prime movers, and away we go. For now, we are temporarily attached (and so, not assigned) to the First Cav Lt Waller says we're Eighth Army and to think that way; we're mobile.

This afternoon, after taking shell inventory, Charlie asked Lt Waller when we were getting paid for all this, and Billy Waller said, "Well, Villalón, see if you can get the Chaplain to punch your ticket for you."

Much hooting at this, and the other batteries (they're First Cav) prob wondered what the hell we were up to.

The war has been on from June 25 to now, Aug 4, so Charlie has a point: we've missed two paydays. We also get two-and-a-half days a month for leave time, so we're accumulating that too. (I sure as hell wasn't thinking of this back at the Osan/Suwon fight.)

All batteries assembled and told one more time: We must hold at River Naktong. Pusan is a busy port but the word is that it's largely unprotected. The Naktong is it; no going back anywhere.

Learned this from runner: K's call their homeland Hanguk (Han-Guk?). Does *gook* come from that? (Hook Frazier was once married to a Puerto Rican; she died in the Philippines while Hook was stationed there. Hook says that Puerto Ricans were called gooks by GIs stationed in the Caribbean).

After chow (two hours ago), another talk by Os: why we fight. There were two Os. One straight from Pusan—and he went right back after his talk—was all hot air. The other O, a 24th Divisioner in the hard fight in Taejon, gave a tough talk; no B-essing there.

He's an Intel and Recon O. Says NK Army is called the Immun Gun, and he called it that as well as NKPA. Said ROKs were fighters. Make no mistake. Many NK killed by ROKs. ROK have a tougher battle than we do because they have no organic tanks. This means they have none assigned to them; that tanks are not in their organizational charts. And, also that ROK have little artillery; that too makes it tough for them. (Capt's name is Thos. Kuykendall; a WWII vet.) Said ROKS fought well with what they had. He knew of grumbling coming mostly from First Cav guys.

After talk, Joey said it was racism on First Cav's part and that we, as Texas Mexicans, know that attitude well. How true.

Last cigarette after chow and walked over to Inf guard. It gets dark only after 2300 hours but was told to go down the hill if I wanted to smoke. Sat down with two other Inf guards smoking away. We were on our second cigarette when we heard a far-off grunt.

"What's that?" they asked.

Told them it was an NK T-34, an animal of a tank. Hadn't heard one since Osan, but the sound is unmistakable.

Talked about tanks for a while and then went back up the hill to try to sleep.

August 5. Early this morning, our Air Force all over the place. They own the skies.

"Yeah," as Hat says, "except when it rains. Then they stay home, stuff their wives and worry themselves silly over the ground troops in Korea."

The Air Force is dangerous, though. They make expensive mistakes: they've fired on US and ROK troops on occasion.

Early chow, and trained new guys on sighting, setting the bubble, wheeling the guns, and spent time on the phones with Forward Obs.

At 0815, another talk from Os and Old Guys. And got a surprise, a new O; his name is Lt Vitetoe, and I was told he's Arty all the way: knows guns, studied, and later taught at Sill. Fought in and out of Taejon, wounded lightly, but now returned to duty. Goes to run B Battery as a temporary replacement, and then he'll come to us.

Talk by Os: NK prepping for assault. Soon. Don't forget night attacks. Be prepared.

Meanwhile, we are receiving more and more supplies. My question is: We've got the equipment and we have the training, do we have the men? Those of us from Task Force Smith days in July have fired and have been fired on. And, we saw what happened to those civilian families when we blew them up along with the Naktong River bridge. I guess the new troops will learn when they see the Battle Police pushing them back to the fight.

No planes overhead from 1200 to 1500 hours, but they were back in business at 1515. Strafed NK, which was massed east of the Naktong preparing for a dash across the river.

The Air Force used rockets and napalm fire balls on hills and roads. To see napalm is to die. Awful to watch, to imagine being caught there. But, as Old Guys say, napalm is bad, but localized. Our high explosives shoot out thousands of steel fragments the size of a fingernail, and spreads them all over the place. Stuff like that puts soldiers out of commission fast. Napalm hot and ugly and, as Old Guys say, psychological.

Anyway, there was the well-fed Air Force blasting away, and they're a big help.

Got to shooting the shit with the guys and the Old Guys after the talk by the Os. Old Guys say that the majority of refugees (back to that again) are city people. From as far away as Seoul, some of them. K is mostly a land of farmers, and peasants tend to stay put. The Communists treat them better than city folk, too. All this after talk got back to blowing up of bridge. Still living with it. What can I do?

August 6. The Naktong is the second longest river in Korea. Told that old Jap survey maps show it to be six-feet deep and one-quarter mi wide. (Have found old Jap maps unreliable; but they're all we have for now). This Summer of 1950 has now turned burning hot and dry, so one can see the sand bars and a long strand of beach. Still, in the Monsoon season last June-July, the Naktong must have been deep enough to drown a giraffe. (Don't remember the Naktong when we took the train from Pusan on way to Osan/Suwon. Prob crossed the Kum too and was asleep at the time).

Other arty units on surrounding hills, but difficult to spot them from here. Prob dug in well. Our Engineers dug an extra spot for us in case we have to wheel around for fire direction. Usual fine job by Engineers.

Saw one guy I thought was a Texas Mexican. Turned out to be a Coloradan; called himself Donald Trujillo. Says his people came from Spain, and then Charlie and Joey asked him if those were the Spaniards that landed in Virginia and then trekked across the South until delivered safely and soundly to the Promised Land. This is the third Coloradan we've run across, and they all claim to be Spanish. Well, that's the first Mexican of any kind I've ever met named Donald.

We spoke Spanish to him, but he answered in English. Skinner and Stang are forever after Joey, Charlie and me about speaking Spanish; Frankie Maguire too, but since he's a shit, he doesn't count. The three of us will prob have it out at some PX beer party with Skinner and Stang and whoever else wants some after this is over.

Worked on the binocs and spotted Lt Brodkey and his new assts: Billy Bromley and a spooky guy named Henry Farmer. Farmer has a huge Adam's apple which bobs like the bubble on the sighting mechanism; and he squints when he talks to you. Bromley is just crazy; there is no other word for him. They've got a great observation post. They usually sit and smoke on the down side of the knoll, wires and phones strewn around them. They'll come on the phone for fire mission or to check the phone usually in this order: Brodkey, Bromley and then Farmer. When we get more Os, they'll serve as Forward Obs, so says Dumas.

Trained binocs on roads and saw much US Army vehicle traffic, but not fired on by NK.

Hat: "NKPA is there, they just won't give their position away."

Two runners came by on way from Battalion HQ. A S Korean agent with them. The Word: NK is gearing up and, despite the Air Force, being well-supplied. AF will continue night bombing, but runners say the bombing is not effective. But since light stays on in summer, liaison planes can direct targets. I've not seen this done. What runners say is not effective is the attempt by big planes to use coordinates to hit known targets. The runners' assessment of night bombing by Air Force: not accurate. Much NKPA traffic at night, though. Hear it when I'm trying to sack out.

One more word on runners: (And one of them gave me a hand-drawn map of Korea, finally!) still looks like a high risk job to me.

The map: our front is extended along our defensive perimeter, called The Perimeter, and it's not large. We have been pushed back, and hence Gen Walker's order about no retreat. None of that Hollywood noise about stand or die; we're holding and we'll hold and then counterattack. But first, we have to see (take) what the NK throws at us.

From the map, K looks like a boot without the sharp toe and heel. Pusan is to the right, the SE corner, and we have a small chunk of what the NK hasn't taken. Our unit's position is to the left of Pusan, or west, and the sea isn't far from us either.

More on runners: A two-mile run is not unusual for them; but written messages may be relayed using various runners. A danger: loss/capture. Another: a garbled message in "oral orders." Special kind of guy to be a runner. Brave, good sign readers, and able to work with minimum direction. An assigned job, but runners I know are volunteers. They're not cowboys, they're just good, hardworking guys. All shapes and sizes, and carry lots of candy for energy (and to cut down smoking on running trails?). Like us, they read maps well and can use a compass with no trouble.

Latest plan: If Immun Gun breaks through (makes a hole in some line), our arty unit will be sent to that spot and fill it with steel. Our trucks, the prime movers, are parked midway down the hill with noses pointed to roads 1) for us to quickly hitch the 105s and 2) for them to move out smartly. These are dirt roads but hard and solid on account of the dry summer. So, if the Immun Gun breaks through, there we go to help out the unit closest to the hole.

Inf and us, as support, are fighting on two ridges: Cloverleaf and Obong-ni. NK wants them. (Nighttime runners came in and we can hear much NK vehicle traffic on other side of Naktong).

Cloverleaf and Obong-ni forming a blister—a bulge—on the line. We were all told that bulges are bad because troops can be cut off from the main body, and this will result in loss of life, equipment, morale, etc. Old Guys say it'll be a big fight. Training new guys harder, and we are training them to switch jobs around guns if need be.

August 7. Runners came in bunches today. Today, on August 7, the 24th Div lost part of Cloverleaf and Obong-ni. That's just a hard luck unit; they're not cowards. We fired all day August 6. Fight started at midnight, August 5.

Still August 7. Big danger would be loss of town of Yongsan, five-miles from us; it has four/five good roads going in all directions. An important location is the word. But, the important center is the town of Miryang; lose that, and lose Korea. It's that serious. Because of my map, I now know exactly where we are. Is that bad?

Os and Old Guys stressing importance of Miryang. Imagine all eight divisional units being told this too.

August 8-10. Hard fighting. Learned that NK crossed the Naktong on August 5, midnight. (As usual, they began by firing their 82mm mortar and long-range guns.) NK crossed at Obong ferry and also used underwater bridges which can't be seen. (Russian trick, say the Old Guys. Look like troops running on water.)

NK firing by battery at US Infantry. This is heavy concentrated fire dangerous to life, limb and the pursuit of happiness. (But we do it to them too.)

Our telephone wires held up; no tanks to chew it up, and no tank is going to climb these hills anyway.

Runner told us a new Div moved into line just before the August 5 midnight attack. Of all the luck. (These are prob the reserves the runners talked about last week.)

That's the Second Div from the States which landed in Pusan on July 31. Some division: they brought no artillery with them. And, it's a mixed bag: reserves, actives, clerks, etc. from Europe, Panama, etc. They were positioned at Cloverleaf with the 24th Div, which means it was the 2nd not the 24th Div which lost part of Cloverleaf. (This I didn't know until this morning.)

Heat ghastly and that everpresent rice paddy stink; that heat must have been quite a shock for the 2nd Div when they moved in, and them coming from up north, the state of Washington. Many Second Div casualties and drop outs due to heat, not combat.

But: Yongsan not lost. The original line is now five-miles behind us, although fighting continues for Cloverleaf and Obong-ni ridges. NK is pouring it on. (Os call it Yongsang not Yonsang, but with no accurate maps, I've no idea of spelling of K towns.)

Miryang is not lost either, but neither side is making headway for command of Cloverleaf and Obong-ni. This is the high ground round the two towns.

August 10-13. Trucked to this place to fill in gaps. Trucked in daytime, since NK air presents no danger. Hard, hard fighting for last four days.

August 14. Rain. No air support for us, but rain and lots of it, gracias a Dios. Roads are still holding up; our arty trucked to support Bns of 9th Inf Regt (2nd Div). They fought well but with the usual malingering whiners and bitchers getting in the way. The 2nd Div did not take the hill from NK, but both sides knew they'd been in a fight.

Stang's contribution to Army humor:
Q: Why is NKPA like a horny GI?
A: Because it just keeps coming.

NK has a self-propelled (SP) 76mm gun. A bitch of a gun. NK used SP 76 to drive 1st and 2nd Bns of 9th Inf Regt off hill. Battle Police caught up with stragglers and redirected them to proper unit. Some GIs were lost and disoriented; others just ran away from the fight. But Battle Police there, and sent troops back to fight. Old Guys say it's these guys who, if they survive the war, go home and brag about how well they fought. Old Guys say this is human nature, that they're a new outfit, and they don't know each other well. No unit pride is established yet due to the makeshift arrangement of the division.

The majority of people, acc to Old Guys, will fight, but they must be shown by example. All this while we're firing, and they're standing there, talking to the Forward Obs, a thumb in one ear, the phone in the other, and carrying out fire mission and redirecting fire. Noisy as hell, but we talk and yell while we work. That, or go crazy.

Strange piece of business: was told that NK had only one tank on the scene. One of those damned T-34s. An Inf crew with a 3.5 rocket put it out of action. One of the Inf Os got on the sponson—the gun platform of the tank—and yelled for the NKPA crew to surrender. Someone from inside the tank fired on the O, and the O got himself a white phosphorous grenade and shoved it through the air duct.

White phosphorous is the worst; we have them in shells and use them a lot. The 2.6 bazooks bounced off the T-34s at Osan, but these are 3.5, a new model, bigger, meaner. Bazookas are weird anyway; you fire the rocket and you can follow it with your eyes somewhat. (The 2.6 rocket, not the 3.5.)

Ordered to wheel guns around for new target and then, almost immediately, ordered to stop firing. Everyone lit up a cigarette and the Old Guys checked the gun barrels, the blocks and sights while we waited for fire mission. Dumas went to the shell crates and stopped two guys going somewhere and told them to bring the crates closer to us.

(Liaison plane spotted US troops coming into 105 range and hence our order to stop when we wheeled; that liaison plane saved those Infantrymen, and they'll never know it.)

Frazier: "Some men will not come out of their holes to fight. And they damned well better 'cause the Immun Gun has a million grenades for those guys".

But, as Hat says, it's human nature not to want to kill or be killed.

Lt Brodkey told me at Aid Station of a Capt from 2nd Div—a weapons platoon O—who ordered him, Brodkey (and us) to direct fire on him, the men and the position. This was to stop Immun Gun from taking the position.

Brodkey refused. The Capt (named Macías; no first name yet) got hold of our Bn HQ and requested same. So, we fired and Macías was right. Brodkey told me he'd say no again. It's Brodkey's judgment as Forward Observer, after all. But the Capt wanted to hold the hill as ordered. So, Bn resolved the conflict; we poured lead and steel on that knob with two fat salvos.

(The Capt is a Weapons Platoon O, but he was leading a rifle Co here. It happens some Os die and some Os fill in, and if no Os are available, the Old Guys, and so on, down the line.)

During the break, Stang also said he thought this was the first time Bn HQ had ordered us to fire, and he found it strange. Told him that was the first time for our battery too.

Here's how we worked the salvos that caught the Immun Gun: on the first one, the entire battery, and we've got nine working guns now, fired in succession: guns 1, 2, 3, etc. And then after this type of salvo, the other type: the entire battery fired at once. No doubt about it, Immun Gun was caught. They came back at us and at Inf with a few rounds of 82mm mortar but that was it. After the salvo, which allowed Capt Macías to hold the hill, the order came to wheel guns around again and direct fire according to Forward Obs new fire mission.

Our lines here are so tight there's little room for maneuvering, acc to runners. Units are bunched up. Gen Walker means to hold, and that's it. Everybody is up here on the line and that's why trucks are so important now: NK can't run as fast as we can drive.

Back on August 12, another task force, Task Force Kean, went into a gulch for close fighting. The gulch was in that bulge I was told about (Cloverleaf & Obong-ni). Much fighting and Task Force Kean sent there because NK was converging on Taegu. Taegu is a point and NK was coming at it from two roads that were to converge on it. Had to be stopped. The bulge was getting bigger and fighting there must have been one massive screw-up with GIs and NK troops fighting all over the place. No idea what happened to Task Force Kean.

It's not hard to lose your bearings here, get all screwed up, etc. For instance, we fired our 105s to our front for six hours straight two days ago, and, at the same time, we also had reports of NK to our left and to the rear of us.

August 15. Chowed down. Threw bandages away. Had got burned by shell casings and went to Aid Station; that's where I ran across Lt Brodkey and learned of Capt Macías of 9th Inf, 2nd Div. Hand is burned some, and I use water from canteen to stop the itching. The bandages get dirty right quick and prob worse for burn anyway.

The Yongsan-Miryang battle. The 9th Inf Regt bled there and was battered, but it held. NK counterattacked twice against 9th Inf Regt sector of Cloverleaf and Obong-ni. A hell of a mission for a green unit. Put up what is called "a stubborn resistance." This means a high casualty count for both sides. But unit held as ordered. Did not rid Cloverleaf and Obong-ni of NKPA troops, though; that's something else.

Runner came by and gave me an up-to-date map of Korea. Traded him an NK O's cap I'd scrounged from a runner who wanted three Snickers candy bars for it.

August 16. We were joined by two more batteries. Still somewhat under strength, but six more guns are six more guns. Standing at latrine smoking when Joey came up: "We now have seven batteries here."

That's a lot of firepower. Joey brought some wax (you take candles, melt them and, when soft, stick the wax in your ears). Saved two candles for Charlie, who's coming over later.

Noise is bad enough with two batteries and worse with five. But seven? This is to be a direct fire battery a few hours from now.

Once in a while, because it's so dry, our firing causes fires in woods. Tanks do that too. Danger to tankers and Inf both. Direct battery fire focuses on one target directly and that's a lot of heat there. Troops under fire can become casualties of both our steel and the fires we start in the woods.

The guns are holding up; sometimes wear and tear is due more to road conditions than to firing missions. A few days ago we fired for six hours straight, and the guns looked none the worse. Old Guys say you can fire a gun for 24 hours straight if need be. Sure you can, but you'd also wind up with a bunch of crazy artillerymen. The smell of cordite can make you punchy after of a while.

August 18. NKPA on run. But not just like that. Yesterday was a full day of fighting.

I was knocked out during the fight, but got up to fire again. (An SP 76 most likely, 'cause they can move around.) I was knocked backward and was knocked out. I opened my eyes, smelled the cordite and stared at the sky wondering: What the hell?

Got up running, pushed Hat out of the way and started loading. Like nothing happened.

Hat told me later he thought I was dead. Jesus!

Told I was out for about two-three minutes, and they kept up the fire. I thought no one else was knocked down, since crazy things happen here. Then found out Joey was knocked down too, and he flew some ten feet, but no bones broken. He too got up and fired when he came to.

I don't remember anything about passing out. Happened yesterday, the 17th. I was ordered to Aid Station and took some aspirin. They looked at my hand and again offered to bandage it. Thanks, but no thanks.

The 17th was a long day of hard, hard fighting. The 2nd Bn (9th Inf 2nd Div) pushed NK from its supporting position. This is important. The 2nd Bn then pushed against NK's right flank and had some success.

By threatening flank, NK had to move; a momentary success for 2nd Bn, but a success, and that was important to the 2nd Div's morale as a whole.

News. I didn't know of US Marines in our area. A brigade of Marines assigned (brought in) to Cloverleaf and Obong-ni assault. This additional firepower gives me a clearer picture of the importance of Cloverleaf and Obong-ni. (Obong ferry is where NK started their offensive. They had also attacked three other points along the line at the same time. Started with mortars, etc.)

Runners brought these news: Marines were hit hard, but with good reason. They had some veterans, but the worst luck; NK had captured one of their radios, an SCR-300, I think, and had the Marines' frequency cold. NK heard and could hear all the radio chatter; knew exactly where the Marines were going, what they intended to do, etc.

The Marine Old Guys must've thought they died and were being forced to fight the Pacific wars all over again. They'd send a company this way and whack; they'd send reinforcements there and whack again. They'd try something else and whack. And then, the runner said, when the Marines asked for air support, they were told it was too dangerous.

Somehow, Brodkey got on their frequency and ordered the fire mission. Our Bn said okay, but the Air Force backed out as too dangerous, and they were both right, most probably, but the Marines were getting whacked during all this. The Air Force has made some mistakes during ground support, but how dangerous could it have been for the Marines anyway? Whatever they tried, they lost men, and they were getting whacked by NK guns right on the money.

To add to this, when the Air Force told Marines they couldn't fire because of danger to Marines, the Immun Gun knew that too.

Despite being in the shit, the Marines took two knobs of Obong-ni Ridge. That and the 9th Inf's attack on Cloverleaf helped. To top it off, the Marines had been issued copies of old, inaccurate Jap survey maps.

No idea of USMC losses, but 50% dead and wounded is prob right, given all they went through. Just their stinking luck that the SCR-300 was in working order. You never know about those damned radios.

That was yesterday, the 17th. On my way to the latrine, I heard a couple of cooks complaining about how rough they'd had it the last few days.

Found that my ears bled a little; must've pushed wax too far in or maybe used too much wax, or both.

Ate some canned peaches. Changed to cleaner fatigues after we greased the guns and brushed the barrels. Left those babies gleaming.

Wrote letters home and wrote in my now fat journal. Lt Fleming says journal is a French word meaning day or daily; so what I'm doing is working on a day-to-day book.

Letters: to Aunt Mati; the usual, we're all fine here, say hello to the Vielmas and the Villalóns for Joey and Charlie, etc. Letter to Aaron: how's first yr at St Boniface's and so on. To Israel. What can I tell him? He was in the Pacific a few years ago.

Found two crossword puzzle books in my kit bag; also four cans of beer I'd left there after the last big drink down. Opened a can and passed one to Dumas and did the crossword with eyes only. Am down to six pencils, all short, and unless I get more, I'm saving them for the journals and for the firing charts for when we register targets.

It's 0300 hours. Everybody's up. Hours all screwed up. I woke at 0200 and wrote the above. Felt like noon to me, prob was for the body. Sleeping and eating all screwed up too.

Vehicle noise we hear belongs to NK moving out and away. Heard one last grunt from T-34s pulling out. Night people is what they are.

As for our 105s, we don't need to see the targets with our eyes. Once we register on them, (and since we write them all down and save the charts) it's a matter of elevation and let the Immun Gun Inf look out for itself.

Dumas asked if I were okay after I was knocked cold. Told him Hat thought I was dead.

Dumas smiled and said, "Yeah, I did too. You looked like someone pulled you backward by the seat of your pants, arms out and flapping like a bird. You're lucky you didn't hit a rock or one of the shell crates."

"And Joey?"

"Oh, no. That boy really flew. Ten, fifteen feet, I'd say, and then, whumph!, but no broken bones either, from what I hear."

That was some concussion, and maybe that's what caused the bloodied ear and not the wax. The knockdown reminded me of Lt Edwards, except that when he got up, he was then shot in the throat.

Runner named Nick Bogden (Chicago, Illinois) told me that Macías was a First John, not a Capt, but that he'd prob make Capt since he's running a company now. His full name is Fred Macías and he's Mexican. Bogden doesn't know what state the O is from, though. He told this to Joey and Charlie, me and to Lt Brodkey, who then said Macías sounded like a country boy when he talked to him on the phone. I almost asked Brodkey what the hell he thought I sounded like, but didn't. The Lt is an okay guy. (The Lt's mistake in rank may have come from Macías' identifying himself as the CO, which he was.)

Bogden is to ride with us to our new position, wherever that is, and he'll be a runner for this unit for a while. Asked me if I were a reader and I said yes.

"If you have some books to spare, I'd appreciate it," is how he put it.

Put in a year at Illinois Tech, an engineering school in his home state. Asked me about my major and said I'd no idea with only thirty odd credit hours in. Said that college people like us back home can now take exams to avoid the draft.

Joey was standing by and said, "A bit late in the day, I'd say."

Bogden laughed and said, "I think I'm going to enjoy my stay in this outfit; of course, no idea how long any of us are going to be here." And on and on until Hat came by and said to take the opportunity for some sack time.

But the hour and the body are both screwed up. It's close to 0500; one more warm beer, and I'm sacking out till wake up call at 0800.

No orders for today yet, but if we're through here, we'll hit the road again.

The Lad's Artillery

August 20. Two hours after Mass: surprise orders. We loaded up and moved out as soon as we ate. The fighting is not over; NK is licking its wounds but sending probing patrols at all hours. And there it stands for now.

The Chaplain quoted from Samuel I this morning, and I imagine it's a tired old talk that arty Old Guys have heard a thousand times: " ... And Jonathan gave his artillery unto his lad."

Well, it turns out I was right for once; we did fire to the front for some six hours, and we did have the Immun Gun both to our left and to our rear. This is screwy, but as Hat explained: "Battles are not fought on football fields where the lines are neatly marked. That's why it's important to stick to the guns. We're in a perimeter, and the enemy (the en) can't penetrate. The higher-ups do make mistakes, but not always, and so it evens out in the end."

As for our driving around from place to place, aside from us, three other up-to-strength batteries are also shunted here and there, but all of this is inside The Pusan Perimeter. We've gone north little by little and are now closer to the 5th Regimental Combat Team (RCT); we may wind up firing for them. We'll see.

Confirmed: The Weapons Platoon O's name *is* Macías, and he's a First John. If he stays alive, he'll make Captain. The runner Bogden, who passed this on, gave me a lot of the stuff I'm setting down today.

To chow after Mass, but fell asleep and sloshed coffee on my hands; didn't feel a thing. Couldn't keep my eyes open, lit a cigarette, almost burned my fingers, so I said the hell with it and went to sleep on the shady side of the hill.

Charlie woke me up; on the move again. No idea where, and when I got to the vehicle area, everyone was loading up. Stang told me I was goofing off, so we had some words on this. (We're both Cpls, so it wasn't a matter of rank.) We got in the same truck, he stuck out his hand, I didn't take it, and it ended it right there.

Picked up an extra battery unit waiting for us, and three of their guys rode with us. One was a Polish kid from East Liberty, Pa. and a Lithuanian from Mauch Chunk, Pa. That's the name of the town, acc to him. His name is Popnick. Guy about our age, 18/19. The third GI is an Irish guy from Buffalo NY, named Davey Doyle. He may turn out to be a problem. The Polish guy, Bernard Pavlovsky, was teaching me a song in Polish, and I then gave him a Spanish translation. Doyle busted in saying, "And what Army you guys with?"

Sgt Dumas was also in the truck with us, saw where this was going and told us to drop it right there.

Met another convoy. We stopped and let it go by; wrote part of journal during 30 minute wait.

Ours turned out to be a 20-25 mi ride, but you can't tell what with the winding roads and all. Looked at the map after we got in, but no idea where we are.

Guessed right about the 5th RCT; we'll be firing for them. A Regt Combat Team is something needed in a hurry and troops are highly mobile (Inf, Arty, etc.) It's different from a Task Force, which may be used for a special mission. I'll ask the Old Guys about this.

Sitting under trucks, and we heard some sporadic fire from both inside and outside of the Perimeter. Prob GIs and NK crossing each other's patrol areas.

Ate hot chow. The 5th RCT guys get at least one hot meal every day if the kitchen truck shows up. Chow's okay.

Same routine: registered on the hills, came up with twenty-two pre-selected targets, and all we have to do is to fire on those coordinates and no time wasted on aiming, etc. Battery that joined us is okay but not good. Prob don't know each other well. That makes the job harder for their Old Guys and Os.

Some ten minutes after we arrived here, Lt Brodkey took his forward observers and spotters down the hill, up a ridge, and then settled on a round dome on another hill. The Signal Corps guys trailed along, phones dangling, and laid wire. We spared six armed Inf guards to go with them.

Lt Brodkey's new Forward Ob assistants, Lts Vic Bricketto and Anthony John, went up the dome after a call from Brodkey. This confirmed readiness of lines, etc.

Lt Brodkey still uses Madman Bromley and Henry Farmer as spotters, runners, etc. Farmer was recently baptized Ichabod Crane by Joey, and is now known as Ichabod. He's a spooky guy; very religious, but he jerks off at night when he thinks everyone's asleep. A Southerner. He and Brom must make a good team, since Lt Brodkey relies on them to do their job.

Changes: Either Lt Vitetoe or Lt Fleming is to be the new Exec and Lt

Waller the Battery CO. (No news on Lt Edwards.) Lt Fleming came by and explained that there remain many leaks all along the line.

"The pounding NK took yesterday was substantial, but since NK still has the initiative, this means we'll remain in place and disable more of their Inf if it shows up."

This is the Army's reasoning for now.

Leaks are bad, of course, but penetration of the line does not mean destruction or disaster. Lt Fleming was most emphatic on this. A pep talk, but no B-essing.

Mobile laundry came in and I retrieved my stuff. Was issued a set of new uniforms etc. since we left most of what we had back in the Kwansai District. I'll never see that stuff again.

The runners coming in from Taegu HQ say this: First Cav in Taegu and in heavy fighting. Taegu is to our rear, but that's the way war is. Gen Walker will not give up Taegu, and that's it. Targets for NK the same: Yongsan and Miryang, etc. Runner also said Gen Walker dismissed a Bn CO on the spot. Boom! Just like that.

Asked, but runner had no idea what's going on with ROK in mountains and east of us, near the sea. Fighting most prob is my guess, but they're on the other side of Perimeter, nearer to the Sea of Japan. (Bless my new Korean map.)

New runners stopped by to trade war souvenirs for money. Told them we had none; our Old Guys frown on souvenirs; souvenir hunting is catching, and then there's always the danger of losing hands/eyes/lives because of booby traps.

Runners thought we were crazy; there's big money in souvenirs back in Pusan. Runners say story about leaks are true. Getting dicey for runners now. This is true in the south. But they say you can get caught anywhere.

Saw Petey Sturmer, the runner from Donora, Pa. Sturmer says First Cav fought NK toe-to-toe. It took the First Cav two/three times to repulse crossing of Naktong by NK. Told him we'd been with the Cav then, and Sturmer said: "Then you must know of the 26 GIs who were machine-gunned to death. Mortarmen, all of them."

Told him no, and he said, "Yeah. Shot in the back. Russian-made M-guns, according to the Os I gave the cartridges to." Petey took the Intel and Recon Os out there and found the GIs in a trench just as Petey said they were.

Sgt Dumas had been standing there unnoticed and said: "You saw this? Yourself?"

Sturmer swallowed hard, and we were all looking at him: "Yes, Sarge. Intel and Recon moved in, and HQ also moved to that hill, and then I had to go up there for further orders. Intel Os said some of the men were castrated. Some were burned before they were shot, according to the field docs."

We watched as Sturmer reached for a cigarette and dropped the pack, about to cry. "Some had their tongues ripped out, cut out, I guess."

By now Frazier and Hat were standing with us and listening.

Frazier: "Where'd you get this?"

"Saw it. Ask your Combat Team patrols. They took the hill and reported it to Intel and Recon."

The Old Guys moved on to see Billy Waller, and Sturmer reached for his right hand pocket, the message pocket, and said, "See you, guys."

Charlie'd been listening along with us and said to Frankie Maguire, "Well, Pisspot? Doesn't much matter which language those mortarmen spoke, does it?"

Charlie stood there until Maguire moved away. "Son-of-a-bitch won't look you in the eye," is what Charlie Villalón said.

The Word: The NK is still capable of launching big attacks. Back to the guns, and all we talked about was what runner Sturmer said about the murders and atrocities, until Frazier told us to drop it. "All you need to remember is that if you surrender, you'll get the same treatment."

That's incentive enough for me.

Later that evening, Capt Kuykendall, the Intel and Recon O who gave a talk a while back, was in the area. I stood at attention, and when he stopped, I told him who I was.

He nodded and said, "Yeah, you're one of Waller's orphans."

I told him I was from Texas, the Valley. Told him of Fort Jones. Capt K said his father was an O too, a cavalryman, and then said he, the Capt, knew the Rio Grande Valley from having lived in Fort Jones, etc.

Asked him about atrocities and about NK prisoners we were holding in our area.

He said the eleven prisoners we held are typical of what is happening to NK now: nine of them are South Koreans impressed by NK into army. Not soldiers at all, minimum training. Happens all the time; armies placing foreigners in their armies is not unusual. Some GIs captured Mongolians in Wehrmacht uniforms soon after D-day etc.

As for NK and uniforms, he said NK used our uniforms, in part, because theirs rotted off. (Rice paddies mostly responsible for that.) Confirmed some NK officers also in GI uniforms and that some spoke English.

Went on to say that POWs are a bother at this stage and that the two NK we have may be let go. The others, the S Korean civilians, could be sent to some town to let them find their own way home. Or, the Army could hire them as laborers; this too most likely.

Didn't understand about letting POWs go, but the Capt says everything is too fluid now to fool around with POWs. Now, if he had a battalion of Battle Police, that would help, but there are not enough Battle Pol to go around. POWs just not worth the trouble after you get as much info from them as you can. Told me to give Lt Waller his regards—no saluting here; he just pointed his finger at me and mounted the waiting jeep.

Our Inf guards are well-armed. There's also a twin 40mm gun—the M-19—that's able to suck the life out of any living thing in those hills. Like a killing vacuum cleaner. The RCT also has a Quad 50 (the M-16). That monster has four 50-caliber M-guns firing at you at the same time. You can forget about going home with that thing coming at you.

Much damage with those two. They have a good range, too. Inf needs them more than we do at this point, so they'll be gone soon.

Skipped hot chow; living with atrocities for now. Stood by guns from 2000 until 2300, and then to the sack. Loosened the boot laces, but did not take boots off; you never know.

August 21. A slow day at the office. Around 0630, sharing some canned pears and pound cake with Skinner, we spotted two liaison planes flying by. They dropped to tree-top height and headed for the camp clearing. They each dropped a canister, and within fifteen minutes, the runners from HQ who had retrieved the canisters went out to other units.

Skinner opened up some and said he was adopted by a family named Lassiter (Lasater?) From Deridder, Louisiana. Went to school there, etc. Went to the eighth grade, dropped out, tried commercial fishing out in the Gulf when he was fourteen and then enlisted at age sixteen. Said the Lassiters were good people, but too religious for him. After a while he said, "I plan to make the Army my home: I like it here." He then got up and headed for the latrine.

I was rinsing my mouth to take out the pear taste when Dumas fell us in.

"Vacation's over, boys. Rafe, Stang, ... where's Charlie? Skinner? Hey, Villalón; yeah, you too. All right, get the guns uncovered and get the guys out for some training. Now!"

Wheeled the guns for practice and the Engineers worked on the digs again. (Got some 155mm shells by mistake and moved them out of the way.) Cleared that part of the area; if we fire for hours, we need room to maneuver. A matter of safety too.

After practice, ran down and up the slope to see Brom and shot the shit with him and Ichabod. Returned to base camp, took my carbine apart, cleaned it, and ran the rod down the barrel a couple of times. Checked my C-rations and decided to eat chow-line food tonight. Lazed around a while and then the word was passed along: NK not dead yet. Although our sector is quiet now, NK began leaking through at other points and is now attacking along a wide front. The 2nd Div is defending Miryang, and the 25th Div is down south; NK is also trying a breakthrough to Taegu Road via Yongsan, which lies east of us.

Guess the ROK under fire too, since this has the look of an all-out attack. As usual, feverish activity here due to training of new guys, but not unsettling nor unsettled.

Dumas's training session this morning was a preparation for this. We got the word after the work was over. The phone guys reported to Frazier that communication with Lt Brodkey and his crew was clear, etc.

August 21-23. Intel guys said the 5th RCT is on the list of NK attack zones, so there went the Quad 50 and the M-19 with its twin 40mm. No firing by us for two days; we stood by guns, ate by the guns, sat by the guns, everything by the guns except going to the latrine. Hurry up and wait again.

August 24-31. Couldn't write all last week. Will reconstruct beginning with 8/24.

Within three hours after big batch of runners left last week, we wheeled four batteries toward the River Naktong itself; Lt Brodkey and the guys scrambled to give phone as well as arm and hand signals, and then the other three batteries spread out to where we were. This done, we fired due west, toward this part of the winding Naktong where NK began its attack. The other batteries fired around the surrounding hills where movement was reported. After this, the 5th RCT went out to drive NK off any high ground it may have taken on this latest dive across the River.

Our first order came through loud and clear: "Fire on pre-planned concentrations."

We fired all morning. Stopped from noon until six, and then resumed again from 2000 to 2200. Some company from the 5th RCT got caught by NK, sweated some heavy fire through the night and fought back, then got by-passed by the counterattacking NK, but the company kept up its rifle fire and finally left the hill. Old Guys said the company prob ran low or nearly out of ammo, but we had no way to get it to them. So, they marched down in good order.

Then, another rifle company from the 5th RCT came in firing away, and we stepped up the "pre-planned concentration." Nothing to it. We knew exactly where our shells were going to land; we're a machine. Hook Frazier counted six duds during our fire.

Cooks came by with soup and coffee. Had some coffee and was sitting down when shells from NK self-propelled 76s passed by high overhead.

Not concentrated fire, though. Range off too, but they were firing all over the place and that makes it dicey because there is no pattern to NK fire. This shelling all over is their pattern at times; it's not an aimed, sustained, concentrated fire.

Offered but passed up on hot meal for a second time. Too tired to eat. Too much to do.

August 26. At 1900 hrs, a runner came by again: NK did cross Naktong, on north to south meander, and came at our unit; this explains our six-hours of firing time yesterday. We shelled death out of our sector, but NK Inf gutty and ran to ridges and some of their units got through.

(Dates all screwed up. August 23 or 24. One NK breakthrough close to here; immediately south of us, and that made another dangerous bulge.)

At 2245 (8/24?), hard fighting went on. This has been a long fight. Hard fought by both sides and more casualties than I've ever seen in any artillery unit: some of our 105mm guns smashed, guys killed outright, many wounded. But no orders to move, to clear the guns, etc.

August 30. Cooks, clerks, everybody put to work unpacking shells for us and picking up empties.

We must've wheeled the guns around some 50 times in nine days of fighting. Slept through cannon fire whenever relief guys came. (Lt Fleming relieved Brodkey every other day, and food was relayed to Forward Obs. Crazy Bromley slept out there in forward ob holes some nine days straight. Ichabod said Brom is crazy, but he wouldn't trade him as a spotter.)

Another foul up, though. We were issued more 155 shells again. Guess Old Guys sent them back; we have enough 105s, for now anyway. Dud situation remains the same: at least half-a-dozen during an average hour's fire.

Runners and two S Korean agents spoke of many NK wounded. Dead, too, I guess. Can't remember sleeping, but nobody stays up for nine days straight, so I must have gotten some sleep. You smell and inhale that cordite enough, and it can can make you see things that aren't there.

Hat happy with firing: no quitters here, is what he said.

NK rushed our ridge ten times. Our Inf guard and Inf company from 5th RCT fought them off. I was either firing or asleep or doing both at the same time.

Brodkey and Fleming often behind NK units when their Inf rushed us up here.

Crazy Brom: "We watched them go up to you guys, and after much small arms fire, here they come down again. Up and down, up and down." Brom smiling when he said this. He's crazy.

Hat: "You did what you had to do. You stuck with the guns." From Hat, this is a compliment.

But it's just what they've been telling us all along: don't desert the guns, keep firing until ordered otherwise. It works here.

Joey and Charlie got some minor burns. (Everyone was wading in shells and the blocks and the barrels do get hot.)

Don't remember getting sleepy. Nor remember being tired or jumpy. And writing this now, clearly, evenly. Too, the night is so quiet I can hear the pencil scratch.

Joey came over from B Battery and brought some coffee. Hook Frazier handed Joey and me two packs of Camels. Told us we'd been in a helluva fight. "We fought for seven of the ten days here."

I had no idea, Joey didn't either. Told today's date by battery clerk, August 30.

The war is now two months and five-days old.

But NK still raising hell south of us. Joey said a guard from the 5th RCT told him the following story: "One of their Inf companies fought for a hill and stayed on it for one-and-a-half days. The NK came back and ran our Inf off; NK then stayed on hill for twenty-four hours. GIs fought for ground again for two straight days; NK retained hill when the US Inf company finally left battle. Then, the NK sat down and watched our guys walk away. Did not fire, did not attack, did nothing but watch our guys walk down hill."

We asked Sgt Dumas about this and he said it could have been any number of things: The hill was the objective, and NK had no further orders; maybe they didn't have much ammo left; too, NK was prob running short of food. Or they may have been tired after the long fight.

Dumas said: "It could have been anything. No use trying to figure it out."

"But what about the atrocities?" we asked.

Dumas said, "No, not in a fight, usually. Atrocities take place during lulls, or pull backs, or when some stupid son-of-a-bitch gives an order and everybody goes crazy."

But this was a fight, Dumas said. He also said the closest to this was a very long week of fights somewhere in Italy. Back in '43. "But this one was worse," and Dumas smiled as he said this.

Joey and I took the hook.

It's an old Army joke: The fighting will increase in intensity when we go back home and start talking about it to friends, etc.

But then he got serious and said we'd been in a hell of a fight. Frazier must've caught the last part of this and joined in.

I then told them I couldn't remember much of the fight anyway. No idea when I ate, slept, smoked or went to the john. Frazier broke into laughter at that one: "Rafe, it's always like that. It's being in the artillery. It does that to you. You go crazy after a while. Happens to the Os, too. Hell, it happens to us Old Guys. It's human."

We went on like that and no one wanted to sleep. Groups of other guys were all huddled and whispering and probably saying the same things we were saying.

Talked until 0545 and all of us had a hell of a big breakfast. Small arms fire behind us was scattered and things settled down after a while, and then it became quiet in our front, the Naktong.

After early chow, I checked the guns, took the shell inventory, looked for the firing charts and, after twenty minutes, found them under a bunch of unopened boxes of C-ration hamburger patties. Turned in report and charts to Sgt Dumas and, when relieved by Stang and Skinner, went off to sleep.

August 31. Sacked out until 1430 and asked what day it was. Woke up hungry and munched on some Grandmother cookies. At 1515 we were told to pack up, but everyone had already squared away the area. Waited an hour; the usual. Convoy waited for Battle Police escort, and we pulled out as soon as the BP gave us clearance.

Driven south on road paralleling Naktong. Hot, humid, and the smell of Korea is enough to drive you crazy.

Hat and Dumas in our truck. Charlie up front with the driver, and Joey and I talked about home. Tomorrow is 9/1, which means most of the cotton's been picked and due to be plowed under by Texas Dept of Ag law. The Valley is just as hot as Korea in the summer, so the cotton bolls must have popped open like popcorn and gotten as big as baseballs.

K can be a beautiful place; it's got hills, mountains, big, big lakes and good-sized rivers. But when the wind blows, the stench will drive you out of your mind.

Still, Korea is beautiful; the Monsoon is something else again, but that must come here in June and July, because August is drier than gunpowder.

During the ride, I asked Hat what Lt Fleming meant when he mentioned the Korean loafers. Hat said, "They're not loafers, they're aristocrats."

At any rate, they wear black, shiny stove pipe hats. I saw a bunch of them among the other refugees along the road. Koreans usually dress in white: men, women and children.

Came to a Y on the road, and we stopped for some M-24 tanks and two convoys of mounted Inf to pass through. They too were heading toward Naktong line. As usual, the Battle Police directed traffic; one B.P. told Hat and Dumas that the previous week, the NK held this road for two-and-a-half days. This was the site of a big hole punched by NK; eight mi deep and six mi wide. From the burned landscape, there's no question that heavy fighting went on here.

The passing convoy was longer than anticipated and everyone was ordered out of the trucks: stretch your legs, smoke 'em, etc. Stang and I walked over to check the gun covers; looked okay, but they do take a beating.

Went back to barracks bag to check on clothes returned by mobile laundry. Nine pair of socks, four handkerchiefs, all six t-shirts and shorts. Khakis at bottom of bag okay with no mildew yet. Had aired everything day before yesterday and again yesterday after battle. Scrubbed light mold off low-quarter shoes. Second pair of boots in fine shape and took these out and replaced them with the ones I had on; was putting them on when a convoy passing through stopped for a break. From the looks of them, the guys riding look like replacement units. Two Cols got off their jeeps and began reading maps. No staff with them, just guards.

Checked straps from my helmet liner: rotting but easy to mend. Joey's helmet has a big dent; result of concussion when he flew through the air. Helmet must've grazed a tree or hit one of the guns.

Reached down barracks bag and got out a couple of moldy paperbacks. Worthless; paper stuck together. Need dubbin for boots and will get some from supply next time Quartermaster shows up.

Checked carbine; okay. Guys on jeeps and prime movers (the big tractors) yelling and waving at us as they drove by. One more cigarette and then decided to take carbine apart just for the hell of it.

Hook Frazier taking leak behind weapons carrier, Hat joined him, and then I had to go. Asked Frazier how he thought war was going and Hook said, "NK can't go on like this. It's a small country, a few million people, not heavily industrialized," etc.

Also said Lt Waller gave him (and Hat and Dumas) info on atrocities on GIs in Taejon: forty more GIs shot/tortured but worse for civilians; five-thousand of them shot.

Asked him if the Lt meant five-hundred, and Frazier said, "No. Five thousand."

Frazier. He learned to read and write in the peacetime Army of the 30s and 40s. Knows his stuff, too. Once showed us how to replace the pin on a hand grenade, how to hold the carbine steady when firing the entire clip on automatic, etc. Hook is the Old Guy who told us the way to escape strafing. A mean cook, too. He'll mix four or five C-ration cans of whatever and serve them like that. It's a dish he calls Cow-Cotton-Onions.

Asked him about Lt Edwards and his wounds; no news.

Convoy finally passed and Battle Police let us through. No idea who we're joining. With handy map at the ready, I've an idea we're going south and still parallel to the Naktong.

Rode up front the rest of the way; the driver is a guy named Bob Martin; an Old Guy, but a Cpl like me. A rummy: red nose and broken veins. Quiet, steady, smokes a pipe. A Mississippian. All the guys here call him Bilbo in honor of some racist politician from Mississippi.

Martin answers to Bilbo; he's a WWII vet. Offered him a cigarette. He took it, and we enjoyed a quiet ride up front.

We took a side road as the sun was going down and stopped in a clearing complete with HQ, medical aid station, newly dug latrines; work done by some forty to fifty Korean laborers helping the Engineers.

Thought this was our destination, but I was wrong; it's an overnight stop; this site is for another arty unit coming in later. Still, we uncovered the guns and set them up and posted Inf guards. (Standard procedure; two hours later, in pitch dark, relieved by the other arty unit.)

Ate some canned peaches and took journal out. Sacking out; time: 2100.

The Pusan Perimeter and Taegu

September 1. This much is certain: the NKPA isn't dead. Runner after runner tells HQ that the NK is gearing up again. Despite our air force, the NK is being supplied; South K agents walking back and forth across lines say the same. Another reason for NK wearing GI uniforms is that theirs are in tatters, and they take everything from POWs and the dead: boots, uniforms, etc. But they are still receiving ample supplies of ammo and rice.

I don't know how much there is in this: We hear that Gen Walker told the 2nd Div "to stand or die." This comes from a runner, although it sounds like Hollywood. (The Pusan Perimeter, though, *is* the last line of resistance and defense. Either hold on, or we're thrown out to the sea. So, we will hold; the U.S. cannot afford to lose face in the Orient.)

Much hard fighting yesterday north of us. This means that the NK is after Yongsan village again. My map shows those five roads in and out of Yongsan; it's a village but important because of the road system.

To the east of Yongsan lies Korea's biggest military air field—Yonil. It's away from us, near the sea and below some mountains held by ROK.

Stood by guns a while and worked on shell inventory. Time to reorder some. An hour ago, a runner came in with news that NK had entered Yongsan, but that the village had not fallen. NK is in the outskirts. Lt Waller says this is critical.

Runner: "I'm the last of the runners to leave this afternoon." Said HQ had pulled out stakes, and that fighting in Yongsan village is house to house. NK pretended to be dead and would shoot GIs as they walked by. (An old NK trick; Os and Old Guys always remind guys to shoot at corpses just in case. Some NK dead are booby-trapped, but this too is old news. So much, then, for souvenir hunters.)

Something called KATUSA in Yongsan village. Don't know what that is; USA for army is obvious, and K must be for Korea. No idea what AT is for. Anyway, KATUSA unit is in Yongsan.

The NK T-34 tanks showed up, but some of our tanks are equipped with 90mm, so this evens it up some.

Must stop. Wounded coming in to Aid Station, and we are clearing ground for them.

September 2-15. This is all very confusing. I saw some stuff and I also learned some from Os and Old Guys who keep us up-to-date. Talked to some of the wounded, too.

Runners first: Sept. 2. After long, heavy fighting, Yongsan village is now rid of the enemy. This acc to K agents and to two runners who volunteered to go there yesterday afternoon and were back here in 30 hours (1900, which is the time now.)

So, Yongsan is safe for now. NK retreated to a chain of low rolling hills west of Yongsan, which means they have to be rooted out by Infantry. (And by tanks, if possible. Don't know which arty unit is there.)

Marines—and this is news to me—were in the Yongsan village fight and began their attack down Yongsan-Naktong Road. (They're going back to Obong-ni, where they had such rotten luck the first time when their radio was captured by NK, etc.)

Marines probably volunteered for that job; that, or HQ assigned it for psychological reasons, which makes sense, since it's an appeal to unit pride.

Wounded. A wounded guy named Joe Haney (Jonesboro, Ark), said the fight with NK was like the French-and-Indian War, except there were no redcoats; all guerrilla fighting by both sides. Haney is a PFC, and he led a squad up a hill and held position until ordered to abandon it.

Second Division doings. Sept. 2: Their 2nd Bn (9th Inf Rgt) was attacked in force some fifteen to twenty mi north of us. The Bn then went into attacking position itself. It was trying to make contact with the 23rd Inf (also of 2nd Div) which was in trouble. Two Inf companies of 9th Regt (plus G Co already there) held hills just west of Yongsan. Not far from us. NK were holding hills opposite.

September 2-15. (Sept. 3) Much rain the night of Sept. 2 and kept raining till today, 1300, 3 September. Then the sun came out broiling. What a country. Rains just like Gulf hurricanes at home, then the sun comes out, and in a few hours, the land turns into a hardpan out there.

Knob hill fight. (We were on the move; we started toward River Naktong.) Got to site, but were of no help; we were bystanders watching the fight for Hill 209. It stands just behind the River Naktong; we had driven through here some ten days ago and here we are again. NK's objective: to take Hill 209, and they kept blasting away.

Runners: GIs up on 209 in a bad way. No water available, and not much food either, acc to S Korean agents. NK using their 120mm mortar, and this is a legitimate bitch of a gun. But GIs held on. Bitter fighting. Then it rained. They soaked their uniforms and blankets, and squeezed them for water to drink. Finally it got dark and quiet, but many NK patrols out there, and there was constant skirmishing, and so, no rescue for guys on top of 209.

S Korean agents to HQ: One-half of GIs on hill are dead. (We had some arty forward observers above a town, on the slope of a hill, but couldn't order fire mission; no clear cut target and so much danger to GIs holding hill that they sure didn't need more firing from anybody, and certainly not from us.)

September 2-15 (Sept. 4). A battalion of the 9th Inf and the 5th Marines counterattacked Cloverleaf and Obong-ni at 0800. They were stopped, but they counterattacked again and this time with success. NK began to retreat. Reports confirmed of two undamaged T-34s abandoned by NK. NKPA retreating along ridges and on backside of knobs and hills.

The North Koreans must have assembled and reorganized later that same afternoon, because they counterattacked in force. But GI Inf went after them again.

Up on Hill 209, a runner reported cries of wounded GIs. NK holding on to some ridges surrounding 209, but it couldn't take the hill.

Much fighting on the slope opposite to ours; we couldn't fire to hit.

All manner of reports coming in throughout the day. Learned that Lt Macías ordered arty on village/settlement that forward observers registered. Forward Obs relayed Macías's message to Bn to level village (common practice since July, and this avoids house-to-house fighting.) Bn turned down the request to level village, and this was strange, since we'd done it many times before.

Old Guys said this was a new policy. I don't know what policy means.

Officers: US Army feeling pressure from European observers. (Well, to hell with that, I say.)

Later this pm, policy was changed and Lt Macías got his arty. (Lt Vitetoe explained to us about politics and policy; that's about as screwed up as taking away our beer rations this week.) That no-leveling-of-villages policy caused many GIs to be wounded or get dead permanently this morning.

Beer ration: Some group in the States complained we were drinking beer, that many of us were underage. They should have thought of that before they sent us here. Underage!

Four hours ago, 2200, NKPA moved against Lt Macías's guys on Hill 209; now called George for the Inf company holding it. This time, the GIs fell back (without orders from Macías), but he used tank support there to blast NK off the hill. After this, Old Guys got the riflemen to come back to the hill, and they fought again.

Runners told us it was a seesaw battle. And at night too, since NK had come right back at them again. This is face-to-face fighting: no shaking hands, but you wade right in just the same.

NK settled in on hill but, oh! those tanks. GI armor chopped up NK and would have climbed hill, except it too steep for tanks. Since fighting took place on the opposite slope, we could hear the cannon fire some, but mostly, we could see the fire coming out of the tubes as it shone on the clouds and the light bounced back to earth. The fire looked like orange, pink and red lightning. It was like a storm of some kind never seen before anywhere.

With the help from the tanks, Lt Macías counterattacked. It was a bar-room brawl, acc to the runners. Hand-to-hand. People wrestling in the dark, rolling down the hill. But, finally, the NK was pushed back. The runners going in and out and back and forth with messages all say they've never seen a fight like this one.

We stood at ready alert in case NK chose to circle around this side of the hill and we remained on alert until an hour ago. But, had the NK tried to circle on this side of the hill, they would have died on the spot. Brodkey registered every inch of this ground, and a child could have given the fire mission; and that's the truth.

We watched parts of the fight from up here. We couldn't see the troops, but we could identify the green tracers from the NK machine guns; no idea how they lugged the M-guns up that hill, but they did. The GIs held, though.

Once in a while, we heard the whump-whump of the Sherman tanks, and that night we saw the northern lights; the aurora borealis the guys from New York kept talking about.

Finally, the clouds broke and hard rain came down on everybody. A runner, soaked to the bone, stumbled in and said the rain didn't stop the fighting. You would've thought Hill 209 was full of gold the way both sides went after it and each other. Jesus.

Three more runners came in and said Lt Macías regrouped and stood ready since NK was bound to come back. It did; we could see the grenade flashes from up here. Two more runners went down our slope to make their way up the hill. What a job!

Both sides fought through the night and the rain. Dawn came and we could still hear firing here and there. Two guns away, a call came in on an SCR-300: a request for arty fire support. The call bypassed our observers, so one of our Os used a special code I'd not heard before and confirmed it was Macías.

Lt Vitetoe: "Fire mission. You've got heaven and earth registered, show us something."

What a release. We'd been waiting to help and we finally got the chance.

We started crashing shells down there; any thought of NK to use reinforcements was nipped right there. With GIs holding and counterattacking, and our firing on this side of the slope, the NK had to abandon its position. It wasn't a matter of personal bravery or resolve, as Hat calls it; the firepower from us was just too much. Added to this, the guys on the hill kept up the fire too. The NK had to give.

But the GIs on 209 didn't stop there. They used the hill as a line of departure, and then the 9th Inf (2nd Div) counterattacked. They were fighting for guys in their unit now, and this is always a help. Looks like every fight now is the longest I've ever seen. God.

September 2-15. (Still Sept 4). At 0100 hours, we wheeled the guns pointing on the knob opposite 209. We stood ready, but couldn't fire. We had no recent intelligence reports as to conditions on the knob. Then, a S Korean came in with some news. There were only two Os and 20 EM left atop the knob opposite 209. (This was part of the 9th Inf Regt and they were in their own fight and not on rescue mission of 209.)

NK strong there too and this had left the guys on the knob on their own. The S Korean said some troops were in shock, others were looking wild-eyed, but as far as he could tell, all could walk. GIs in daze from thirst, hunger and the firing they'd gone through.

S Korean agent: "I heard the NK Officer order to attack the hill, and I waited, but no attack NK came."

The two Os on the knob told the agent they were leaving with their men; they were going to break up into four-man squads. Do that or die—no food, almost out of ammo, and the guys were in bad shape. The S Korean agent says a paralyzed noncom was left on the knob on his own say so. That was all the agent could tell our Os. (I hope to have more news on those guys on the knob.)

Ate at 0130; loaded up and prepared to go to a sector just south of us. Must be a bigger battle yet. Hat and Dumas say they don't remember Italy or Belgium fighting as long or as bitter as this one. We left in good order, but everyone frustrated: we did very little.

A few trucks remained behind for possible survivors and anybody else that comes trickling down from the knob.

Drove for two hours and stopped; area was just vacated by another arty unit. Guns set up, and got a chance to sleep from three to 0430 when tanks woke me up. Tankers get up as early as cooks and bakers. First, they start up Little Joe, the auxiliary engine that warms up the main one. Then Little Joe goes off and main engines kick on. After this, they've got to gas up. Takes time to get a tank going.

Not sleepy. Hit the journal and felt ready to meet the day.

September 2-15. (Sept 5). On this day, a heavy battle all along the Perimeter. The River Naktong bulge lies immediately to our front. The Marines did not forget Obong-ni and went back with the 4th Inf to get it.

All this was done in heavy rain. I know the Monsoon is a July event here, but this rain is no slouch. Rain or not, the NK counterattacked, and this time we helped stop the counterattack. We saw NK digging, after which more heavy rain followed.

Obong-ni pretty well secured is the word. (Marines helped win it back, and this afternoon they were pulled back and ordered to the port of Pusan.) Got a second Marine cap in a trade for my short Army cap.

Marines were being sent back to Pusan, they said. Strange.

Just learned of the following Sept 1 event. The NK broke through in the bulge but did not exploit the advantage. Os say two things stopped NK: 1) poor communication and 2) supplies. Our triple A helped: Air, Armor, Artillery.

The big difference in the war now, (Billy Waller's words): " ... is that US Army can regroup, re-form and counterattack faster than NK."

"Just look at us," he said. "How many miles have we covered giving supporting fire and direct fire?"

Lt Waller is right; still, K is not a big country.

Another big hindrance to NKPA is also its lack of air power and not having a mechanized force of consequence, so says Lt Vitetoe.

(Lt Brodkey was out for two days with heat prostration; he'd given his water to Brom and Farmer during the long stay in the broiling sun. He's okay now.)

The fighting in this area doesn't stop, and it's all due to that bulge. The 23rd Inf Regt got separated from its parent Div, and got pushed back with its back to a major lake. A case of fight or drown or both. Being cut off, they were in isolation.

Its sister regiment, the 38th, came to the rescue. (We were in support, but barely.) This is now the third screw up: got sent some more of those damned 155mm shells. Wasted time moving them out of the way so we could work our 105s.

During above mix-up, the NK overran our position for a short time, but we remained in place with the guns and the Inf guard firing until Eye Co of 38th Inf retook our position. An M-1 I'd picked was no good, but I'd kept two carbines from the last fight, and they worked well.

During NK infiltration, we also spotted some of them wearing GI uniforms.

Runners said fighting in the South has been going on beginning with August 31 to now.

The 38th Inf Regt, which came to our rescue, was itself surrounded by two NK divisions. (This is one reason why we were overrun.) The rapid counterattack by the Regt is what drove NK off our hill. No more retreats by GIs. There is "no place to go."

(Old Guys: "Remember, NK divisions count from 6000 to 7000 troops; ours are 16,000 plus." Meant to reassure us.)

The following happened on Sept 5-9. We were told, repeatedly, "No retreat, no place to go," every time we fired, so we fired and fired. Our front was still the River Naktong and that bulge looking at us. On the 5th, our fire was deadly accurate, from all reports of the S Korean agents. They and our runners said the sight of NK dead along the Naktong was horrible. Many dead, and many mutilated by arty fire. (Runners talked about flies covering entire bodies out in the field. Lot of bad shit there, they said; shit water on rice paddies too and flies on corpses, etc. The medics will probably show up to give us shots; Lt Waller says diseases and infections usually rank higher than combat casualties.)

Three days before, the NK had punched a hole through the 25th Div position south of here. They took a place called Haman; it's not on my map.

Then, the 24th Div was broken by NK as well, and the Div headed for the rear. The 25th Div under severe attack itself had to come in and regain the lost ground. Agents and runners reported a great slaughter by both sides in this counterattack, but the 25th Div restored the position.

The 24th Div had been reconstituted earlier but still did poorly. (All Os talking about best fighting done by the 27th and 35th Regts of 25th Div.) Our old friend, the 5th RCT, came down here too and helped stop the threat.

Leaks by NK all over, but air power is a big help in containing leaks and also a help to ROK (this from HQ clerks who know).

Two solid weeks of fighting all along the Perimeter, and we're all punch-drunk.

Another bulge again and the First Cav in one crisis after another all along valleys and hills and, worst of all, the rice paddies.

Told this on Sept 5 also: the threat along three quarters of the entire Perimeter has eased. But not in Taegu. The 8th Army moved its Taegu HQ and signal equipment to Pusan.

Important: Gen Walker remained in Taegu. He didn't go anywhere. Being driven in a jeep here and there. He stayed in Taegu much like Col Warrington, and Gen Dean remained in Taejon until the Col was ordered to lead the men out (thus saving a sizeable fighting force).

Still no report or word on whereabouts of Gen Dean. Dead? Missing?

There is much fighting going on in Taegu right now. Many casualties too. Battery clerk said that the first 100 men to assemble in the morning is the fighting force for the day.

And now, of all things, our own 105mm ammo is becoming scarce. NK better not hear of it, is all I can say.

Heard the following on Sept 10: Twenty-seven of the 30 EM stranded on the knob opposite Hill 209 made it through. Both Os too; one of the Os was captured and kicked in the head or hit by a rock; NK removed his boots and ID, and then threw him in the Naktong. But the O wasn't dead and later walked back to camp with the S Korean agent who found him.

The other O was wounded and was left on the slope where he fell. Woke up hours later, got his bearing and waited until morning to walk to our unit. The EM, some severly wounded, made it back with help from S Korean agents and from buddy GIs.

September 2-15. (Sept 12). Taegu is still in danger because NK controls Hill 324; this is the key to Taegu. Frazier said we may go with another arty unit there and then ammo can catch up with us. Things on hold for now; runners say NK picking up their dead (a high count due to our shelling) but not assembling or gearing up for battle at this point. We're very, very low on ammo.

Left at dusk; sun barely showing through, and it must've rained somewhere around here; we caught the end of a rainbow on a burned out hill to the right side of the road.

Parked and set up an hour's distance from Taegu; the guards were posted and the guns set up. Kitchen truck drove in and we thought, at first, it was an Ordnance carrier with our shells. Hot chow; Joey and Stang said if they ate one more powdered egg, they'd start cackling.

Ate in a hurry, covered and hitched the guns and drove down an unusually dusty road; so our convoy was given away by the dust, but no one fired on us. Acc to my map, Hill 324 is the highest in the area; it's so flat here, it's possible to see Taegu and the hill from seven mi out, which is where we are stopped.

The 324 commands the terrain of the Taegu Valley. My map also shows the hill mass to be one mile long. That's dangerous territory for an attacking Inf, since the slopes are steep, steep, steep on all sides.

We passed the afternoon and the night on that one spot and then entered Taegu from the East. Waiting for ammo which did not arrive anyway. First Cav Div came out here with us; they were part of our convoy (the 3rd Bn of Cav's 7th Regt). Effective fighting force: 500 to 550; the NK is supposed to have 700 men at arms.

Because of ammo shortage, we did not give any arty preparation prior to attack by First Cav. We saved what we had, 1) in case of NK breakthrough, and 2) for counterattack if that happened. An Inf unit found some shells in their convoy and brought us a truck full, but it was the same 155s again.

So, with no arty support from us, the Air Force was called in. The air strikes started at 1100, and we saw the 3rd Bn massed for maximum rifle fire. The NK had to mass up too; it's only natural.

And the NK again started with their 120mm mortar; from out here, we could also see the green tracers from the NK M-guns.

Many Os went down in this battle; the two Os left had to reorganize two companies of the 3rd Bn. They did so and led the way. EM fought well and on own initiative, was the report. They also had plenty of Old Guys to help.

Watching a battle is not worth squat. You want to help, to fire, but it was no go here.

Os and Old Guys gave a great performance in Taegu. It was that "no place to go" attitude all over again. The slopes were steep as I just knew they'd be, and under much heavy enemy fire. But the troops kept moving up.

The GIs got nearly to the crest of 314 when the enemy counterattacked. The NK Inf just rushed out, helped by those monster 120mm mortar of theirs. (No arty from us.)

Our unit waited to see what form the counterattacks would take; GIs pulled back and NK retook crest. Immediately after that, the air strikes began again and raked the crest. I lost count of the number of air strikes. (Some Navy planes there too.) The crest became full of smoke and we all thought: Fire! It's damned dry despite the hard rains all around.

During all of this, we stood by the guns and waited and watched, and being told of battle by runners, etc. But, hell, we could see it for ourselves ...

Was told of wounded O who with a small group of guys yelled at the other available men to come up with him. "There are enough of them here for everybody."

This sounds like Hollywood to me, but this is supposed to be true. I believe it; fighting makes you do crazy things. And, he isn't the first O I've heard of who has said this to inspire his men.

The crest was taken by GIs, lost and retaken three times. All Os either dead or wounded in this fight. Old Guys took over and, with EM shooting, bayonetting, they swarmed all over the hill. At the third retake of the crest, the NK lost integrity, disintegrated, cut and ran.

The GI's suffered 229 casualties in two hours of combat. Most Os dead or wounded; all runners and S Korean agents coming in with this report.

We didn't fire, but if NK were to regroup and come up with a serious counterattack tonight, we still have the supply of 105mm shells we started with.

Wounded runner came in. Medics rushed up and ripped and cut fatigue top off him and began working on the kid while he gave Col Conner the report; the Col was holding a map and standing by our No 2 gun talking with Maj Lewis, the Bn Exec, and with Billy Waller.

Runner: On the third retake of the crest, four GIs were found shot and bayonetted, with their hands tied. Uniforms old and tattered, and all four were shoeless. Must have been taken POW earlier in Taejon or God-knows-where.

Runner and another wounded S Korean agent: One O was found tied hand to foot; he was burned alive by retreating NK. (Body charred, blackened and found near 5-gallon can of gasoline.) Many enemy dead wearing GI uniforms and boots and helmets; using M-1s and carbines, too.

"No place to go."

September 2-15. (Sept 12). Fighting still heavy in some parts of Perimeter, but things don't look as bad as they did in Jun, Jul, Aug, and part of Sept. (Told that pockets of many en troops will be isolated, and that they will then look to get back to their own lines. This is what NK was doing when it found itself cut off from main unit; NK need supplies just like anybody else.)

Still no issue of beer. If (and when) PX catches up with us, we can *buy* some. Except for Os and Old Guys, most of us are all under twenty-one.

We scrounged for beer among guys and loaded what we had in a weapons carrier, and the driver took the beer to the guys who attacked and took Hill 324.

No beer. Jesus, what a country.

Sept 15, and up-to-date with journal. War not over, but we're getting stronger, and more supplies while NK is being supplied as well as we are.

Heard about KATUSA again. It stands for Korean Augmentation US Army. It's the joining of ROK soldiers to our units or maybe vice versa. Don't know how this would work. After all, who speaks Korean?

Saw myself in a mirror a medic was carrying. I look as old as the Old Guys. Beat. Other guys do too, but did not notice until I saw myself. Lack of sleep, food, jumpy, nerves, too many cigarettes (no beer, says Charlie), etc, etc.

All of us look as if we've been on a drunk for a year straight. Chaplain came by, and even he looked beat. We asked about beer for the troops; he had nothing to say.

Lt Waller got the word on 105 ammo: Some was diverted and, in some cases, we plain ran out. But, supply should get back to normal soon.

Tried those greasy Vienna sausages. Threw them up. Opened some old WWII K-rations and found some instant coffee. Bit pieces off like candy and chewed that awhile. Went then to kitchen truck and got some hot coffee.

Tried the WWII K-ration cheese; no taste to it. Wrote two letters home, but there's no mail in or out of Taegu. Told Charlie that the Army owes us pay since June. We'll hold out for the interest too, he says.

Funny fighting in Taegu. Air strikes, rifle fire, all small arms, and since no tanks here, and us with no ammo, it was strange. But the fighting went on just the same.

Stang came over and we talked things out, shook hands. Said he heard Bernard Pavlosvky wounded badly; I hadn't seen that battery in two weeks. Pavlovsky is now back in Japan, if he's alive.

Fighting going on still, but Special Services personnel in area. Got me some books, a baseball glove and a softball; no baseballs. (I was wearing my second Marine fatigue cap and traded it with a Special Services guy for an extra softball. My glove is a Vern Stephens model.)

Asked the Special Services guys what they knew about the beer situation. Said it was some anti-alcohol group back in the States.

As the Old Guys say, "The world is full of assholes and they're all red and tight."

2145. Fighting continues, and I'm hitting the sack. Folding up my poncho and will use it as a pillow; if it rains? We get wet, is what the Old Guys always say. (Ask a dumb question, etc.)

Hat said to expect much training once ammo comes in, just to get timing right again. He sat down, we talked a bit, and we smoked a couple. Asked about the journal, wanted to know how it was coming along, and he then moved on to check the rest of the men.

About to put journal away when it started to rain. (Korea is a strange place: the rain always bring with it a big chill, and then, when the sun comes out, it burns everything and everybody.)

Lambs Without Blemish

September 15. Hit the sack at 2145 hours last night and slept until 0500; woke up to rain. Fall hasn't hit yet and the trees around the site hold water so that any shaking of the leaves brings another hail of rain. Worked in the area; supposed to be waiting for another arty or Inf unit. Guys mostly smoked and read comic books.

Finished reading a condensed history of the U.S. Navy; read about Decatur, Jones and Farragut, but the interesting ones are the brothers Perry: Oliver Hazard and Matthew C. Interesting to see if Japan has papers available on Matthew C. Oliver H. died young, 34, of yellow fever, down in South America somewhere.

Joey and Charlie and I got to speaking Spanish and then went into English and then mixed both as we always do. Hook Frazier says his wife, a Puerto Rican woman, used to do that, and it drove him crazy. No children in that marriage, according to Hook, but he keeps in touch with P R in-laws around Christmas time. Slow day at the office.

September 16. I don't think this war will ever end. What Joey calls "A not-so-merry-go-round." Woke up 0300 and ate something; started to work at 0330. Raining for thirty-six hours. Powdered eggs at 0600. Lt Waller gave us the word: we're still the 219th Field, but now belong to something called I (pronounced Eye) Corps.

"The folks back home" have no idea who fights in a war. To them, everybody fights. I thought so, too, but now I know: the tooth fights, and the tail sees to supplies. Hat put it down in numbers: for every fighting man here, there are some seven to eight who supply us: quartermaster, ordnance, signal, chemical, etc.

By 0730 work began to pile up; rain kept everyone going here and there. I spent most of the day tending to ammo crates, digging ruts to drain the water off and away from work area, checking and tightening the gun covers, etc. Then, in the rain, three patrols came running in: NK coming at us with a sizeable force. About the same time the phone rang, and we rushed to the guns.

NK attacked on a wide front which included us, and we forgot about the rain and started to fire until NK decided to pull back.

Not a serious probe by NK, acc to Old Guys; just keeping us on our toes. No one killed or wounded, and the rain went on as if nothing had happened.

September 18. Today's fighting took longer than I thought; the 17th was also a busy day. The 5th Regimental Combat Team, (5th RCT), had moved in and was told to take hill 268 on September 16. That's the day NK came at us suddenly and then abruptly pulled back.

(Today we began with support fire in a driving rain. It proved to be a long fire for us and for all the batteries lined up on the neighboring hills.)

Yesterday, by noon, every battery was giving direct fire; two South Korean agents and a runner were wounded by the wild firing coming from both sides. They were brought in by jeep and tended to at the Aid Station and released.

The 5th RCT took hill 268 after two days of fighting. They reported that NK dead on hill came to hundreds. Os and Old Guys went to verify. The Army still photographers were driven to the base of the hill right after the fight.

Well, "the folks back home" should see what 20 dead bodies look like. Then, they could work up to 50 and then a 100 and then 200-300 with arms bent, legs off, and half bodies here and there, some guys slammed against tree trunks or parts of them hanging from branches. After this, we could take the taxpayers by the hand and walk them through the 420 NK killed and wounded on hill 268. Make them see how their tax dollars are being spent.

A town called Waegan (not on my map) was flanked by the 5th RCT. (Must stop writing to see to shortage of 105mm shells again; on the other hand, we have no shortage of PX toilet paper; trouble is, toilet paper won't stop NK.)

September 19. Waegan. The 5th RCT fought for three straight days. We fired for four consecutive days, but we're keeping an eye on the shell supply; no word why we're short on shells.

The 5th RCT continued to be engaged in a savage fight from all accounts; as for us, we were firing at close range. The NK had set its line in front of Taegu (good old Taegu), and the RCT broke the NK's front. With this, the unlucky 24th Div was then given the site at the River Naktong. (The 24th Div was again given more new men; that's no good for any unit. Takes replacements time to know each other, but time is something we don't have.)

Took out some old firing charts. We were here earlier when we were heading east toward Osan and Suwon with Task Force Smith; that was a long time ago.

September 20. Things are moving very fast. Attitudes and war are changing too. This morning, the 5th RCT took town of Waegan, which means that the NK is out of our area for a while or waiting to counterattack.

No news on casualties of 5th RCT; bound to be high, though. They have fought long and met tough resistance.

First runner: First Cav meeting bitter NK resistance in hills surrounding Taegu. Second runner: First Cav not advancing. The defense by NK is now termed *fanatical*. Many losses for First Cav, but worse for NK, what with our arty and air power against them.

Load up! Load up! Moving on. Must stop here.

September 22. Taegu hill captured. NK leaving their dead behind. The stink is horrible. First Cav did a hell of a job. From up here, I can see more than I want to: dead horses and oxen (and two camels), and many, many dead and wounded NK Inf; many T-34 tanks smashed and burning. NK cannon pushed into ditches and abandoned. More bodies of NK on the sides of roads. Boxes and boxes of all types of ammo. (Some ammo boxes are the ones we had abandoned earlier.)

Skipped chow. Two batteries in readiness to move out, but we were told to stay. So we go around scratching our behinds with nothing to do but wait. We work on guns or go crazy with boredom.

NK on the run is the word. Runners streaming in with news. I walked up the hill for one more look at the NK dead, and after that, worked two more hours on the guns, the journal, and then got in the sack.

September 22. It's official, NK is on the run. Gen MacA launched a surprise invasion on the western coast. Not far from us. NK folded up here and began to escape trap. Things are more relaxed now. No fighting in our sector.

Cleaned and greased the guns, took shell inventory, etc. Skinner and I checked each block of every functioning gun and tagged two for Ordnance removal.

Half supply of 105mm came in. *Half.* Signed for shells and equipment and wrote Aunt Mati; read some more naval history.

Unit hit with a surprise: no beer again. No beer to be issued to us until further orders, etc. "The folks back home" don't want their boys to be drinking on the job. Twats! What a country; we can kill hundreds of NK and South Korean refugees, but lips that touch liquor etc. What a crock. The Army just got around to issue the news formally through a General Order, and that makes it official. (About as silly an order as the one reminding us to take precautions against the heat in Korea: "The Officers and noncommissioned officers in charge will see to it that etc etc … ")

Two long days of rest here; Special Services dropped off books, comic books, baseballs and gloves. Ate some canned pears. After this, cleaned my boots and aired the second pair, applied dubbin and let it set; put on clean fatigues. A playboy.

September 23. Beer issue on again. That was quick. Would like to see the papers from home regarding this little screw up.

Hot chow and were told at chow line to be ready to move. At 1600 we hitched the guns, loaded the gear and rode west. Headed for Taejon. Told NK liable to put up resistance there, so we're loaded for bear with additional units, but no new issue of shells for us.

(I now know where Osan/Suwon are; close and just south of Seoul. Inchon, where the recent landing took place, is northwest of Osan-Suwon and southwest of Seoul.)

We're doing well now, but I won't be forgetting the days of Task Force Smith and the misery we took there.

Did not see, but heard of NK truck jammed with ammunition and retreating NK blown up by a 3.5 bazooka. This happened in the town of Chonjin. Runner said explosion caused a crater the size of a box car. Truck and the men disappeared; all that was left was the crater.

"The folks back home" should also see what one of our 105mm shells does on impact: won't be enough of you there to put in an envelope.

Runner told us a funny story. A truck driver, a scrounger picking up parts for our vehicles, drove up to what he was told was an occupied/safe village. The two-and-a-half-ton got a flat on the outer rear tire, so the driver got off to fix it. There he was, working on the spare, when he spots some soldiers marching up the same road. The scrounger takes another look and recognizes the troops as NKPA. Right away he gets on his feet, waves at them, they stop and wave back, and then he gets in the cab and gets the hell away from there.

The runner said the scrounger was laughing when he said this, but then said he'd like to get his hands on the throat of the patrol leader who termed the village as safe and clear. What happens too is that NKPA uniforms wear out and the NK use ours out of hand, and thus much confusion arises from this.

Liaison plane flew by convoy and dropped message canister near HQ trucks.

Convoy stopped. Orders changed. Veered off Taejon highway and ordered to River Han; the last natural barrier to Seoul. The Han also winds southwest of the capital city, and that's where we're going. I don't think we'll be that close to Seoul, though. Still, that's a lot of territory to be covered by a bunch which was nearly pushed into the sea when we were bottled up in the Pusan Perimeter.

September 24. The breakout of the Perimeter is now complete, and it is being called that, the breakout. Runners are now coming in by jeep, since they have to keep with us and other units.

But it's still the NK's war. I saw photographers and moving picture cameramen recording this: some 500 ROKs buried waist deep with their hands tied behind their backs, bayonetted, clubbed, beaten and shot. We then saw photographs of eighty-six GIs also buried the same way and in the same condition.

Dumas: "From what we've seen of the NK, they force the prisoners to dig their own holes."

Driven over much territory in a few hours. Isolated pockets of NK are now operating as guerrillas but considered no great danger, we're told.

An Intel/Recon O told us South Koreans civilians are against NK, so NK must fight for everything and can't, don't and won't expect help from South Korean countryside. All the Old Guys told us this was a bunch of bull; most civilians will cooperate with any army.

September 25-26. Crossed River Han, driven northeast and found Seoul recaptured; a mess. We'd fired for fourteen hours without let up, and other arty units did likewise. Seoul, the capital city, is now a dump of broken concrete. Much smoke and many fires still on. Told that Seoul population before the war was one million.

Resting here. Seoul refugees coming back. Yeah, but to what? Many, many horror stories about NK torture and killing of South Koreans. I've seen what they do to combatants already; no need to see any more.

September 28-30. Reorganization; consolidation. Getting some replacements. Troops talking about going home. Old Guys took us aside and told us to forget it. Each one of them reminded us we were at war and to forget about going home.

"Just get it out of your head."

Hard to accept this, but we'll see if the Old Guys are right.

Changes. Lt Fleming has been transferred temporarily to 2nd Div Arty. Same sector with us, though. Lts Waller, Brodkey, etc are still with us. Got a battery commander, Capt O O Chandler. Billy Waller goes back to being Exec. Lt Brodkey requested he keep Crazy Bromley and Ichabod Farmer. Lt Brodkey also got two new 2nd Lts to work with. The other replacements, Lts V Bricketto and A John, died at knob hill fight when unit was overrun, acc to runners. Will ask Crazy and Lt Brodkey about this.

We're Eighth Army once more and attached to the 2nd Div. Might get to see Lt Fleming again. We're Waller's Orphans all over again, but we're still the 219th Field.

October 7. Spent last five days training replacements. Dull business, but has to be done. Worked half days and read most of the mornings or afternoons after work.

Told that tomorrow we cross the old South/North Korea boundary line, the 38th parallel.

One of the replacements wound up in Charlie's battery; a kid named Yzaguirre from New London, Tex, wherever that is.

October 8-10. We train. Old Guys see to it. Keeps us from going nuts. Issued OD pants and shirt; getting chilly. Nights are cold already. ODs go under field pants. Issued two pairs of gloves per man. We're to trade our blankets for Arctic sleeping bags.

Old Guys: "Don't zip them up; sleeping bags are death traps if zippers freeze." They should know.

I kept my two blankets; just in case.

Old Guys: "If Korea gets real cold, and it promises to do just that, we'll go into 5s and 3s: T-shirt, woolen undershirts, wool sweater, O D shirt and field jacket; that's the five. The three consists of long johns, O D trousers and field pants. That ought to hold the wind."

We'll see.

October 12-13. Driven just east of the North Korean capital city of Pyongyang. Some Eighth Army unit took it. To stay overnight here before we go north again tomorrow.

Bummed a ride with Recon/Intel guys and drove around Pyongyang. Looks better than Seoul, but it doesn't look as if it were an attractive city when intact. Saw two North Korean refugees; we stopped them and they bowed and got on their knees. Walters, the driver, covered them, and I motioned for them to get up. Gave them a cigarette each, and then they motioned for us to follow them. With this, Walters and the other two Intel/Recon guys brought out their side arms and cocked them as the refugees led the way.

There, behind a pile of rubble were three GIs hacked to death and one O dead, burned with gasoline. Walters raised HQ on the radio, and directed the Graves Registration people to come to where we were. Jesus!

Back with unit and spoke to Dumas about dead GIs; he wasn't surprised and told me to forget it; you'll see worse, he said.

I don't see how.

After late chow, foot inspection. Old Guys stressing foot hygiene. With winter coming, this is most important. Os are responsible for foot care. Chewed out by Bn and Regt (and goodbye promotions) if they lose troops due to poor foot hygiene.

October 14. First Cav is south of us. We crossed the River Chongchong; it's to North Korea what the Naktong is to South Korea.

Big rumor: The Chinese are in the war. Told that First Cav was hit by Chinese not NK. An ambush plus a skirmish, but no mention of casualties on either side. Dumas grunted when he heard *Chinese*. Not surprised, I guess. We're bound to know soon. Runners, line crossers and agents are our best sources for this.

As for us, we're heading northwest to the River Yalu which divides North Korea from Manchuria. Os tell us that both Korea and Manchuria were under Jap domination for years. Korea was called Chosun or Chosen by the Js and Manchukuo was their name for Manchuria. Since the Koreans call their country Han-guk, who named it Korea?

Lt Waller said he didn't know; Old Guys say Korea is also a Korean name, maybe it's a classical name. One thing is sure: the Old Guys all agree that Koreans don't like the Japs one damned bit.

We asked the Old Guys about the Chinks reported to be in Korea. They said that since China is now communist, the Chinese may be here as volunteers.

Joey then said, "Volunteers just like us, right, Sarge?" Everybody laughed, and Hat then said Joey was close to the mark.

We sure don't have much to do now. Once in a while we'll stop, work the guns, but for the most part, going North is a free ride. NK sends no patrols, no probes. They're not, as the Army calls it, "engaging us."

October 21. Runners: this is not a rumor, guys. It's Chinks, all right.

This one runner, Richard Henderson from Lima, Ohio, says he saw them.

Not the mustard-colored NKs, but green to gray Chinese uniforms. Said so to Bn HQ which passed word on. Henderson said probes by Chinese are not in force, but as for being there, you can start placing bets.

Inventory: Nine pairs of socks; one pair long johns; gloves, two pair; one pair mittens; woolen sweater; two OD shirts; one pair OD pants; two field uniforms; the scarf; and a field jacket. The T-shirts I bought at the PX back in the Kwansai Dist are 100% cotton and warm. Boots in great shape. Down to one M-1 and one carbine; issued the carbine and picked up the M-1 back at the Pusan Perimeter two months back. Ordnance gave it a going over and returned it in good working order. Heaved barracks bag back into truck and took out knap sack: books and shaving stuff, etc.

Our CO, Capt Chandler, is an arty specialist and served as a top instructor at Sill. Joined us recently. Billy Waller says the Capt served with another 105 howitzer unit in the Perimeter; we're lucky to have him, acc to Lt Waller.

Lt Brodkey. From Philadelphia; that's Ellie Cohen's hometown. Educated at Cincinnati U. Hell of a Forward Observer. Gutsy job being an FO. Told Joey, Charlie and me he was Jewish; we told him there were two Jewish families in Klail when we were growing up: the Goldens and the Perlmutters, who later moved to California. He says there are many Jews in Phila (He calls it Philly.) Says Cincy is a big Catholic town.

He's a curious guy. Asked if we spoke Spanish and we said, "Sure, Lt. All the time."

Said our English was very good, and we told him we were Americans, just like him. We call ourselves Mexicans, we said, and our fellow Texans call us that too. Wanted to know if that bothered us. At this, Charlie said it depended on *how* it was said. Talked like this for over an hour after late chow. Big smoker, Brodkey. Probably that job he has.

Guards posted at 1500 hours. Gets very dark very early. We're higher than some parts of Canada acc to Hat.

Slept next to the guns and was on guard duty two hours on and four hours off. I think we'll continue moving north or northwest tomorrow. At inspection today were told to put all warm clothing on top part of barracks bag.

We've been waiting here for a day and a half for gasoline, rations, ammo, etc. It's the supply lines according to our Os; they're too long.

Oct 24. After supplies came in, we pulled out at 0845 and rode NW toward some river. Stopped frequently, got off the trucks, told to stay alert, etc. Back on trucks. Did this all the way toward river.

Heard many patrol skirmishes along the way. Because of the hills (hundreds of them), there's poor communication between many parts of the Eighth Army. Every unit is isolated in its own zone.

Old Guys say zones for advance and retreat are designed and assigned for each unit. That way, says Hat, every division or corps stays in its own zone for better organization. Says, though, that with hills, zoning becomes difficult because hills make for poor communication.

Frazier, in the truck, said, "All armies work that way; it's the best method for moving big numbers of people where and when you want them; Chinks, NK, us, all armies do this."

Still, he said, with poor communication between outfits, as in our case due to hills, it's easy to disrupt the flow of personnel.

So, it looks like we're in a mess, but there is order to it. It's when ranks break and lines fold that confusion hits in a hurry; but Os and Old Guys know how the Army works in situations. I don't bother the Old Guys, but I like to know what's going on, how they do things.

Still, it's not my kind of life.

Lt Brodkey came by, and we talked about pre-selected sites and registering targets on the ridges and bridges, the hills, etc. All of a sudden he asked if we faced discrimination in Texas.

Oh, hell yes, we said. But that's something we can't let ruin our lives. He said he too was discriminated against because he is Jewish. I said that in Texas, in the Rio Grande Valley where we come from, he'd be what we call an Anglo. The Lt laughed and said there'd be some Texans who would look at him as a Jew anyway. And so on, etc.

Told him that we'd gone to Mass at the big Rom Cath cathedral in NW Tokyo once and saw some people sitting in two marked-off sections; to the right, the Epistle side, as one looks to the altar. That, at end of the Mass, a fiftyish-looking Jap Catholic talked to us. When we asked about the people in the boxed-in benches, he said they were Korean Caths, and that they couldn't and didn't sit with the rest of the faithful.

Brodkey was surprised until Charlie said, "Hell, Lt, I don't even know where the Klail Anglos go to Mass or if they even have a church."

After this, Joey said the Anglos's church was St. Anne's and that the new Anglos went to Mass there. And that the old Anglos belonged to Our Lady of Mercy parish, the Mexican church.

All this talk of discrimination reminded me of both Frankie Maguire and Davey Doyle and their crap about telling Bernard Pavlovsky and me "to speak English, goddammit."

Joey then said Stang and Skinner were like that at first, but that Charlie told them where to get off, just like he did first to Maguire and then to Doyle.

Brodkey then asked if Pavlovsky was Jewish, and I said that Bernie was Polish and Catholic and that he may now be dead or missing, or, God help him, an NK POW. We went on like this until the Lt went to see some Signal Corps guys about wire and phone supplies.

Right after chow, Stang came up and said he heard us talking and said he knew all about Jews "because there were some in his hometown" in Pennsylvania. I still don't like Stang, but since we're on the same gun crew, I don't stop to argue or to educate him.

From this to a makeshift latrine and Joey, Charlie and Stang and I drank a beer there before going back to the area.

Prepared to hit the sack. Brrrrrrrrrrrrrrr cold. That sun goes down and the temperature goes down with it. If it snows, it snows, and nothing we can do about it. Roads still in good shape, and we're moving right along. We move out again tomorrow morning and have a spot assigned for travel in our zone.

October 25. Well, it's Chinese, all right. Our Inf guards caught three of them. Young guys like us and sent to Intelligence down in Pyongyang. The war's over for those guys. (Runners and South Koreans were right: many Chinese are here; a matter of time before they join right in.)

Morale and discipline. Talked to guys in other convoys during breaks. These guys will be the first to die. Some of them are throwing their steel pots away, just like that. (On one detail, Hat and I and the other gunners picked up eighteen helmets and gathered them in a weapons carrier.)

October 26. Reports of more Chinese in area but no engagement with them. They pull back, and we keep moving north. Os tell us to be on our toes. Much horsing around by some of the guys at chow line. They're dreaming about "home" in Japan. Our Old Guys tell us to forget that. "You want to stay alive, you stay on the job."

Spotted four guys at chow line I'd seen once before at the Perimeter. Arty guys too, but untrustworthy. Hook Frazier told me that when our hill was overrun (I can't remember where that was exactly), the guys from that outfit didn't pick up their carbines to fire. They stayed inside their trucks. Hook said NK could've fired a clip at the truck and hit any number of them. Just lucky there were no NK on the road at the time.

As Hook said, "What the hell do they think the Army issued carbines to them for anyway?"

Frazier pretty matter of fact: These guys won't survive. "Trouble is," he said, "they may take some of us with them."

After chow, Charlie brought me two packs of Camels, and we smoked away from the road and the knoll we're on. Got to take precautions, and it's good practice anyway.

Charlie got a note from his sisters; his father is doing well, they all send their regards, etc. Charlie's mom died about the time mine did. Dengue fever complications is what they told us. Joey is the only one of us whose parents are alive (like Charlie, he too has a sister named Adela).

The Old Guys ordered us to unhitch the guns, set them up, and then we re-hitched them to the trucks etc. Worked at this for two hours, changing crews, mixing the guns, etc. We were a bit rusty, and needed the practice.

Good exercise too. It's cold and getting colder. Will hit the sack after I eat some peaches (it's now 2000 hours) and will add one note here: Sporadic small arms fire to left and up ahead earlier today, around 1500. No NK to be seen, so the firing must be between our patrols and the nonexistent Chinese volunteers.

October 26. Three more Chinese walked in, arms raised, unarmed, and surrendered. Eighth Army insists Chinese not here in force; well, "in force" or not, these guys are here, and I believe what my eyes see.

The Chinese POWs sneaked in and surrendered to Lt Brodkey in the forward ob sites and some in the Inf guard were sent to bring them to our area. Puffy-looking pants and jackets. No helmets, just some warm-looking caps with ear flaps. So, in they walked and stood there until a jeep drove up carrying a Gen, and a Capt (Staff) walked right behind him. Photogs then snapped pix of the POWs, arms raised, and with the Gen "talking" to them. All of this staged for the newspapers and "the folks back home."

Well, if this is so, then how will the Gen explain to "the folks" that these guys are Chinese and not NK?

(We've got reporters in the back area and some come up to where we are once in a while; mostly they hang around with the HQ Os.) They, the reporters, think they'll be home for Christmas. Old Guys told us to take bets we won't.

The young Chinese were whisked to HQ interrogation. Our area a-buzz for a while. Guards were increased, and jeeps and men sent out to roads and hillsides. Capt Chandler got the Os and the Old Guys together and then they gave us the poop: The Chinese are in the war, even if no one has notified Eighth Army.

October 27. Skirmishes the past two days. They're Chinese all right, all right. Our Inf probes as does theirs. Cold, cold days and nights.

Hat: "If we're cold, the Chinese are cold, too."

We didn't fire yesterday or today; stood by guns; watched Engineers dig into cold ground. Tough job.

October 28. Much firing by us at some hills where Chinese, or NK, spotted by low-flying light planes. We still have trouble maintaining contact with other Eighth Army units; it's these hills. At noon today I hitched a ride in a truck and was driven to see the Yellow Sea. The winds were blowing hard all the way. Radios and other equipment packed in the back and delivered to unit operating in that sector, most probably a Signal Corps unit, since they work on SCR-300s and 608s or 680s(?) which I'm not familiar with. Driven back with Frazier in a jeep; now *that* was cold. The driver was a Texas Mexican: Ray Zúñiga from Sanderson out in West Texas.

Saw nothing but hills all along the way. Frazier said it was a hell of a place to fight; no mines on road, though, and this, said Hook, 1) is due to speed with which we advanced or 2) the Chinese are planning to use these same roads when they try to get us the hell out of here.

Back to base camp and saw Inf patrol bringing in two more Chinese

POWs.

October 29. The Chinese may not be here in force, but they're here. South Korean agents reported to G-2 and then Intel/Recon guys gave poop to Capt Chandler. Be careful. Chinese are there even if we don't see them. The NK is there too, resting after frightful beating, but there nonetheless. South Korean agents have got the worst job in this man's army. But the Old Guys say they'll turn on you, so don't trust them. Line crossers is what they are and they bring info to us, but probably bring info to the Chinese too. Probably so.

Much colder now.

October 30. Woke up next to guns. Sheet of ice all over blankets; gun tubes look like big olive-green popsicles. Battery assembled before early chow. We marched in close order drill for ten minutes to get the kinks out. We also ran in place and all of us were ready for the latrine after exercise.

Coffee tasted good. When Army coffee begins to taste good, so says one of the cooks, Johnny Tirpak (Clifton, New Jersey), that's a dangerous sign; it means you'll wind up liking the Army. Tirpak is good friends with another cook, Teddy Koy from Montclair, also in New Jersey. The third guy from Jersey is Martin Flaherty, called Matt. They're young guys for cooks, I think. They all love to fire the guns, and once in a while we let them load and fire.

Tirpak, at the chowline, when we have hot chow, will wear his football jacket that reads Clifton Eagles. Looks weird out here in North Korea, but so far no one has said a word to him. Cooks are something like Army medics, independent as hell. He and Crazy Bromley should meet each other; they'd make a good pair.

Read half of *Good Night, Sweet Prince*. Passed it on to Lt Brodkey.

After late chow, Hatalski and Dumas told us to be ready to give either support or direct fire at any time from here on out.

"On your toes" is the word.

Just before turning in, Bromley told me there was a short fight between Stang and Ichabod. They went at it as they were returning from the chow line. Turns out Stang was riding Ichabod pretty hard about his masturbation; without a word (Bromley here) Ichabod swung his mess kit and whacked Skinner in the groin. Stang will probably lose his two stripes; Ichabod Crane has none to lose. Brom says Stang misread his partner; Henry Farmer looks spooky, but he's no chicken.

Asked Bromley what *he* thought about the Chinese being on the scene etc. Said it didn't mean a thing, since we'll all be stuck in Korea for the next twenty years.

Crazy shit.

Sun going down at 1545 hours.

October 31. Supply lines very long now; we had to stop and regroup, consolidate, etc. so that Eighth Army can be grouped closely for better communication. Eighth Army is in force here in Western North Korea.

Don't know what the following means, but we're assigned and attached to the 2nd Division. Many changes in division, they say. Heard that Lt Macías was promoted to Capt and transferred to a Weapons Platoon as CO. Asked runner about him, since I've not met or seen him. Runner didn't know him.

The 2nd Div now has its own Divarty, so we're here to help out wherever; our two batteries are the oldest in Korea in point of service; we've been in this since July 5 with Task Force Smith. From here that seems like a long, long time ago.

Nearing the Yalu
November 1-14, 1950

November 1. It's official; the Chinese (and they are now called CCF for Chinese Communist Forces) are here, and they ambushed some First Cav units yesterday afternoon.

No idea of casualties, and we don't know if CCF is here in force, but they're here to help out the NKPA.

Communication remains poor. It's the hills. It doesn't matter how high we raise the antennas, the SCR 300 can't do the job. So, our Inf guards have been doubled and our guns are ready, although we've not had to use them for anything lately. Very cold. Darkens early every day.

November 2. Firing is back in style, but Chinese forces do not stop to fight. They run in and out of the hills and side roads; they go up and down ridges, and it's now you see them, now you don't. Our patrols walk into ambushes and lose one or two guys. Then, our patrols set ambushes and kill or capture some of theirs, and so it goes.

The Chinese disappear into the mist, as Joey says. We're up here on this hill with our 105s still at the ready and we hear occasional, sporadic small arms fire, mostly to the east and west.

Went to latrine and smoked a cigarette. On the way back, I pulled out the wool pullover from my barracks bag. I'm now wearing a T-shirt, the pullover, an OD wool shirt and fatigue jacket plus the field jacket. It's that cold here. OD pants and field pants still warm enough, though. Gloves are a big help. This morning I cut up an army blanket and made an extra scarf each for eight of us. This is for future use and just in case it gets colder.

A medical orderly came by and said the temperature was sitting at 20 degrees F.

Noon. Was told that some ROK units dashed up to the Manchurian border and filled a water bottle from the River Yalu for their President. No movement in our sector. This is a waiting game.

Old Guys tells us to be ready for anything now.

Sgt Dumas also told us that Lt Waller's heavy cold turned into pneumonia and he was sent back. (To Pyongyang, the North K capital; this is where

Chinese and NK POWs are also sent for interrogation.) Lt Vitetoe is to replace Bily Waller as Exec for a while.

Lt Brodkey. A hell of a good Forward Observer. Doesn't rattle, and this helps us not to get nervous. He and Brom and Ichabod are out there with the two new Forward Ob Lts. With Lt Brodkey, it's business as usual: calm, accurate, etc.

"Show 'em your best, B Battery," is what Lt Brodkey said. The two new Lts wanted to check us out, and we showed them our stuff. It was a good drill for us and got the blood flowing. (Old Guys say the shit is ready; all that's needed is for someone to dump it in the fan.)

We've been ordered to hitch up the guns and move out. Must stop here.

An hour's ride. Roads were okay and hard. A continual series of esses. You can't see ahead of you. Crossed the Chongchong River and much of it is frozen already. The Chongchong winds so that it looked like we were doubling back or retreating all the time.

Got to new base camp and the Engineers were there waiting for us as usual. Some of our new guys are bitching and whining. The usual malingering drones, but nothing they can do about it; they're here, and they'll stay here.

Many 2nd Div guys are new; they have no idea how many dead or wounded in Korea since Task Force Smith days. As Frazier says, "They'll learn."

Base Camp all set up, given hot chow and extra blankets.

November 3-4. Dawn of the 4th. Early yesterday morning we moved on again; this time, to a series of hills overlooking the River Chongchong (which is now behind us again). We set the guns in place. During ride here, trucks maintained convoy speed and drove with blinders on in the dark. The wind cut through now and then above the steady hum of jeeps and prime movers alike. This wind will cut your soul. It's a tough place and time for a fight.

Put to work right away. Don't need light to set up guns. Our outfit can do this blindfolded, and our hope is that the new guys can learn the job. We checked the blocks and sights and practiced wheeling the guns around in the dark. Good to stir about a bit. Ate a can of peaches and was smoking a cigarette when Old Guys and Lt Vitetoe assembled our battery to give us the word.

S Korean agents report: CCF is massing in force. But Eighth Army HQ says it's just a show of strength by CCF. A psychological ploy so we won't go farther north. The Lt then said, "To hell with that, you men stay alert for anything."

November 5-6-7. Stood by guns, cleaned them, ate, went to latrine, smoked, read, stood at the ready, got in some sleep, trained the new guys, etc.

November 8. Yesterday, sometime, a large CCF unit ambushed the 3rd Bn (8th Regiment, First Cav Division) on patrol. CCF had set up a strong roadblock and waited for patrolling Bn to walk back to Base Camp. Hand-to-hand fighting followed. Bn suffered big losses. All of this from three messenger runners and one S Korean agent line crosser. CCF hit and ran.

Big ROK losses too. The Bn may been the unit that passed through our lines on Nov 5th or 6th.

Sister Regiment of the 8th Cav Regt, the 5th, was also attacked while holding bridgehead on Chongchong. The 5th held, and we were placed on alert and ready to move south of the River.

The 24th Division (that unlucky bunch) was north of the Chongchong but was then marched south. With the First Cav holding the bridgehead, the 24th crossed with no difficulty.

Told of another ambush. Said to have lost 600 men; that's a high figure but said to be confirmed; not a rumor. It's still a high figure for me. (That's more than a battalion, I think). So, it was a big ambush and then? CCF disengaged and left as fast as they had come in.

Of 600, not all killed; some wounded, others wandered off, prob froze to death. (I don't know, but a task force is usually made up of a big number like that. Still, six-hundred is what everyone says around here). Old Guys say to wait for "The Word."

Many of those guys have also been declared missing. This too from runners and S Korean agents operating in the field.

So? Part of Lt Vitetoe's words regarding CCF presence included a quote from Gen Walker: "We should not expect the Chinese Communists to be committed in force. After all, a lot of Mexicans live in Texas."

I don't know if I will live through this, but one thing I do know: God's not bringing those 600 from First Cav back to life, no matter what the Gen says. As for us, we're still Texas Mexicans, 8000 mi from home.

Noon. Three NK POWs brought in. Every time I see NK POWs I wonder if they're the ones who tie up GIs and shoot them.

Must stop here. As soon as the 24th Div finished passing through, and the road was clear of their units, we were ordered to go north again. Guns hitched, and the Battle Police handled our convoy's route. Crossed the meandering Chongchong one more time.

November 9. "Colder'n shit, colder'n shit." This is Skinner's refrain. These are Siberian winds up here and everything freezes. Follicles on my nose, for one. Now using my cut-up Army blanket as a scarf to cover my neck and using my GI scarf to block nose and mouth. Get sick up here, and you stay here.

On the move again. Guns hitched to prime movers, and we headed NW somewhat. Some Eighth Army elements went NE. If hills sold for a penny, we'd all be millionaires.

Got to Base Camp. Engineers already there again, and selected firing spot for us. To latrine and a cigarette. Spotted two liaison planes. With all the hills and gullies running into each other, no idea what they see from up there. Our patrols down here see a lot; patrolling stepped up and aggressive. Going up and down frozen hills, patrols are reporting CCF all over the place. Eighth Army HQ intelligence says otherwise.

Hear all kinds of rumors at chow line. We're pulling back; no, we're not. Few CCF out there; no, they're in force. And so on. Well, someone is screwed up. Either the Chinese are here in force or they're not. If you've got reliable patrols, you better believe them. Hills are so plentiful, patrols must go on foot, no other way; no jeeps, etc. Returning patrols say you can hide 100,000 Chinks up here and still not see them.

We're just holding here. Alert and ready, etc. Most of Eighth Army is consolidating (along River Chongchong). The 24th Div, which passed through area going south, is on reserve for us. The First Cav is just east of us and gathering supplies.

Lt Vitetoe said our supply trains are getting too long and strung along too many miles and, as he says, "Hence our need for consolidation."

November 10. This routine is getting old: cold, guns being set up, checked, barrels seen to, Inf patrols going out, and everything and everyone in readiness. The more we stay, the better the supply situation gets for us; but the more we wait, the worse it also gets: dull, dreary, gray days, and that wind that'll cut you in half.

Went to my kit bag at 1000 hrs for some reading. First time I've had the hours to spare. No idea what books I picked up from Special Services. Reached in and started on the first GI paperback I pulled out.

1340 hrs. Read parts of a novel called *The Loved One* by a woman I've not heard or read before. A strange piece of writing and prob beyond me. No idea that many English actors living in Hollywood.

Getting dark already, 1450 hrs. Hot water barrel on, and I dipped two cans of C-rations for late chow. Can of hamburger patties and a can of lima beans and ham. Ugh. Prior to Army, I'd not eaten one lima bean. Nor much ham either.

North Korea is an icebox.

November 11. Armistice Day but no celebration, and who the hell would even think of one? Lt Vitetoe told me that E Waugh is English and a man. One of England's better writers. Rattled off some five to six titles. Went on to say that *Loved One* is a parody of some type; a satire, etc. To look at it that way. Told him I'd give it another try.

Earlier today, Hat, Frazier and Dumas got our battery up at 0530. Hot coffee. Hot water barrel on and hung some wired C-ration cans in barrel. Breakfast. Traded Stang some Grandmother Cookies for pound cake.

After morning chow, went through two-and-a-half hours of work (registering hills, contacting forward observers, etc). Bushed and hungry, sat down to eat my cake at 0900. Could have eaten the can itself. Os always eat after we do. They too eat C-rations, but they eat standing up: pull down tail gate of prime movers and have their Cs served on metal plates and with individual spoons, forks, etc.

Capt Chandler usually walks around area. Stops, asks questions, talks to you. No B S and all business. How do you find firing now v last summer? What are the differences? Who decides on what to do on any given day (load, aim, fire)? A quiet guy. None of our Old Guys knew him in WWII. May have fought in Pacific; he's no regular, no 1930s O. Guess he's Dumas's age: late 30s. But asks the right questions, so he knows his stuff.

Still cold. Early morning exercise was good to get the kinks out. Been quiet for 2-3 days. No small arms fire; nothing.

Patrol brought in two more NK POWs in their mustard yellow uniforms. To be sent to Pyongyang for questions, is my guess.

I remember the mortars raining down on us south of Pyongyang. Good thing NK didn't have much artillery when we met them on the way north. What little I saw was enough for me; reminded me of our own battery; crackerjacks, like Hat calls us.

Charlie came by to collect mail for home; told him I had none. Said truck would leave for Pyongyang in two hours. Must stop here to write Israel and Aunt Mati.

November 12-13. Old Guys not letting us get rusty. Hat took me aside and put me with one of the new batteries. They've got a ways to go. They're not interested in practicing. Much whining. Lt Vitetoe is no screw-up; knows he's got some crapheads and training is the only way to wise them up.

Worked with them from 0700 until 0930. Told them of Battle Police (they'd not heard of it). Told them Battle Pol a tough job but effective and necessary: conduct traffic and pick up stragglers who run away from their guns, etc. Prob thought I was lying or making up stories. They'll learn.

They talk big, too. To them, North K and Chinese will be no trouble.

Live and learn, I say. Relieved by Butch Stang and told him guys needed much work.

Lt Brodkey did one hell of a job on pre-selected targets for us. Crazy and Ichabod are good workers, but I still think that being a forward observer 1) makes you a bit screwy or 2) you're already that way and the job fits you.

Engineers came by. That's another tough job (they fight, too). Talked and traded rumors while we worked around them. An Old Guy with the Engrs was at the River Naktong, and I told him our unit saw the big bridge full of people get blown up. He called it The Refugee Bridge. Told me not to dwell on it; those things happen. That's easier said, I told him.

"Look, Corporal, it's not the first bridge. The Union Army did it in the Civil War. Bound to be other examples." (Didn't get Sgt's name.)

Hot chow. Going to latrine is a job and a half. One thing about freezing weather, though, it sure cuts down on flies.

Os and Old Guys inspecting mess kits and hot water; diarrhea is always a danger.

Checked canteen. Half of it is ice and so went to thaw it. Smoked a Camel and one of the whiners on latrine duty showed me a cigarette lighter made in Japan. Looks like a pack of Winstons but same size as a Zippo lighter. He says you can get them in Marlboros and Salems, etc.

The Japanese make them out of beer cans is what Frazier says.

This reminded me of Kazuo Fujiwara, the Jap SW Pacific vet now living in Nara.

Here we are, I told Frazier, five yrs after WWII and this Jap vet is still wearing a khaki uniform. In winter, too. Hook wanted to know what got me off on this and told him Kazuo had a metal leg from his knee down and that the false leg looked like it'd been made out of beer cans.

Told Hook that Kazuo had fought in New Guinea but lost the leg in a swimming accident: a shark bit off a big chunk. Told Frazier that after recovery and out of hospital, a Jap Army Lt gave him fifty whacks with a cane.

"That was a tough army," is what Frazier said. From this we went on to his service in China in the 30s. Talked a bit of his life in Tienstin and Tsingtao and Shanghai where he served with Dumas.

Snow. Started at 1200. Not hard, but wind causes drifts to collect against guns and shell crates, etc.

Medical orderlies came by: checked throats for soreness. I know one of them, a guy named Hill (Robert D., from Grand Rapids, Michigan). Not an Old Guy but older than Joey, Charlie, me, etc.

Features remind me of a payroll clerk back in Japan. A guy from Providence, R.I. Same pinched mouth, doesn't look like he has a tooth in his head. Robt Hill has seen action, though. He too was with us in the Pusan Perimeter and says that one time, some South K refugees spotted his Red Cross armband and ambushed him for medicine, gauze, etc. Asked what he did, and he said: "Jesus! What could I do? I stayed there and tended to them a while." (My throat's okay, acc to Robt. D. Hill.)

Started to read *Loved One* again. Best to go chapter by chapter. Although I do see the humor now.

November 14. Small arms fire early this morning. East and west of us. (Patrols most likely.) No news though. Joey and I went to latrine. Told me Hat put him to work with new battery. Looks like Hat is putting everybody to work with those guys. Trouble, is what Joey called them. Asked if I wrote home a few days ago and said yes.

Well! At 1330 two jeeps pulled up. Field grade Os plus a Bird Col and a Brig Gen. The Battery fell to, and my name was called out: a Purple Heart. (For the small pieces of High Explosive wire I caught during Task Force Smith days last July.) What a trade: I get a Purple Heart for that piece of shit, and a family at home gets the medal for someone who's not coming back.

Hat told me not to worry about the Heart. Keep it, put it in your barracks bag and forget it. Did just that.

Gen and Os ate with battery. We worked some 30 mins for them while they watched and talked. They then went to Capt Chandler's tent for a while and left at 1430. Delivering medals and inspecting the troops, is my guess.

After work, and to celebrate the Heart, Hat brought two cans of beer and I opened them with my GI can opener; a handy little item. Beer freezing but not fully frozen. I know one thing: I have no cavities; that Pabst beer was cold.

With time on our hands, I checked my stuff: uniforms, shoes, socks, gloves, etc. Following Old Guys' advice about winter wear. They fought in France and Belgium, and into Aachen, Germany and all agree it was cold there and hard going. Korea may be worse, but cold is cold and a careless army is a dead army, etc.

Our battery: we've been together so long we can work the guns with one hand tied, says Skinner. So, the new new guys were sat down and we went through practice fire for them for thirty minutes. I don't think it sunk in.

Apart from five Os and 20 EM we lost in Osan/Suwon fight, no losses except for Lt Edwards, who was wounded later, and now Lt Waller and his pneumonia. (Billy Waller never told us much about Lt Edwards's throat wound; prob didn't know much more than we did.) So, all of us know each other and work well. Old Guys say this is important and that's why we must keep after new guys in unit.

Stood by guns until 1700; tired and hungry, ate, worked on journal, and will lay out unzipped sleeping bag, two blankets, and will sack out. Time: 2100.

The Free Ride North

November 17-18, 1950. On the move again; we were driven straight north to a recently vacated area. On the way to this place, we crossed the River Chongchong at least twice; this spot had first been occupied by another Eighth Army unit which is a day and a half ahead of us. No idea where the Chongchong lies from here; we left a main road, and we are now into some hills.

We set up the guns smartly; it's been some time since we've seen any NK. The rumors again are that the Chinese may enter the war.

We unhitched the guns from the prime movers, stacked and counted the shell crates, made sure we'd been sent no 155s by mistake, and after this, an eight-man armed guard escorted Lt Brodkey, Crazy, Ichabod and the rest of their crew to some Forward Observer sites; most likely Engineers probed holes for mines before anyone settled into them.

Lt Brodkey is a fine officer; he knows what to do. He's been with us since Task Force Smith, and all the gunners say he's one gutsy guy.

The Signal Corps guys were right there, trailing along.

After the loss of Lts Bricketto and John (who weren't with us very long), Lt Brodkey was assigned two new Forward Obs Os. They haven't shown up yet.

We checked the field phones: okay. The SCR-300 radio is a strange, unreliable animal. The cold and the wet make it go haywire, and this gets hairy in a hurry, since we live and die by communication.

Read some more Thurber. Couldn't stop laughing. Lt Vitetoe came up and asked what I was reading. (Some of my laughter a result of nerves, but he is a fine writer.) I'd read some Thurber pieces for monologue competition in high school; this, though, is an entire book by him.

Joey and Charlie came by. The Engineers finished their job on the gun emplacements, and we have to check their work. (Stopped at 1450 and it was already getting dark.) More light snow and that *wind.*

After we worked on the guns and policed the area, I talked with Joey and Charlie and Hook Frazier. What does an Army do, we asked? For instance, we've been moving north some time, no firing by us, and it gets dull and deadly unless we're put to work; it's mostly eat and drink, and then some more work for practice.

Frazier said that was about it, action and inaction.

Charlie said that for him the Army was "mostly fighting and being scared." That, he said, is what the Army is.

The three of us then looked at my map. Joey and Charlie traced copies of their own, and we're pretty sure of where we are. The Pusan Perimeter is a long, long way from here.

Korea is not a big country, though. The old boundary line, the 38th Parallel, for instance, is about 150 mi wide, and that's it, but it may be narrower at other spots.

Frazier reminded us that the train ride out of Pusan to Taejon on our way to Osan/Suwon seemed long, but only because we didn't know where we were going. Osan is south of Seoul, and it is a long way, but this is by Korean standards. So, Frazier said, once we retreated east across the Kum and the Naktong, and the Perimeter was encircled, we were in a very small place.

Charlie then tried to remember some of the GIs killed during Task Force Smith. He asked me to check the journal, which I did, but I could find no names for those guys except for John Standing Bear and Will Prothro who'd been with us in the Kwansai District.

That, said Joey, is what the Army is.

Task Force Smith was something. We could have all been killed except for Col Smith's leadership. Killed, and in no uncertain terms.

We'd been issued only six shells of HEAT and, although we had enough High Explosives for the NK Inf after that, it was those tanks! Jesus. We talked about being scared and remembered the panic of some of the Inf and of some of the arty guys, too.

Frazier then checked the guns and asked which group had the duty for the night. He lit a cigarette and said, "Save your matches; use this one to light yours. With this cold, you better hang on to your matches for later." He listened to our talk for a while, but this must be old stuff for him.

Speaking of guys in panic, Hook Frazier then said, "Running away is not the Army. It's human nature."

We then talked about weather extremes: hot and cold. Talked about refugees too and how NK killed so many of them. This took us to the murder of GIs and ROKs by NK, and from this we went to the Chinese helping the NKPA.

None of us, somehow, as if by agreement or understanding, mentioned home or the idea of going home for Christmas.

Talked about the good times in Japan. Talked about Sonny Ruiz, who had been in Lt Merritt's battery, which didn't get picked to come with T F Smith. (Joey said Col Smith's name was Charles, but that Col Drake called him Brad. The Brad may be for Bradley or Bradford, since the Col's name is Chas B.) We then talked about Col Drake and his leg wound. Prob back on the line by now. A good officer, and a brave one too. He and the guys damaged two tanks, and him wounded and bleeding.

The talk went back to Sonny Ruiz. He may have been in the Perimeter defense too. We told Frazier about Sonny's mom being a bit crazy since Chano, the oldest son, was killed in France on D Day. She speaks no English and my Aunt Mati or my brothers usually help her out with papers to be signed, notarized, etc.

Joey then said that Chano served with the Second Div in France. Joey also said that Chano and Sonny were full brothers, but that Chano used his father's name, Ortega, and that Sonny used Ruiz, his mom's name. Frazier asked if this were a common practice, and Charlie said he knew of a good number who did that. I mentioned Freddie Silva, who was in Quartermaster back in Japan. I said Silva was his mother's name and that his sisters used Olvera, their dad's name.

That got us to talking about home a while as we walked to chow. I skipped it, though, and drank a beer from Joey's stash instead. I then went off to tell Skinner about the duty roster for tonight. After this I went to see Sgt Dumas.

Dumas said that Hat and Hook were wounded on D Day, met at a field hospital and were back in the fight by early July. Later, Hat won a Silver Star and Hook won his Bronze for valor. Told Dumas I'd not seen either one wear their ribbons in their Class A uniforms. Only at parades, Dumas said. Guess Dumas has some medals too.

Told me of Jap Gov changing laws on prostitution. Women could be sold, but by 1940, only relatives could sell them. Then, Gen MacA abolished selling altogether in 1946. Dumas also said that he and Hook had lived most of their lives outside the US. The Army is home for them. Frazier did marry, he said (the Puerto Rican Hook told me about); Dumas is a lifelong bachelor.

He's a man in his forties, although I first thought he was Waller's age, early thirties. Black hair, heavy five-o'clock shadow. Knows mortars, machine guns and artillery. He and Hat were in Tienstien, China, in the 1930s. They were kids then, he said.

The Chinese are a strange people, he said, and while there, he and Hat picked up many phrases to get the work done. After the war in Europe, he and Hat were back in China from '46 through '49. He talked about the whorehouses and how different they were from the Japanese ones. That there was much rioting in China in '46 and '47 when the Communists were taking over the country. From China, they were sent to the Kwansai District, where they formed the cadre that trained us.

China was dangerous, he said again. After WWII, everyone wore side-arms: US navy seamen, young kids like that, wearing dungarees, white T-shirts and a big 45 on the hip. Crazy, is what Dumas said. Saw one act of murder there. Some Army Company Clerk was typing away when a Chink lobbed a grenade in the orderly room, and that was it for the pencil pusher. The Chinese Army under Chiang then came in to investigate the incident and what they did was to line up the ten Chinese GIs who were guarding the area, make them kneel down, and then whacked each one with a 45 slug.

Dumas started his army service with the old horse cavalry at Fort Riley. I told him of Fort Jones in the Valley and said he'd heard of it. Served in Texas, but up in El Paso, Fort Bliss. Told him El Paso was some 800 mi up river from the Valley.

"Yeah, it's a big state, all right," is what he said. Dumas then said the Army was a good life and that fighting (combat) was just part of it, but, he said again, that's what armies are for.

He then walked to his kit bag, drew out a bottle of liquor and offered me a drink. I stuck to beer and, after my second, I hit the sack and was working on the journal, when Skinner came up and said Stang and I were to relieve him and his crew at 0500.

November 19. Early reveille: 0430. Chowed down and relieved Skinner. He stayed around for a smoke and said an Inf unit marched through our area around 0230. Went up and down a hill and may still be there, for all he knows.

Guns. Guns behave differently in the cold. Once they're warmed, they operate okay. But, the chief danger of firing in cold weather is that we can get sloppy. It's always dangerous near guns anyway, but the cold adds to one's fatigue and leads to mistakes. I discovered that the wax I use will not crack in the cold; the body heat must keep it pliable, is my guess.

The Engineers came back. We continued working with the guns and with some new guys. Skinner brought coffee for all of us. The Engineers said there was much movement by First Cav; part of it is still to our right, but we can't see them because of the hills which separate us. According to the Engrs, another part of the First Cav is holding the bridgehead, and our main force here has now completed consolidation.

Asked an Engr Old Guy if he'd heard anything about our situation up here, and got a shocker: he sees five to ten Chinese POWs a day. His conclusion: either we attack or the CCF will and then be on top of us. (Dumas once said that if there is one thing armies don't do, it's to stand still for long periods of time.)

I figure the Chinese are just as cold as we are. Their fitness depends on their Os and on the ability to carry out orders, much like us.

Not hungry again. Two days now. This is a bad sign. So, I went to Joey and hit him for two cans of fruit cocktail and ate that. I prefer peaches to pears and pears to cocktail. Pound cake is still my favorite, but not for every day.

Relieved at 1400, but not sleepy and did not hit the sack. Stuck around the guns and got busy with the firing charts and reading arty manuals. Went back to Thurber after a while and read "What if Grant Had Been Drinking at Appomatox."

Lt Brodkey came into the area for a talk with Capt Chandler and the other Os, and I later told him of Thurber; likes him, he said, and asked me to pass him the book.

Weather: it's cold all the time, twenty-four hours a day.

November 20-21. Biggest rumor now is that we'll get turkey for Thanksgiving. Who cares?

Spent two days with the other gun crews from the neighboring battery. The Old Guys are pros, but the EM are difficult to work with. They believe they'll be home for Christmas.

With that attitude (Hatalski here), "They'll be home for Christmas in a box."

But there's not much one can do to break those people out of their shell. If we go back to fighting, I can see these guys bugging out. In practice, they went through the motions. The way I see it is that they do know how it's done. The problem is to see that they do it.

They're not prepared mentally, is what Hat says. No matter how many Old Guys you got or how good they are, instilling pride in the job and the unit remains the hardest part.

That's a new unit; they don't know each other. Worse: their idea of combat was that free ride north after our breakout of the Perimeter and the landing at Inchon, which was a huge help.

"What's the big idea, Corp?" is what they say. "Bucking for another stripe, that it?"

Those guys are my age, but they're children all the same. This type of troop is the most dangerous, acc to Frazier. Not serious. Immature. Will most prob run away and leave us exposed.

Their Old Guys tell them to shut up, to wise up, but there's no breaking that shell. If these are the guys who are to protect our rear, flank, etc, we're in danger.

Again Frazier put it best: "They're all going to die, that's for certain. Trouble is they'll take some of the experienced people with them."

Amen to that.

Two days with those guys, and I was ready to face the NK. Prob the Os' fault at some point.

Before Lt Brodkey went to his Forward Ob post, he gave me a big book called "Manhattan Transfer." Tried reading it, but I can't make heads or tails of it.

Pulled out a C-ration can and what did I get? That horrible beef stew, what Crazy calls "the slow poison."

November 23. Thanksgiving Day. We were supposed to have turkey for chow and did. Saw my first cranberry sauce; looks good, tastes awful. A message to the world from Gen MacA. "Big push is coming in Nov," (thanks for telling the Chinks, Gen) and then it'll be home for Christmas.

That's dangerous talk.

Politics is what Hat calls it. It's a way of saving his ass, and him a General.

For the record: Thanksgiving Day in northern Korea is colder than it has ever been in this century. All this from Signal Corps O who reported in this morning.

We stepped up the practice with our guys and with that other battery. Placed some of them with our gun crews, but no idea how they'll do if we get into a fight.

Stang and I worked on the same team this morning, and he asked me how the turkey tasted. Slightly burned, I said. He said it was probably frozen to start with, thawed, and then cooked again. After working with Stang, I traded places with Skinner's crew and we were back to the old routine. You can go crazy or you can freeze if you don't move.

Capt Chandler had the Os and the Old Guys check our feet again. Medical orderlies came by to look at our feet. What a job! Got to put those socks and boots back on in a hurry, it's that cold.

Got together with Charlie and Joey. Asked for news, rumors, anything. Talked about money in Japan bank. (Not our money anymore, since we're to give it to Natsuko's little brother, Hiro Watanabe.)

Talked about the School for the Blind where Hiro goes to classes, and remembered the Catholic cathedral in that part of Tokyo. That part of the city was not damaged much by bombing, not like the ports and the housing as one comes in from Sasebo and Yokohama. The Japanese really caught it there.

Well, Nagoya, Kobe and Osaka also got it bad, but not like, nothing like, Hiroshima and Nagasaki. None of us made that trip out there, and I wouldn't go there for a million dollars a day.

I'd told Charlie and Joey about the old carpenter in Nara who was working on the restoration of Admiral Yamamoto's house. The old man was from Hiroshima, and he invited me there any number of times. That I should go there and see. Not me, I was too chicken, too ashamed, something.

Joey: "Look, we'll all be taking visions and mind pictures of all the crap we've seen here without having to add any more with a visit to either Hiroshima or Nagasaki." Amen.

The talk turned to our Japanese girls, the terrible fire near the Ernie Pyle theater, and the death of Natsuko, Mosako and Hiro's sister. From this, back to the money we'd deposited for little Hiro. Charlie then remembered we'd also left some money with old lady Yoshiko Ogura in Tokyo. Neither Joey nor I had thought about her or the money until Charlie mentioned it.

The talk got animated. We talked about the cancellation of the beer issue back in September by the temperance people, and how that didn't last long. Remembered what the Old Guys said about eating candy: good, fast energy source. (We've all got Baby Ruths, Powerhouses and Snickers. Frozen, but they taste better that way.) We'd all bought a bunch and stashed them in the kit bags. Talked this way, and then we heard small arms fire, so off we ran to our gun crews to see what we could see.

Hat had his binocs on the Forward Obs and said things looked okay. While we were there, we moved the guns, checked the tires, etc. Cold. Cold. Cold.

This waiting around can drive you nuts. The Os know this and so they put us to work when they can or they talk to us "about the job at hand."

Some radio genius wired up a hell of an antenna and caught Armed Forces Radio Service, a Thanksgiving treat for us. Charlie said Stan Kenton's Progressive Jazz is still going to take a while for him to get used to. The disc jockey played some Goodman with Charlie Christian on guitar. The disc jockey rattled off the names of the other musicians., and he followed this with Waller's *Honeysuckle Rose*. Charlie asked me what *honeysuckle* was in Spanish, and I couldn't come up with it until Joey said it was *madreselva*. Which then took us to that great tango by Gardel, and then we stopped. Just like that. Start talking about home, dances, songs and etc, and it's the stretcher bearers for you.

But soon after, Joey and Charlie nudged me as we stood there listening to the radio.

Joey: "And how about the 'onlies' and the Jap big bands at the whorehouses? American music, and always heavy on the saxophone section. Remember, guys?"

Charlie: "Wouldn't mind being in Big J right now. Hot bath, a great lay, being spoiled to death by your 'only' and a massage. Jesus. And then just sitting and looking at each other, enjoying each other that way. Best time of my life. What say, Rafe-boy?"

Joey then said that if anybody was going to make it alive out of this damned war it was going to be the three of us.

Damn right. To bed and prob more of the same tomorrow.

Pain, Darkness, and Cold

On November 25, the CCF struck the whole of the Eighth Army in the western Chongchong River. Runners tell the same story over and over: much fighting, day and night. Moving out; God alone knows where.

November 26-December 4. Got the hell kicked out of us. No idea what "the folks back home" have been told, but we of the 2nd Division have been battered hard. All of the Eighth Army came under attack, and it must've been by a CCF main force which has been hiding, playing cat-and-mouse, and giving everyone fits while we drove on and on in this horrible, horrible place. A good part of the 25th Division was hit and belted around like an over-the-hill fighter.

Admitting it is better; we can start to work and get over the shock sooner. Like having a scab, Lt Vitetoe said; he then said we'd been defeated in this battle, but not in the whole war.

Five days of hard fighting; five straight days of retreat. Scariest days of the war so far. Beats anything I've seen here since June. No idea what happened along the entire line. I know only what I saw here, and that was bad enough.

To begin with, Capt Chandler was killed by sniper fire. Stepping out of his tent after a runner brought in a written message. Only casualty of the first day. Lt Vitetoe, as Exec, took over.

Reason for my mix-up regarding our position on River Chongchong is that we *were* on both sides, and the whole of the 2nd Division was too.

But everyone is isolated here. A thousand hills; hills running into hills, the place looks like an accordion on its side. And ridge after ridge too. Engnrs had a hell of a time finding a spot for us, until the Air Force spotted a flat surface, and Engnrs went there and got to work.

As part of Divarty, we set up an entire battalion of 105s. A Bn of artillery is hell on earth if you are on the opposite end of the gun barrels.

The Chongchong is shallow in our sector but very, very cold and frozen in most spots. Must cross it by vehicles, otherwise you freeze and you stay here in frozen Chosen.

To our east (and a bit north), a mud hut village called Kunu-ri; the village has two roads, north to south, and is considered important. A village called Suichon lies up ahead. West of Kunu-ri, the Yellow Sea; to the east, mountains.

Later learned of two ROK Divisions positioned to our right. Our old friends from the Pusan Perimeter, the 25th Division, were holding the line. But it was the mountains: the units were bunched up here and there but there was no direct communication. Relied on runners who were in danger of freezing to death, catching pneumonia, getting shot at by us, by CCF, etc. From our gun emplacements, we could see the Chinese gathering strength and moving out of harm's way under a ridge, a hill, something. But they were there all right, hundreds of them.

We were directly behind two rifle regiments of the 2nd and providing support for them; the closest village to us after Kunu-ri was another mud hut place: Kujangdong.

Hills, hills, hills. Ridge, ridge, ridge. Phone wires couldn't reach due to distances, and day after day each unit remained in isolation.

The CCF hit us the day after Thanksgiving. No pull backs by CCF this time. No fading away. Instead, they stormed, swarmed, slashed across Inf and of course they set up a rock-solid roadblock behind our lines. But I'm not telling this right. (I made no notes during the last five/six days.)

Here is the result of the last five/six days: Our 2nd Division was defeated in detail. CCF punched a hole. I don't know how wide yet, but it was said to be six miles deep. CCF took the hills and ridges, and they then set up their roadblocks.

We heard heavy firing all through the night of Thanksgiving plus one. I saw NK and CCF green tracers crossing our red and pink ones, some of the tracers were in front of us and others to our right and left, but all at a distance.

Our unit was not in a firing position, so we were told to stay alert and wait.

We waited as told. Fighting went on all night. At dawn, both sides were still at it. We were ordered to move onto a road in a march convoy to give support fire to Inf units. Spent hours inside trucks with guns hitched so there'd be no loss of time if order came to move out that night.

The order did come, and we slept in the trucks as they moved to form part of another convoy; best sleep any of us was to have that week.

When it began to lighten up, the trucks stopped all of a sudden. We stopped to pick up stragglers from the 2nd Division (9th Infantry Regiment). No helmets, some no ammo, no grenades, no canteens. Just like early fighting in June/July. Running like crazy men and abandoning their wounded. Hat and I picked up some of the wounded and were helped in this by an old Gen. He asked for Col Keith, and Hat led the Gen part of the way, then came back to finish getting the wounded into the trucks.

Don't know how many wounded we piled inside the six-bys; some guys not wounded but in no condition to fight anyway: Wild-eyed. Shaking. Shivering from the cold and crying. Others ready to fight, though. Caught up with Company K, and Company L guys and Os all mixed up; there was no unit integrity and the Os tried in vain to sort each other out. The men didn't know their Os and vice versa.

I almost gave up. I slipped and fell on the ice, face down, helmet came off, and I would have stayed there and frozen to death, but Hat tapped me on the sole of the boots and said, handing me my helmet, "Here, you may need this."

Nice way to put it, but I was tired and just didn't care to go on anymore. (Alas, I am so faint I may not stand; My limbs under me doth fold).

While the truck stopped to pick up two wounded guys and then got ready to move, we received direct rifle fire. We scrambled out to fire carbines and M-ls. All of a sudden, the Chinese stopped firing and Lt Vitetoe sent Inf guards to patrol hills to left and right. We waited by the trucks, but there was no repeat of fire by Chinese.

An hour later, the Inf either cleared the hills of CCF or the CCF moved on, and once again we mounted up and proceded. Our patrols had skirmished some but returned okay. We then met with the 2nd Bn; these guys had not been hit at all. They had been separated by those hills, so the Bn was intact as a fighting unit. They joined the march.

Dawn. Cold and clear but no Air Force despite the blue skies. Suddenly there was a fog cover, just like that, and we got in the middle of a hellacious fire fight. Ordered not to stop and to drive by the fire fight so we could stop to pick up wounded just ahead.

This is crazy, but I remember that all of a sudden, out of nowhere, on the side of the road, there were thirty Chinese POWs, dressed in white winter uniforms, marching under GI guard. Lt Vitetoe told guard to check CCF for weapons and found none, then gave order to Sgt in charge to release the Chinese right then. The sergeant pointed to a hill and up the Chinese scampered, and this new Inf unit joined our group.

Other strange things. I saw stragglers here and there and then, I'd see a disciplined unit in good marching order following a convoy of passing trucks. At one point, the Battle Police rounded up some stragglers and put them in marching order with the Inf passing by.

Our convoy then drove to a side road, drove up a hill, we unhitched the guns (there was firing all around, and all over the place, but here we were, as if on practice fire, unhitching the guns and waiting for orders) when Frazier and Dumas ran up to us and pointed to a Chinese unit out in the open. Bam! Bam! Bam! And that was the end of them as a unit. Our troops on the road deployed and waited for us to drive back onto the road.

Back on the road, the firing picked up as we drove forward, and then it got quiet again. People having private wars, it looked like. Then, more stragglers, etc. And GIs coming out of hills onto the road firing as they ran and not turning their backs on the Chinese.

Then we stopped. Two Inf guys ran up to see what was what and returned to report: Two trucks were on fire up ahead holding up convoy. Some Inf guys got off the trucks and, we with them, pushed the trucks off the road and down a hillside. Then, back to our trucks.

Confusing scenes. We moved out slowly and saw Inf guys leading tanks. We moved to the side of the road to let the tanks and the Inf go by. (Had to be the 2nd Division since this was our sector.) Saw more Chinese POWs left on the side of the road by our Inf. CCF already disarmed and they sat there amid all the noise, yelling and fire. Ahead of us, two GIs, stragglers, said they'd been captured by Chinese and then led out to main road by CCF officer and squad of CCF enlisted men; they were disarmed but the CCF let them keep their cigarettes, wallets, etc.

Back on the trucks once more and got to the bank of the Chongchong again. Water freezing, and the troops on opposite bank using M-16s, the Quad 50 caliber M-gun vehicles, and tanks, plus any available carrier to ferry stranded GIs. We got off the trucks, stood by, sat and waited for them to be ferried while some of our prime movers were also used to bring the troops across.

We unhitched five of the guns, turned two of them to the hills behind us and three ahead, across the river. When the first trucks got back, we were then ordered to rehitch all of the guns. Firing not too heavy here at first. Some Inf GIs impatient and attempted to cross on their own: freezing water, and they became casualties immediately.

Sporadic sniper fire from ridge. All of a sudden, the Quad 50 crossing the river to get Inf back, stopped, pointed its four 50-caliber M-guns and fired for two minutes straight. That quieted the snipers.

With all guns hitched again, we drove to the northern bank and enjoyed fire support the whole time. We unhitched the guns one more time and stood at the ready.

Got dark; fighting got confused, so both sides had to stop. At the same time, the Inf guys were still being ferried over. I then saw 10-12 Inf guys who jumped into Chongchong; not deep, but they too became frozen casualties and unfit to fight once they crossed.

Saw also two of our tanks destroyed while ferrying troops, and still another group, 20-30 GIs, sitting on the side of road, disarmed and released by Chinese. They wandered into our area and Lt Fleming told them he'd try to contact their CO.

Their Old Guy hobbled with a wound, lined his troops and waited for Lt Fleming's orders. We then got some abandoned M-ls from our trucks and passed them out to those guys.

I think we went without sleep for twenty-six hours this time.

Woke up next to my gun, given coffee by Dumas, who said, "Keep down; sniper time, pass the word."

I also remember from yesterday that some Infantry guys tried to get on tanks while the tanks were moving. Can't be done—maybe in Hollywood, but not here. Also, saw at least two tanks traverse tubes and knock wounded GIs off tank unintentionally. And that's "goodbye, Johnny," 'cause tanks kept going.

Riding tanks is dangerous anyway. Looks good, like parachute troops and Rangers look good, but most of the guys we met from those outfits were misfits, weird types.

Turkish Brigade. It was abandoned in confusion but it kept fighting. One big mix-up by Turks: they shot at ROK thinking them Chinese. Most of the Turkish Brigade in heavy combat; no idea how many, if any, survived. From somewhere, Hat got a Turkish long knife to open M-l ammo crates and the Turks helped themselves.

Don't think anyone knew what was going on. There were Chinese units to the left and right of us; we'd broken through one roadblock just south of us, and when we looked up front, runners came running by to say CCF were also coming right toward us from the north.

Lt Vitetoe gave the order: "Infantry guard, deploy; gun crews, stand by." Meanwhile, guys were still being ferried across from this part of the Chongchong.

Hat and Frazier and Dumas pointed to the Inf, and some fifteen of them began unloading the shell crates from the weapons carrier behind us.

We fired. Nothing to it. Loaded up, fired; moved guns to side, wheeled around as needed, and fired again. Guns kept jumping up and down since they were not dug in, but we just fired like crazy until Dumas ran up and told us we'd run out shells at that rate.

But despite noise and confusion, etc., Inf is always in the worst position.

Stopped the fire, rehitched the guns and got to the edge of the river again. Ordered to move, this time to give supporting fire south of the Chongchong again; we set up and fired for two hours straight.

Hitched the guns again and ordered to recross the river to north side, once again to give supporting fire for Inf being ferried to south side. Good sized Inf unit in good marching order passed through us, going to rejoin some bigger Inf unit.

Then, three gasoline trucks were standing on the north side and our prime movers crossed the river and gassed up. More magic: 105mm ammo in trucks parked and waiting for us on side of road. Ate some pork and beans and given hot coffee. (Had put cans of pork and beans on empty shells and this kept the cans from freezing altogether.)

After this, hitched guns again and recrossed river. Since we were next to last in the order of retreat, we stayed on the side of the road and unhitched and stood by guns ready to give either supporting or direct fire as needed.

Then, what looked like the whole 2nd Division appeared on our side of the river. We hitched the guns one more time, crossed the river again and were then re-issued the order of withdrawal by units. We were seventh of eight in the marching order, with the Engineers in eighth place. (Engineers probably last so they would blow up bridges, mine the roads to slow up the CCF, etc.)

As soon as the first unit began to cross, we started to fire. The first to go was the Infantry to cover the hillsides and ridges. Then a Recon outfit was the second in the marching order, with 2nd Division HQ after that in third place. We were firing during all of this and the CCF was firing back; there was no slacking by either side.

Sounds crazy now, but the convoys were on regular march order: one, two, three, etc. (Good discipline shown by EM and Os and units on the whole; I've talked with over fifty guys since this, and everyone admitted being scared to death. I was too, and I don't see/understand how any of us survived.)

The Recon outfit then followed but were preceded by Battle Police. The two ammo trucks were with us with the Engineers right behind us. Our two batteries, Joey's, and Charlie's and mine, were attached to the 23rd Regt Combat Team (made up of 2nd units), and we were then joined by a tank unit and one AAA battery which had been idling on a side road waiting for us.

The Pass was a narrow road, and up ahead, we could see the arty gun fire against the dark sky: pink, red, orange, yellow, bluish green. On signal, we turned our guns around and began to serve as rear guard.

The road we marched on was the MSR, the Main Supply Road. The lst and 2nd Bns of the 38th Infantry Regiment were then sent to clear ridges west of the MSR. The 3rd Bn had the same duty but east of us.

These are tough jobs: the flanking patrols which clear ridges. Without them, we go nowhere.

Sat and waited; slept some and then got up in a hurry. Roadblocks up ahead and they were stopping the units ahead of us.

Tank on fire. This time, one tank blocked the entire convoy. Then, the prime movers took over and pushed the tank over the side. Firing fierce by both sides, but guys on prime movers kept at job and pushed the tank down the embankment. Firing on all sides. Vehicles whizzing by. Firing by CCF from both sides of road. Convoy had to slow down. We were way, way back of the convoy and watched all of this like a movie.

Suddenly Lt Brodkey calls for direct fire. The Old Guys and Lt Vitetoe gave the orders and went to work. (Brodkey's voice calm as always: "We've got pre-selected sites here. See chart four.")

This takes two seconds and bam! bam! bam! there we go again. Seemed like we fired for hours.

We were in that same damned narrow Pass that Frazier pointed out in Oct and Nov. Supposed to go through it. Firing; tanks afire, blocking road; trucks stop. Little forward movement. Chinks firing, a madhouse. Some GIs fighting like madmen; others ducking the fight and hiding behind bushes. The convoy stalls, lurches and moves on, over and over and over.

Morning. Blue skies. The Air Force shows up and helps, but can't do it all. CCF all around, hundreds of them. Air Force concentrates on CCF behind us.

Some Infantry had no unit of command; guys in trucks from different units and Os continued to have a hell of a time with troops they didn't know. Os tried to rally guys, but some guys wouldn't get off the trucks.

We could see this through binocs, and then some GIs trying to board trucks were being kicked off by other GIs. Then, five Old Guys armed with 45 automatics began pushing GIs around, assembled them into a group, set up a skirmish line and forced these guys to fire at the hills. This quieted the Chinese fire for a while; some of the guys got their spirit back, and then, out of the trucks, more GIs scrambled off and began to fire; but there were still more guys inside the trucks than out.

At the same time the Inf guys up ahead stopped to fire at the hills on both sides of the road. Lt Vitetoe got us together. "Hitch the guns and grab M-1s, carbines, whatever. Fire and run, fire and run."

So, with the guns hitched and secured, we began to run and fire, etc. The Engineers started moving out and they too were firing up both sides of the road toward hills and ridges. When we got to the point where Lt Vitetoe wanted us to go, our other trucks stood in place waiting for us while the Inf stragglers unloaded the ammo; then, just like that, two runners rushed out of the side of the road with new orders for us: "Fire all of the ammo you've got on the ground. All of it."

Vitetoe asked who gave the order and one of the runners said: "Col Keith himself, sir."

In the middle of all of this, a little liaison plane had spotted CCF, and we couldn't miss. The runners disappeared, but we had our orders and Lts Vitetoe, Brodkey and Fleming gave the orders to make ready. Dumas and Frazier waited for Hat and when Hat gave the word, the cooks, clerks and the Engineers next to us started opening the shell crates, and the stragglers formed three lines from the ammo trucks to our batteries.

Took no time to do this, and we were ready. Fire for effect, and there we went. I forgot about the troops trying to make it out of the Pass and concentrated on the firing job at hand.

Frazier kept count: in twenty minutes we fired over 3200 rounds of 105mm at the advancing Chinese. Forward observers right with us on top of tanks, trucks, and jeeps directing fire and readjusting. Two clicks down, fire! Up three clicks, C battery. Fire!

Ichabod and Crazy were the closest to us. Two gun, left, fire; three gun, right, hold it; three gun, fire. And we fired. And we fired.

Thirty-two hundred rounds in twenty minutes! Paint burned and peeled off guns. Breech blocks were blackened by the heat. All of us yelling, shouting—more ammo—let's go! Clerks, cooks and Engineers, shaking their tails and feeding us ammo. Fire, fire, fire. Forward obs yelling, "Forget the clicks, just fire. Fire! You'll hit them from here." All of a sudden the ammo was gone, and Brodkey was looking through the binocs and standing on the hood of our truck. He said, "The Chinese have stopped their advance." (Just like that.)

Part of our Regimental Combat Team acting as Infantry guards were yelling at us, like a game. We saved the RCT, but we saved ourselves too. And the Chinese stopped advancing. It was great. The CCF must've thought we were counterattacking.

The Engineers followed close behind, and eight hours later, when this part of the Pass was cleared of burning trucks, disabled tanks, etc, the Inf then mounted up and rode away. The Chinese had stopped, and since they had no trucks to chase Inf with, it was a matter of driving away and leaving them far behind.

The 25th Div's 24th Inf Regt was reorganized somehow, and it was placed to serve as our Inf escort in the rear guard. With the Engineers behind us, the Regt firing right and left made a sleeve for us to go through, and we headed toward the Pass again.

The Eighth Army was shot to hell from what we could see, but it did not disengage; most units kept fighting.

Checked my watch and found it stopped at 0100; asked for the time:

0220. We, of the 219th Field, were the last element to come through this part of the gauntlet with Kunu-ri and Kujangdong behind us but with some Chinese roadblocks still ahead. Got some sleep inside the trucks despite the lurching and stopping and moving on.

The hardest jobs for us:
1. moving,
2. trying to give supporting fire, and
3. defending guns at the same time.

Other CCF elements engaged us on the hills and ridges, but a big chunk of advancing Chinese units was stopped by our 3200 rounds on the ground. The remaining ammo in the trucks was untouched, and we made ready to move, since our arty column was then ordered through the Pass.

What a mess. The Engineers with us picked up a dozen new stragglers, but these guys were full of fight and lucky for us, since we were caught in another fire fight.

There were two more roadblocks, but we also had the abandoned M-1s and carbines for small arms fire.

We moved out around 0245. Marched in the dark, under fire. Saw more tanks and trucks on fire and these too were pushed down the hills. We made it out of the Pass; the two roadblocks were bloody affairs but we broke through and rode away dead on our feet.

Our 17th day arty was in good shape; the 37th arty kost ten guns; other arty outfits in so-so shape.

Then once out of the Pass, we discovered that we'd removed the blocks and sights from our guns and placed them inside the trucks, covers and all. We did it automaticaly, like the Old Guys and Os said we would.

We fired the 3200 rounds on the ground, and as crazy and tired as we were, we had stopped to remove the blocks and the sights. We also thermited three of ten barrels, but I don't remember any of this.

Blanked out and blocked that out too, but guns were secured and that's what counts. Guns were well served is what the Old Guys and Os told us at the assembly area.

Morning. Blue skies. The Air Force shows up and helps, but can't do it all. CCF all around, hundreds of them. Air Force concentrates on CCF behind us.

Some Inf had no unit of command; guys in trucks from different units, and Os continued to have a hell of a time with troops they didn't know. Os tried to rally guys, but some guys wouldn't get off the trucks.

We could see this through binocs and then some GIs trying to board trucks were being kicked off by other GIs. Then, five Old Guys armed with 45 automatics began pushing GIs around, assembled them into a group, set up a skirmish line and forced these guys to fire at the hills. This quieted the Chinese fire for awhile; some of the guys got their spirit back, and then, out of the trucks, more GIs scrambled off and began to fire; but there were still more guys inside the trucks than out.

At the same time the Inf guys up ahead stopped to fire at the hills on both sides of the road; Lt Vitetoe got us together. "Hitch the guns and grab M-1s, carbines, whatever. Fire and run, fire and run."

So, with the guns hitched and secured, we began to run and fire, etc. The Engineers started moving out and they too were firing up both sides of road toward hills and ridges. When we got to the point where Lt Vitetoe wanted us to go, our other trucks stood in place waiting for us while the Inf stragglers unloaded the ammo; then, just like that, two runners rushed out of the side of the road with new orders for us: "Fire all of the ammo you've got on the ground. All of it."

Vitetoe asked who gave the order and one of the runners said: "Col Keith himself, sir."

In the middle of all of this, a little liaison plane had spotted CCF, and we couldn't miss. The runners disappeared, but we had our orders and Lts Vitetoe, Brodkey and Fleming gave the orders to make ready. Dumas and Frazier waited for Hat, and when Hat gave the word, the cooks, clerks and the Engineers next to us started opening the shell crates, and the stragglers formed three lines from the ammo trucks to our batteries.

Took no time to do this, and we were ready: Fire for effect and there we went. I forgot about the troops trying to make it out of the Pass and concentrated on the firing job at hand.

Frazier kept count: in twenty minutes, we fired over 3200 rounds of 105mm at the advancing Chinese. Forward observers right with us on top of tanks, trucks and jeeps directing fire and readjusting: two clicks down, fire! Up three clicks, C battery. Fire!

Ichabod and Crazy were the closest to us: Two gun, left, fire; three gun, right, hold it; three gun, fire. And we fired. And we fired.

Thirty-two hundred rounds in twenty minutes! Paint burned and peeled off guns. Breech blocks were blackened by the heat. All of us yelling, shouting—more ammo—let's go! Clerks, cooks and Engineers, shaking their tails and feeding us ammo. Fire, fire, fire. Forward obs yelling, "Forget the clicks, just fire. Fire! You'll hit 'em from here." All of a sudden the ammo was gone and Brodkey was looking through the binocs and standing on the hood of our truck. He said, "The Chinese have stopped their advance." (Just like that).

No idea of date or time of much of the above. Have decided to set down the followng now before I blank it out.

Shits who kicked wounded GIs off trucks; GIs fighting until last round was fired; Os getting blown away off tanks, trucks, and roads, and getting up to fight again. Old Guys taking over from dead Os. Some Infantry running away. Others sticking with unit and firing as they fought their way through the Pass. Much yelling at times; silence at others but continuous roar of noise from tanks, trucks, arty rifle and mortar fire. The CCF pitched in with its bugles and whistles, day and night. Cymbals, too, I think, but bugles and whistles, for sure.

Am now sitting here on the British lines. This is where we wound up, but all according to the plan of retreat, say Old Guys. British unit called the 27th Bridgade. Gave us hot food and coffee. They too were separated coming through the Pass and stopped here to reorganize.

A British Old Guy just came over; wanted to know if I were a reporter. Gave me his name, Alfie Cosgriff, Irish he says, but born and raised in England; in Yorkshire, a place called Huddersfield where James Madison, the actor, comes from, he says. He asked if we were the guys that caused the earth to shake the night before. Said that was the best exhibition of firing he's ever seen since Africa.

Will stop here; I think I've had sixteen hours of sleep in five days. Hand beginning to shake. Hit the Irishman for a cigarette; sloshed coffee on my gloves, my hand was shaking so.

I don't think I mentioned the brutal cold once in this entry, "but Lord how these weathers are cold! And, I'm ill-wrapped."

Our unit is going south to consolidate. A big retreat; most likely a catastrophe, a disaster, and the war is not over.

The Eighth Army did suffer a big defeat. Still, a hell of a test, and Os and Old Guys say we make the grade. No heroes; just men in combat.

The Old Firm

December 5? Our original unit has been scattered. Haven't seen Charlie since Kunu-ri/Suichon fight; he and his battery transferred out as fillers to go help a newly reconstituted battery out of the Pass. Joey in another battery now, but still in same battalion. The Old Guys, Hat and Hook, sent off to Joey's battery and, like us here (Dumas and me), training replacements. Skinner and Stang with us and running their own crews.

The Os: Lt Brodkey here and he's got Crazy and Ichabod with him. He lost the two new Lts during Pass ambushes. Lt Vitetoe went with Hat and Frazier. Billy Waller back from hosp and assigned as battery CO, but no captain's bars yet.

Didn't take long for CCF to consolidate. Our trucks left them far behind after Chongchong River ambush but here they came again.

Some light combat with both sides probing here and there.

Many skirmishes, much patrolling, and we hear sporadic fire when CCF snipers sneak in when our arty fires. Our snipers sneak in when CCF arty is on the warpath.

Our new guys training "on the job," but we're not engaged in pitched arty battles. CCF hurting as much as us, but they're without good supply lines, according to Os.

New division near us, the 3rd. The 3rd fought in Italy and elsewhere in Europe, and some of their Old Guys still with Div after all these years. As the Old Guys say, "You can always count on the Army not to count on the Army." The 3rd has been fighting in Eastern Korea; some of their arty guys say that was a mess too.

Still colder'n shit as Skinner says. Rice paddies frozen; no stink, thank God. Convoys on narrow roads splatter mud and ice when driving by. Freezing cold, and it's only December. (Still, I remember the summer heat. Hard to believe Korea can be both burning hot and freezing cold in same year.)

Were issued parkas for coming Jan/Feb/March cold. Tried mine on and returned it. Warm enough, but too heavy and bulky. Issued a winter cap with flaps. Beats the helmet, but that steel pot is something I'll never throw away.

Newly-issued pile cap is great for work; light and warm at same time. Got a new type with flaps and button snaps for them. Something like the old-timey aviator caps one wore as a kid against earaches.

Four CCF Inf wandered in alone, unescorted, unarmed and hungry. CCF clothes: warm and light weight. Look bulky, but that's due to pouches and sewing patterns on pants and jackets. Shoes of straw and rubber. Explains why CCF removes boots of GI dead. Wear soft caps, bandoliers and usually carry two mash-potato grenades. They also carry pots and bowls.

In June/July Osan fight, NK wore mustard-colored field uniforms. Easy to spot and to distinguish from CCF. CCF also wear white camo uniforms, and I've seen some of their trucks painted white as well.

The following is probably true, but I have no way of proving: Casualties for Eighth Army at Kunu-ri gauntlet came to 8000 dead, wounded, prisoners, missing. Sounds high to me. As for CCF, they too died in great numbers. But 8000 American casualties?

Dec 6. (At least I think it's the sixth.) Patrolling continues. Got two-and-a-half days off and slept some 14 hrs straight. No idea of exact date; asked some of the guys, but they didn't know. Woke up hungry after long sleep. No kitchen truck, so I dumped some Cs on the hot water barrel. P/beans and wieners. Always cautious of wieners since Vienna sausage episode.

Went to see Dumas after chow. Time: 2200. He was working on firing charts. If CCF comes this way (we're overlooking a road junction with some mountains to our right), we have pre-selected firing sites marked, and they'll catch hell down there.

My map shows this road, and it's the likely road for CCF to take. Our perimeter is some 17000 yards in circumference. Arty can handle that okay, but up to Inf to hold.

With this time off after six months of fighting, I've written letters home and I also sent a Red Cross telegram from Seoul on our way down from Kunu-ri. By now, Seoul may be back in CCF/NK hands again.

Once, when we were back in the Kwansai District, I didn't write home for six months. We'd been having great times in Nara, sailing in the Inland Sea, and just helling around when a Red Cross guy showed up wanting to know if I'd been in the stockade or something. He said my family was worried, etc. Well, I had no idea I'd not written home in half a year.

Dumas: "Since our outfit's been engaged for six months, we've been due for light duty."

Still, training is training, and it's work. But it beats the hell out of being scared out of your mind. Fighting just takes too much out of everybody.

Dumas: "Chinks aren't supermen; they're going through hell, too."

Told him I'd been thinking about Japan a lot lately. Dumas said it was having the time to think that's doing it. It's not bad, he said this two or three times.

"Gets your mind off this shit, Rafe."

Took one of his cigarettes and told him of the Jap Army veteran who lost his leg to the shark in a New Guinea beach and who now lived in a stairwell.

Told Dumas about the two-story stairwell. Some friends of his moved it to the side of a two-story whorehouse and he lived in the hollow of the stairs. He earned extra money playing an accordion, but he drew his money and his meals from sweeping next door at the Temple of Pleasure Emporium.

Dumas looked at me and said: "We'll probably leave this country as poor as we did Japan."

After this, I went back to the area and settled down for some reading: *The Red Badge of Courage.* Many people will like it, but I wonder if combat vets will to any great extent. Still, it was a war and not much different from this one when it comes to dying.

Read *Best Plays of '46-47.* Good stuff. Easy reading, plays. It's an annual series, but Special Services had but the one volume.

Lt Brodkey. He read *Badge* in college and said his prof was enthusiastic. Brodkey liked it then, but found it different now. Had wanted my opinion, but I hadn't read it at that time. Kept *Everyman* and *The Second Shepherds' Play* and returned him *Manhattan Transfer*, unread. Told him I would try it later. The Lt is a methodical type; had not noticed before, but he stutters now and then.

December 7. Back to work. Pearl Harbor Day plus nine years; I was going on eleven at the time. Started day off by training some replacements and was told that part of our unit moved toward Wonju, south and east of Seoul. Fire mission: a valley filled with NKPA and CCF battalion-sized units.

A liaison plane reported that our battery caught some CCF patrols during our practice fire two days ago; hell of a way to lose a life and hell of away to introduce new gunners to battle.

Bitching natural, but overdone by these new guys. One new guy transferred here by mistake. A Texas Mexican named Jacob Mosqueda was with us 2-3 days, and is now where he should be, in Joey's unit.

Dumas told me the story on Negro arty guys. They belong to the 500th, which also got caught in the Pass. Told me they ran away twice when their CO volunteered them as Inf to help truck convoy. Negroes kept separate from us; they have their own units. I've no idea how I'd behave if I were an Amer Negro in the service. Separate, but in combat just the same. Am told most of the Os are white in those units. Don't know if this is true or if it makes a difference.

Mail trucks pulled up to area and spent time with us.

Now 1900 hrs. Received two letters from Aunt Mati. Nothing new: praying for all of us. Says she has no news about the war except for headlines, etc. Her letters are two months old anyway.

Kitchen trucks rolled in; assigned to this outfit. Hot chow. Was given mess duty: inspecting hot water for hygiene, checking mess kits for cleanliness, etc. Rookies know about GI shits, but you still have to watch them.

OK to bitch about the weather, but whining about why we're here is out. Dumas was joined by another Old Guy (Russ Hocks) and they talked to the rookies. Rooks not interested. Well, I'm going to watch my hide with these new guys.

But they'll learn if they live through it. Takes time for them to see the truth of what fighting is. The learning part is scary since they have to learn to work as a unit. You mention unit pride to these guys and they sneer at you. We'll see.

Questions: What will they do when CCF comes at our Inf, punches a hole and then comes right at our arty? Hocks and Dumas having a tough time convincing them of this. I've tried to train two gun crews the way I was taught: change crews, change guns, mix up the crews, etc.

These guys are getting there, but they're not there yet.

What happens if CCF attacks tonight? What if some of these guys are scared of the dark?

Some good signs. They'll cheer when they hit a target area Lt Brodkey sends over the phone. But fighting is what armies are about, and we still have to see what they do when CCF goes into offensive.

Spotted a Bird Col wearing a parka. Okay for him, but he doesn't have to open crates, shove steel in the tubes, etc. Temps may hit zero and parkas are fine, but the secret is not to expose too much skin to the cold.

Some rookies full of questions about fighting. They know nothing about ambush at the Pass, and Task Force Smith is not even a name or a memory. Hard to talk to them about this as it is to write Aunt Mati about what we do here.

What is harder for them to understand is how arty guys can get killed even if we're behind Inf. Talk about CCF snipers, rockets and CCF arty scares them, but it doesn't sink in. They remind me of dead guys in Oct and Nov who thought they were tougher, better, than the Chinese.

Reminded Dumas I still had 18 hrs coming to me and went to see Joey. Had talked with him via SCR-300 yesterday; he said that truck after truck load of wounded coming through from Seoul hospitals. (All Pass casualties.)

He asked about Charlie, told him I didn't know; I thought he was in his, Joey's, area. J. says no.

Must stop. On way to Joey's unit and will hitch a ride.

Dec 8-9. Much fighting near Seoul. We were moved south of Wonju some. Just before we drove off, Stang and Skinner were assigned to C battery; they were to wait in place until picked up by quarter-ton truck to take them there.

December 10. Fighting started for us today. Pulled back again. Eighth Army whipped, but remains whole in many parts. Asked Dumas if we were going back to Pusan. Said he didn't think so; said we'd be in a hell of a fight soon, though.

Talking with Lt Waller, and I described the old-looking Brig Gen I'd seen at the Pass. Told the Lt that the Gen had helped Hat and me pick up wounded and put them in the truck; Lt Waller was at the Pyongyang hosp with penumonia at the time.

Speaking of Gens, had forgotten about Gen Dean until a runner confirmed today that the Gen had been a POW for some months. A South Korean agent with the runner gave an account of civilian betrayal of Gen Dean. No idea if old men like that can survive.

Dumas said Gen Os treated differently from EM POWs. Asked Dumas if that courtesy was also extended by NK.

"Good question," is what Dumas said.

Dec 12-20. Three days of fighting, hard and heavy by both sides. Our new guys are better, but they still haven't been tested sufficiently.

Dec 22-25. Gen Walker killed on the 23rd; no hard feelings from me. What good would that do anyway? He's gone, and I'm here. As for the Mexican crack he made, if he were alive today, he'd still feel the same way, so what the hell.

Christmas Day. Bitter cold. Mail trucks tried to get in, but stopped by cold, bad roads and CCF artillery.

Dec 26-January 3. Told of much, much fighting in Seoul. I thought Seoul lost to CCF a while back but it looks like that's not so. We formed in an area below Seoul, and this looks like delaying tactics all over again.

January 5. Joey called. Charlie was supposed to be among wounded in trucks from Seoul hospitals. (Last 2-3 weeks.) And now presumed dead. Joey confirmed this through runners. To be buried in K permanently? Joey doesn't know. Thought I'd write his dad and sisters but had no idea what to say. Talked to Dumas who said Lt Waller would write to Charlie's dad. But also said for me to approach Waller first, since there is no official confirmation.

This, too, is the Army.

Training and combat are the best medicine. Training serious now, and we hear of fighting, hard fighting, just south of us. Not bothered by having a battle south of us. We also have had to fight our way east and west. As the Old Guys say, a direction is just that, a direction. This isn't World War I with trenches, etc.

January 6. Ammo trucks rolled in and we spent the morning and noon unloading, checking crates, taking inventory. The 105mm crates are now clearly marked so as not to confuse them with 155s. Inf guard climbed trucks, gave the signal, and ammo trucks moved out toward Joey's battery.

The Os said we'd be fighting hard beginning tomorrow. Large CCF forces moving south, east and west. Given hot chow and our Inf guard put on two hours on and four off. We were fed in place, and I took my gun crews aside: cover crates in case of sleet or snow, we'll check guns one more time, and relax. CCF will be here tomorrow, and there's nothing to do but wait for the Os to give the orders.

January 7-20. Two weeks of absolute shit. Thirteen days of sporadic fire, too. Heavy here, weak and light there, and then hard fighting. Shifting of ground but no retrograde movement. Os said to prepare men, that we will not retreat much anymore. This is it, etc.

We fired and fired. CCF fought and moved on a wide front. We fought back, but CCF pushed on, but did not, as Os say, push us around. Big difference in that.

Was told that Gen Ridgway replaced Gen Walker last year and is now making a point of visiting every unit. Drops in like a hawk. Said to have fired some Light and Bird Cols on the spot, acc to runners; but no hard news on this. (Lt Fleming helped me on spelling of Gen's name from Ridgeway to Ridgway.)

News got around: 8th Army is to hold and to be ready for a push. No choice. We fought in an easterly direction; familiar place, and the bulk of fighting was done here since CCF had been trying to punch holes in this area.

Dumas: "This is the biggest concentration of artillery I've ever seen. Check the men's ears, Rafe." Dumas said he'd never fought for two weeks straight. Said CCF food and ammo supply trains must be getting through despite Air Force, etc.

Hard fighting again two days ago, but no retreat by 8th Army. Many

CCF wounded/dead, but they're still in front of us, and in force. Since we're not retreating and since they are keeping an eye on us, patrolling, etc, Hat says this is called "being engaged."

Our build up something else. Getting ready for a push of our own, just like Pusan Perimeter. No question on this.

Dumas ordered sleep for everyone; we went out to check the Inf guards. (Cold. Wind whistling down to zero temps.)

Whining by the troops down, a good sign.

January 24. Rested for four days straight; wrote home. Hat and Frazier and Joey back in our battery. Battalion got beefed up and, drank a few beers with the guys. Tanks moved in our area; I talked with tankers. Two Texas Mexicans, Cayo Díaz and a kid named Balderas; Díaz is a tank commander, Balderas a cannoneer, etc. Two Mexicans from California in same outfit: James Osorio and Benny Pulido; they're farm kids, too.

Checked guns and crates.

January 27. *We* started our offensive on Jan 25. (Became an adult, 21-years-old on the 21st.)

"Killing is the name of the game," said the Os. "Forget the real estate."

"We're after bodies and blood, and our arty is the agent," said Waller.

Much talk (sermons, almost) of "inflicting bodily damage."

Well, high explosives will do just that to Inf. We've also got VT, variable time fuses, which do more harm than high explosives. Still, you fire eight shells of HE, and the stuff flying out there looks like fleas and mosquitoes coming at you when the shells explode in front, behind and among the troops. Frightening shit, HE, but VTs worse.

IX Corps is west of us. We're remaining here, east of IX. Not much forward movement: one to three miles a day.

Cautious but murderous fire and movement to front. No cowboying like last year. What is taken is held and the CCF dead are left behind as evidence.

January 28-February 1. Lost or misplaced journal but found it 18 hours later in chow area.

Worst fighting ever. I swear.

Got screwed again. CCF was hurt badly on some parts of fighting line, but *we* got whacked. CCF Inf unit came straight at us and overran our Inf. Forward obs isolated for day-and-a-half, and Lt Brodkey then led Crazy and Ichabod and three other guys back to our area.

As usual, Lt Brodkey saved the firing charts and brought back the telephones; can't leave those behind for CCF.

High casualty list. Lost *all* the new guys. Dumas and I wounded lightly.

Said fuck it, and didn't report wounds. Above left eye again: CCF's and NK's favorite spot for my wounds.

Had abandoned area to CCF, and then ran into an ambush (both the battery and our Inf guard). We were driving up a narrow highway some four mi west of a village called Hoengsong. Rocking along, not fast. We had no flank guards and no idea why Inf not on job. We seldom move (at times impossible to move) without these guys.

One reason for ambush was that a ROK outfit was hit hard. The unit dissolved and we had no flank guard as a result. Was told of this last night at chow.

Well, our battery was to give supporting fire to ROK unit supporting us, but we were beaten to the punch by CCF. Ambush took place at CCF favorite time: 0200.

During fight, big roadblock, took 15 guys with me to unhitch guns. There was firing all around. Wild firing: M-guns, burp guns, M-1s, name it.

When the convoy first stopped, some guys stumbled out for a piss, half asleep, and CCF firing all the while. A mad house. Given orders to fire straight ahead; some of our guys were hit by us and by CCF both.

Daylight came early but CCF didn't retreat. Stayed by roadblock, so we fired like hell. Dumas, a rookie and I were the only ones from the gun crew alive at daylight, 0500.

A relief column came in and broke up CCF roadblock, and the Inf took after CCF with liaison planes leading the way with radio-ground communication.

Next day (yesterday) our convoy moved southward again. (To get away from CCF and then to regroup to come back at them.)

Lt Vitetoe wounded slightly on left leg, right hand and foot. Refused evacuation; went from Aid Station to Clearing Station, and returned to unit.

Lt Waller: "The column stopped when the leading truck was blown up by a direct hit, and this delayed the rest of column on a narrow road."

Just like the Pass.

Much firing, and this time I thought I'd gone blind. My steel pot was turned around and some steel dug a gash well into the pot liner above my left eye again. I knew I was dead.

Slow reaction time on our part, but this due to long fight earlier in the month.

Learned that our Inf guard fought well and two of them led the relief column to the fight scene. The relief column was led by Bird Col. Fighting started again by 0800; CCF prob figured we were on chow line and not waiting for them.

The Bird Col: "No retreating. Stand here, men." And he himself was right there, showing the way.

I passed out briefly and woke up on the ground. Felt okay. Medic who patched me up had received a face wound. I got up, asked permission to rejoin the gun crew and found Dumas and the rookie alive. His name is Kiel.

Medical supplies dropped later this morning, and medics brought in by chopper and truck convoy. Air Force zoomed by and dropped bombs west of us where CCF must've gone after ambush.

We three are the only survivors from the battery. I *earned* the Heart this time.

Reports: Some arty guys ran away again; got chopped by CCF fire and by ours, this last inadvertently since our guys were not supposed to be in that firing lane.

One arty Capt so angry he mounted a Quad 50-cal by himself and fired at CCF less than 70 yards away. Must've killed and wounded some two hundred by himself. Reminded me of O at Pass I saw knocked off tank only to get up half-an-hour later when he woke up to start firing again. Got knocked off second time and came right back. No idea what happened to him at Kunu-ri.

The Quad 50 Capt should get something for that piece of action because it allowed the Inf Old Guys to settle the men down and get them in skirmish lines in rapid time and ready to fire.

Situation: We're in a big CCF punch hole and there's no plugging. Confused fighting this morning all around, but not near us yet when day started.

At exactly 2300, last night, bugles and whistles again. The stock on my carbine busted, and I picked up an abandoned M-1 and some ammo off a jeep and joined some guys behind rocks. Good thing we did—CCF mortars hit in front and behind us. Much fighting and firing. Mortars veered off to our left, but we stayed and fired behind the rocks.

Another Bird Col drove up in middle of the fight around 0100. Brought additional reserves, and we were to serve as plug for CCF punch. Fierce, fierce fighting. Lost sight of Dumas and Kiel as we were to act as Inf. We were assigned on the spot to different units and areas.

Didn't know a soul, but joined guys in the fight, and as a Cpl was given eight guys to lead to the right of me and did so until 0140. The Bird Col also joined in in the fight.

The Col ran around, standing up, not crouching, rallying the guys. All of a sudden we're in hand-to-hand shit. Grenades, people jumping in and out of holes, running into CCF, firing, etc. Confused, madhouse fighting.

Could hear Bird Col yelling, "Kill 'em, men. Kill 'em. Fire, fire. Keep firing."

Much fighting. No let ups, many mix-ups, much yelling. More hand-to-hand fighting, head-to-head shit.

Fighting stopped all of a sudden, and CCF moved off; we reorganized immediately, set up a defense perimeter, and since no kitchen trucks here, we ate cold C-rations in place.

Young Os and Old Guys: there'll be another fight tonight. On your toes. Stood by and rested; a chance to catch our breath.

At 2000, after hours and hours of last night's and this dawn's fight, told to wait for night-time air support, which scares the hell out of everyone. At same time, some 200 yards to our right, green tracers of NK M-guns opened up. Also some small arms fire which sounded like M-1s; probably captured by CCF since firing coming from their side. Old Guy led six-man patrol to pick up stragglers.

Junior Os and the Old Guys that were left led the charge. We massed for fire power, no artillery just arty guys acting as Inf, and here came the Air Force napalming 200 yards to the right of us where the green tracers of NK gave away their position.

I swear half of our guys were crazy from all day and night fight, especially after coming on heels of two weeks of fighting before that.

At daylight, 0500, the CCF and NKPA in retreat and leaving their dead and wounded behind.

That Bird Col was still walking around, talking to us. He asked me if I Inf. Told him I was arty. Remembered him as Col cradling the private at the Pass and said so.

"You in that too, son?" is what he said.

Before he left, he told us that five-hundred-thirty artillery-men and supporting Inf had been killed in the two ambushes. He said *killed,* not casualties.

HQ tent set up, and he went in for breakfast chow.

Kitchen trucks drove in and we sat down to eat hot food; someone gave me a beer. About ten minutes later at 0615, Gen Ridgway shows up. (Close to six-feet; balding.) Walked up to all of us, we got on our feet; he smiled and told us to sit, enjoy the food. As he talked, there was sporadic fire away from our area, and he stood there until the Bird Col reported to him.

Gen Ridgway to the Col: "Our soldiers have counted 4000 confirmed CCF dead. Their offensive here is broken for now." (Voice is matter-of-fact; no dramatics.)

He and Col must be old friends; Gen R put his arm around the Col and waved at us as we remained sitting on the ground, resting, eating, etc.)

The Gen was back after chow and spoke to assembled group; a quiet voice but electric, too. "You men have my respect." Turning to the Col he said, "Paul, I'll not forget what all of you did here today. You won, and you did it hand to hand." With that, back to his light plane to see another unit.

Some French here with us; they too look as bad we do. Traded cigarettes and handshakes.

My wound is light; a piece of wire again. The headache is prob due to the chunk of shit that went through my steel pot and liner. Am okay, but strayed from outfit after second ambush. Told to wait for either medics or for my unit which must be close by. Requested transportation or direction to my battalion. Given directions: hiked three miles and saw many CCF dead along the way, so many I almost stepped on them. It was thick with dead in some spots. Enough to drive anyone nuts. Some of the bodies were frozen stiff.

Ran into US Army photographers and newsreel guys. One civilian among them wanted to snap a picture of me with my helmet off and with the CCF dead behind me. The Signal Corps guys told him to lay off. The civilian insisted. I told him to fuck off and I headed toward my Bn.

Got there and reported to the medic tent. Medics said I was okay, and I was then sent along with thirty-forty others to a back area Aid Station for observation, rest and a hot meal.

February 2. I'm to be in the hospital area for three days. Eye okay but puffed; look like a beat-up boxer. Dumas drove over and we're to be assigned to a seasoned arty unit again. Said Hat, Frazier and Joey are one unit away from us.

"They caught hell, too, Rafe." And then, "Remember the rookie? Kell, was it? He's okay and resting at the Clearing Station."

"Kiel, you mean?"

"Yeah; well, he's all right."

With that, Dumas left some cigarettes and some letters from home. Got an early St. Valentine's Day card from Babs Hadley. Said she'd also sent one to Charlie. Jesus.

February 5. Bandages off. Resting on cot, not on cold, cold ground. Eye fine. Purple Hearts here by the carload. Got me a cluster in a little two-inch box to go with one of the Hearts I lost a while back.

Released and starting over. No barracks bag, mine lost in ambush. Issued new clothing, shaving gear. Ordnance gave me a carbine, new model.

Quartermaster filled out second form and got *new* stuff. Extra pair of boots, new steel pot; grabbed some C-rations and beer. Was issued plastic sun glasses. Unwrapped ODs and two field fatigue pants/jackets, new gloves, etc. Signed for everything as always. Best dressed man in Korea.

Undressed behind crates and left old shit there. Refugees will scrounge around and find this stuff just right.

February 9. Given three days off; trained some; got timing back; it's great to work with guys who know the score.

The 8th Army is to attack the River Han. No idea when, of course, but CCF occupies Seoul and also Pyongyang

As always, much probing "to inflict bodily damage." No nonsense or grandstanding by Ridgway: kill the CCF, and the real estate will take care of itself.

Reporters and photogs in swarms now. Os say best thing is to 1) either talk to them or 2) pretend ignorance. (It's better to look a fool than to prove it to a newspaperman.)

Hatalski: "If they want stories, they should go to some back area and listen to the assholes there."

Was told that CCF started new offensive east of us yesterday, at dawn. CCF not beaten, but how many more men do they have?

Our unit was not in second battle of Chipyong-ni, which was another 8th Army disaster in Dec or Jan. Told that Marines are close by. Our Inf from former defeat at Chipyong-ni is waiting for a second chance at CCF.

Our arty unit is together again. The recovered guns from ambushes are with us again and no rookies in this outfit. Stang and Skinner are here and Brodkey's got Crazy and Ichabod in tow.

The old firm is what Billy Waller called us.

Five Days at Chipyong-ni

February 13. Morning of the first day. A lot I know; we were driven to Chipyong-ni—not to Wonju as rumored—and we formed part of the 23rd Regimental Combat Team.

A French battalion stands next to us, plus other support units. Not far, the 500th Artillery and their 155 howitzers were set facing north and east, the same as us. (What we want to know: Will they hold and not run away as they did at Kunu-ri and again at Obong-ni?) I also spotted a battery of Self-Propelled guns (SP) along with our arty Bn which makes for strong fire support; up to now, and in this sector, we're the only ones with 105mm howitzers.

Three-hundred yards to our rear, the Engineers quickly laid out an air strip. This means we're to stay here and wait for a fight to develop. Runners say the combined CCF/NK force coming is the main force; I've not seen so many line crossers, runners and agents in and out in any one place.

As we drove in this morning, we found the ground covered with ice and clinging to the trees. Much snow on hills, too. Our hill rises no less than 500 feet, acc to my old Jap map. Early this morning, just as soon as we got here, we registered other hills and ridges and bends of a road some 1500 yards away not shown on our firing charts; despite freezing weather, we worked like hell, got the phone wires laid out. Contact was made with the forward observers, etc, etc. (Later discovered other firing charts showing we'd registered most of the hills during our drive north last October.)

Engineers reported that the ground was frozen anywhere from ten inches to one-foot deep. They were forced to pile drive crow bars using a winch before they could begin digging with spades. Guns need to be dug with all this ice around, otherwise they'll buck up and down. Worked with Engineers who told us temp stood at 5 above, but all of us sweated anyway. (Gun emplacements proved to be sound during wheeling exercises.)

Our Inf guys not good at digging. They pile up rocks, some dirt, etc. Most wounded Inf guys come as a result of poor fox holes.

Chipyong-ni remains as before when we were last here: a village with a railroad nearby, trestles, some old gold mines, railroad tunnels, etc. Using my binocs again, I spotted the 155mm guns of the 500th to our right. We're separated by Inf support units.

No unit is isolated here, though; during the Oct-Nov drive north last year, it was a helter-skelter, bronco-busting ride with little contact possible between the 8th Army units.

This is to be a Perimeter battle, acc to the Old Guys. Big battle shaping up, and we're to make a stand here; we'll be surrounded but not trapped. Chipyong-ni important because if we hold, we threaten all Chinese and NK forces south of the River Han. Then, if we're successful, we can use this place as a jumping off point for a new offensive north again.

Old Guys and Os explained about a perimeter-type fight and defense, but I didn't understand the part about being surrounded. Old Guys said that's what this perimeter defense is. Big, big perimeter; not as big as Pusan, but big enough. If we hurt Chinese and North Koreans enough, we'll be in better shape for our offensive that's sure to follow.

We're usually told everything by Old Guys and Os, and so we're not in the dark. And if captured? We tell all we know, just like CCF POWs tell all they know. No Hollywood heroics here; everybody knows the rules. Besides, what do we usually know except for rumors, etc.

During talk, took out my map and Hatalski pointed to our situation. We are surrounded and the battle will last until someone quits. (I think that the longest any of us can fight—the CCF and us—is a max. of three/maybe four days; after that, both sides peter out. A body can only stand so much.)

Hatalski: Twenty miles from here it will be quiet. Farmers will be working plots and breaking up rice paddies to air out the ground before it refreezes again; the K women will be cooking; the kids will be playing inside the huts and no noise of war over there. War, Hat said, is always localized.

Many troops in perimeter who are just as experienced as we are But, I still don't trust 500th Arty, since they've run away twice that I know of. With units so close and with Inf close to the 500th, the Inf guys will keep them in place this time. Where can they go, anyway? We're surrounded on purpose.

Sgt Dumas came by with hot coffee. Dumas: Roadblocks and fireblocks will keep us inside the perimeter, and CCF will try to keep relief columns from coming in. (Dumas also said we may not need relief, but both sides try everything). There's always air transport, he said.

All our units under constant contact with one another. Wires holding up this first day and communication is in good shape. Patrols went out in all directions some three hours after we got here. Orders are for everyone to pull back to the perimeter at night. The ground has been mined and the mines have been charged, barbed wire laid out, booby traps placed and trip flares ready. Our job is to wait.

Talked to Frazier and told him that despite being surrounded, I felt safe in the perimeter.

"No battle lasts a hundred years, Rafe," is what he said.

During noon chow, whistles and bugles again, and we set to work. We fired our 105s for five hours, and the Air Force also bombed a large force of CCF coming toward us from the north and the east. Some of our returning patrols were pinned down temporarily by CCF ground fire, but we got them out of trouble with our arty and with some Inf guys leading them away from the wire, the traps, etc.

Duds: Of the first eight shells fired, three proved to be duds. This is a continuing problem, but, as Old Guys say, there's no way to know beforehand, so just keep up the fire and the rhythm of the unit.

Like the Os said: Both sides are probing, and the battle won't begin until the CCF is ready. CCF will attack and most prob it will be at night. Our fire today is a sign of CCF gathering strength.

Stang: "Bugles and whistles, bugles and whistles."

Strange sounds of bugles and whistles and cymbals started at 2000 hours. Very dark, very cold. Battle not near us, more to the south.

At 2230, we came under attack. Mortars and arty from CCF. They start their attacks this way all the time. We under heavy fire, but also heard increased firing at southern and western sectors of perimeter.

Couldn't see where we fired, but since we'd registered everything, it was a matter of firing at pre-selected sites. We fired at will from 2230 until 2400 hours.

This is how it started: CCF Inf first walked into the mined field, then they stepped on the trip flares and booby traps and some CCF became entangled in wires. Flares lit up area where CCF started attack. Then, suddenly, it became daylight. The 500th shot their big light flares and then our Inf heavy weapon companies started their M-gun and mortar fire. Flares so bright, night turns into day for a while. Inf M-gunners could see CCF clearly when firing.

Damn Quad-50s raked ground and first wave of CCF went down. (You get wounded here and not recovered by your own. You freeze to death.)

Our unit caught hell from mortar and arty fire, though. One CCF burst started a fire on some dead trees and then two of our guns were knocked out and we suffered many casualties/dead/wounded. (CCF has big mortars and good arty along with their Self-Propelled guns.)

Quiet at midnight on first day of fight. No smoking allowed, so we sat or stood by guns, and CCF started to fire again at 0130 and we fought until 0530. CCF did not make it to our hill, but kept probing all night long. Our Inf guard up here were kept busy by accurate sniper fire on them and on us.

After morning chow, sporadic fire followed from 0800 to 0900. Two runners came by and said CCF penetrated 2 mi south of us; runners coming from there. Enemy was later repelled, and runners returned to our area followed by two South K agents.

During the night firing, the French Bn marched through our unit to go after Chinese forces which had taken a high hill we'd clobbered earlier. Despite our fire, CCF stayed on hill, and it was up to the French to rid the hill of CCF.

Lt Waller told Hat that CCF had to cross a wide open field to get to hill, and that CCF took it anyway. So, the French ran up the hill and raked the upper ground with M-gun fire. They then marched back, called for more artillery from us, but there was no CCF response. Chances are CCF just marched down on backside of hill.

Firing proved just how much firepower we have. As Dumas said, "To lose a battle in this perimeter, we are going to have to screw up in a big way."

This was a pep talk, but what he said was also true. We're well-armed; we're also surrounded but not unprotected.

Were brought coffee and fell asleep until French went out again and raked high ground with M-gun fire. I have no idea what happened in other sectors of the perimeter. As usual, we're reminded that we're not the only people engaged.

Report from runners: CCF has fireblocked our area to the rear. The taking of the hill was a diversionary attack.

Blocks work in two ways: to prevent our Inf from coming to rescue us or to prevent us from leaving. But this is more important: We're to stand here and fight. We're not going anywhere. It is now 1100 and will go to sleep.

Second and Third Days. (Lost a day of sleep.) Rousted at 1300 hrs. Hungry. Hot coffee. Cold pork/beans. Got binocs out and saw this: Two M-19s (these are dual 40 cal M-guns) plus six M-16s (the Quad 50 cal guns) and a number of Self-Propelled guns (SP) now placed around our sector of the perimeter. Must have moved in during our rest period. (I can see 400 yards to the left and some 300 to right before hills and ridges block the view.) If the CCF Inf come at us, they'll die in bunches.

Worked on guns, checked blocks and sights, (reported crack on breech-block of No. 2) and took shell inventory. Given hot consomme from kitchen truck. Told of much firing by our unit while we slept, but none of us woke up. (Couldn't stop eating; ate three candy bars and two cans of peaches.)

Stood by guns most of the day and to sleep at 2100. Rousted again (at 0300 hours) and saw this: Flares lit up sky, French marched out of position and went after CCF using bayonets. CCF fled.

French saved our battery's bacon and the 500th's too. Saw CCF as close as 20 yds to our right (infiltrators only, not a massed force) and some at 60 yds to our left. We stood by guns firing M-1s or carbines, but it was the sweet Quad 50 caliber M-16 that provided the firepower.

The 500th was penetrated again. Fighting intense and up to Quad 50s to regain lost ground. Told that our Quad 50s fired 10,000 rounds. Sounds about right.

The following took place at 0600 hours. French, again with bayonets, charged and ran after CCF unit, caught some and, this time, dragged them back as POWS for interrogation. Spooky coordination. First, it's pitch dark, then the flares go up and entire area lights up like twelve noon, and from our hill we can see CCF and our guys and the French out in the chase when flares come up. French stop, fire all around, and then start chasing and grabbing CCF prisoners again.

We gave small arm support from up here while French Inf was running to CCF position. We couldn't fire 105s because French too close to CCF.

Good light also due to flares dropped by C-47s. These flares are called Fireflies. Spotted some CCF running on and at bottom of railroad trestles. Good target of opportunity, but not enough CCF to fire 105s at them, so Inf called for mortar fire.

Fighting broke off on my way to breakfast at 0900 hours. Saw 100 of our guys on the ground, others leaning on guns and some standing. All wounded. Blood clots in a sec because of cold. But wounded being attended too fast. Aid Station tents being steadied against cold wind by tree trunks, pieces of railroad ties, rice bags, etc.

Counted additional 200 wounded at Collecting Station. Most probably came from area south of us which saw much fighting the first two days. Counted some four dozen choppers taking out serious cases. The rest were marched to thirty waiting ambulances; others not as seriously wounded climbed by themselves aboard the three two-and-a-half-ton trucks. All were then taken to Clearing Station and from there to Field Hospital inside perimeter.

To latrine. Sneaked a smoke with some of the guys. Battle not over. Morale is high, since being surrounded is one thing, trapped another. Repetition of this is supposed to mean reassurance.

Supplies come in by air and CCF has no air force here to speak of.

Ate little and then decided to scrounge for pound cake from a medic; traded him second copy of Gene Fowler's *Good Night, Sweet Prince.*

Back to work: breaking up frozen ruts, kicking ice off caissons and tires, also removing ice formed on tarp cover of shell crates. Sleet stopped a while ago. Engineers (and Signal Corps guys) at work again on mending defense features (barbed wire, phone lines, etc) after last night's and early dawn's fight. Got inside truck with Joey, wrote on journal and shared a cigarette. Looked outside of truck and watched 20 C-47s dropping supplies.

Two runners came by: Main Supply Road (MSR) clogged with new CCF fireblock and needs to be cleared. Brit Brigade ordered to go there and clear it, acc to runners.

Stood by guns four hours; saw more phone lines being laid, barbed wire replaced or added to existing line. Relieved and tried to sleep; couldn't and decided to calm down by cleaning carbine. After this, I got Lt Waller's 45, stripped it, oiled and cleaned it, and still felt ambitious. I then cleaned Hat's and Frazier's carbines. Hat said I should sweep and mop the kitchen and do the dishes too. He then said what I needed was a cigarette and a book.

I was nervous and that due to not enough sleep, he said. So off to afternoon sack time and saw eight of our guys sleeping under a truck. Slid under a quarter-ton truck, thought it too cold to sleep, but must've passed out, since I woke up two hours later. Woke up hungry.

Standing by guns, both Hat and Dumas said CCF will attack us again tonight and tomorrow morning, if they have enough men.

Relieved by Stang, stuck around area, read some and at 1400 hrs watched US wounded evacuated. Count is 500 in all. To be attended inside perimeter.

Some will be back in a day or two. (Our Regimental CO was wounded in the calf, but he refused evacuation. Bound to be replaced, though. Lt Fleming says CO has been here in K as long as we have, July '50.)

A long third day. Os and Old Guys and us sat around guns for talk.

Lt Waller: "Armies meet to fight at same place because all armies want roads, railroad accessibility and high ground to dominate view of area. Both sides gear up, staffs (ours and CCF's) bound to come to same conclusion as to where to fight. Someone points at a dot on a map and orders go out on both sides and troops begin to assemble. Perimeter fight such as this is not new, only new to some of us. It's similar to Pusan Perimeter," he said. "We're surrounded, but it's not the same as being trapped," etc.

Lt Vitetoe: "What makes us fight, what makes CCF or any army fight, goes back to the subject of pride, mutual respect among the unit and trust between the officers and the enlisted men." He said that GIs who go into shock are not cowards. "Many will come back to fight again."

My question: "Why did some guys run at first Osan fight, and why did some guys stay to fight NK Infantry and tanks? Why did some of our arty guys up on the hill cut and run, and why did we stay on the hill until ordered off?"

Hatalski: "Boils down to inner resolve, moral courage which is not the same as physical courage. Question is not who will fight, but who will stay and fight. The answer is moral courage and trust in each other."

Skinner said all roadblocks rank with the blowing up of civilians on Naktong River bridge.

Lt Waller: "Matter of degree. Blowing up of a bridge will last longer in the mind than actual combat. The Kunu-ri and Pass ambushes were frightening for all, but they'll be forgotten.

"The bridge was a static picture. The mind retains this clearly or nearly so. Kunu-ri was like a movie; you'll remember small scenes but not the whole show."

Joey: "I was scared to death at the Kunu-ri ambush. The cold gets to me, too."

Dumas: "Kunu-ri was the first big ambush for our unit—a longer row to hoe. How many of you remember the number of times we crossed the Chongchong River in relief of the Infantry? Did you know we went back and forth four times ferrying Infantry and wounded?"

Stang: "All I remember is being cold and scared and helping load the wounded inside trucks with Rafe and Sergeant Hatalski."

Frazier: "That's it, but keeping to the job during ambushes at Kunu-ri is no guarantee you won't crack in the future. We've got to recognize that trust and security are morale mainstays."

Lt Vitetoe: "The CCF says American troops won't fight at night. We're showing and proving to the CCF they're wrong."

A pep talk, no question, but being told about our situation is a hell of a lot better than living and dying in ignorance.

Asked by Lt Waller what we thought, I told him I admire the patience of wounded and the work done by medics.

Stang said he was scared at first Osan fight last July, but also too scared to run. After he saw US Infantry in shorts, shoeless, abandoning their ammo and rifles and stinking like shit from running in the paddies, he swore he'd never run.

Skinner said he kept his eye on Joey Vielma and did just what Joey did up on the hill. Dumas said this is a good technique: keep doing your job.

Joey: "What if I'd taken off, bugged out?"

Skinner: "Shit, I'd've beaten you by a fucking mile."

Much laughter, Os too, and pep talk broke off.

Fourth day. Looks like the heavy fighting is over at Chipyong-ni. Woke up to hot chow. On the move again. Dumas reported that the 155mm crews that dissolved at Hoengsong was the same unit (the 500th arty) that bugged out last year at Kunu-ri.

Before loading on trucks, our unit reorganized and took in twenty transfers; we learned that the gun crews and guns we lost consisted of another batch of new guys who joined us recently. Didn't know their names. We had to train them, since they were not arty guys; they were mostly service troops that had to fill in as line troops here at Chipyong-ni.

Our unit has been reorganized and re-equipped. Lt Waller in HQ to find out if we of the 219th Field are still part of the 23rd Regimental Combat Team. Ordnance guys just left us and removed another busted block along with a broken sight from the No. 3 gun. Block had a dangerous-looking crack in it. Dumas said the other gun we lost was also due to a cracked block; gun exploded at the time of firing and put five guys out of the fight; one died right there and four came up with multiple wounds.

"Chinese rockets—Dumas talking—coincided with the firing of the other faulty gun; this is what helped kill the other gun crew. But it was the cracked block that did most of the damage in both cases."

After Ordnance left, some Os and Old Guys from Division HQ (notebooks and pencils) came up ready to ask us what we saw at Chipyong-ni fight. We all lit up and sat or stood by guns smoking away while we waited for Billy Waller.

The interrogation started as soon as he came back.

All of us agreed that our Infantry Bns fought well. That the French and their bayonets made CCF run, etc.

Two Old Guys forming part of investigating group are old friends of Hat's and Frazier's. The Old Guys asked me if I saw GI POWs, and I said yes. They also wanted to know if they fought after rescue by our troops. Told them some did.

Joey said that most POWs he saw did fight. Senior O asked if we saw atrocities on GI POWs.

Skinner and I stepped up and said no, not like what we saw when we fought NK in last six months of 1950, when we saw GIs burned to death, or buried alive and bayonetted with hands tied behind their backs, and so on.

Stang: "Well, there must've been NK here too, since GI POWs told us some of their dead had their ring fingers cut off, their field uniforms stripped and boots removed."

The major asked if I always keep a journal, and I said I did. He then asked how long I'd been writing, and I said since coming to peacetime Japan in '49.

After the inquiry, we were given flat beer said to be from a Seoul brewery. Despite the teeth-chattering cold, we had some and saved some.

At noon chow, our Regimental Combat Team was relieved by units of the First Cav. Lt Waller said the 23rd RCT has been disbanded and everyone in it is to return to their regular 2nd Div units for reassignment; but first, he said, we of the 219th, have been promised three days of rest in some back area. (But not before Ordnance comes in again, rechecks the guns, the Os sign for them and their replacements, etc.) Always something.

On our drive, we picked up a good number of stragglers. They'd been caught in some fierce fighting at Wonju on the same dates we were in Chipyong-ni. Some of them were former prisoners, and they said the CCF treated them okay; it's a good thing the NK didn't get their mitts on these guys.

One of them told a curious story: He's a guy about our age, and he's called Lee Branson (Douglas, Arizona). Branson said he was walking along (and alone) the Hoengsong-Wonju road and that he met a sizeable CCF group going the opposite way. He was disarmed on the spot, and he then went on his way and they on theirs, and that was that, he said.

Other stragglers hooked on with some South Korean line crossers and brought back intelligence reports on names/numbers of CCF units, etc. One of them, an Old Guy, led four stragglers, all armed and with much abandoned US ammo for their M-1s and carbines they'd picked along the way.

Since it snowed during most of the ride, we had to stop for over an hour because the strong winds produced a blizzard, and the drivers couldn't see the road.

The stopping gave us a chance to eat some hot C-rations we'd wired to the trucks' engines, and then, out came the beer, which we shared with the stragglers.

At least three of the stragglers suffered from frost bite, and their hands looked like hell. If they didn't take care of their feet while on the run, it's goodbye to the toes, at least.

Been promised some days off; rest area duty.

Hoengsong

February 18-19. Capt Bracken joined the 219th on 2/18; he'll be the CO for our battery again; this is his first command since the war started. He's the O who calls me Tex, for God's sake.

Were promised some days in a rest area after last January's long, hard fight, but this was cut short.

About six days ago, some US Army and Marine Corps units were caught in an ambush on a twisting road between the towns of Saemal/Hoengsong; we were assigned to a death count detail to recover the dead there. We'd been promised some days in a rest area, but this was cut short, and we learned why when we got to the Hoengsong road.

The battle must have been a horror; as we drove up, we could see nothing but devastation: burned trucks and tanks; jeeps and weapons carriers also burned and on their sides or blown upside down.

And the dead. No idea how many, but for a short route, the death count will rank as one of the highest in the war. Some of the men with us broke down right away, and I've no idea why I didn't break down with them. That I didn't doesn't mean I'm brave, God knows.

The cold is unbelievable; colder than last Nov-Dec in northern Korea; brutal. But noted that glass melted and embedded in some GIs in trucks.

Before we started out as a group to help with the recovery of the bodies, a runner brought news about the gauntlet at Kujangdong last Nov. This was the first hard news regarding Charlie Villalón; we were told he was killed in Kunu-ri along with three other guys during the crossing back and forth of the River Chongchong. My guess is he prob died saving someone who didn't deserve it.

I have no idea how long I'll be able to sit and write about what goes on here; words fail when I write the word "horror," and the word itself means little unless one speaks of bodies that are torn, burned and unrecognizable ... but even that becomes tiresome and repetetive, which is what war is: repetetive. How many ways can a person die, anyway?

Some continue going to Mass now and again, and I do too, but I refuse to go to confession.

Receiving absolution for killing doesn't make sense to me, no more than being wounded, surviving and then seeing someone die, next to me or across the way ...

Add Charlie Villalón's death to this, plus my state of mind at the start of the death count detail on the Hoengsong road, and that completes the picture of early February.

On the first day of the death count, I got off the two-and-a-half-ton truck at the assembly point and threw up. Tried a cigarette and got the dry heaves immediately afterward. I then wandered off, canteen in hand and rinsing my mouth. Done in, I climbed in the back of a covered weapons carrier, had a good cry, and that brought some peace.

Feb 19. The Hoengsong fight/ambush took place about a week ago while we were fighting at Chipyong-ni. Today we joined the Marines and went back to the Hoengsong Road for our dead. No wounded here; no one survives in an open field at ten degrees F.

We found the dead well-preserved due to the cold. This made ID easier too. Graves Registration Os and enlisted came with us. I counted eleven dead Os, all ranks, with the highest being two Majors, and all the Os within 50 yards of each other. Leading small groups, I'd say.

The bodies were frozen, and this too made it easier for us to stack them. We then lined up the dead on the road while the trucks waited their turn to load them up. We were asked to identify guys, told them we were artillery and found seventeen from our battalion. Graves Reg EM recorded the names as we handed them the dog tags.

Joey identified seven from a 37th Field battery, and I came across three others I knew: Dutch Evitts, Robert Boatwright and Richard Delaney. Their outfit had been been through the Naktong bridge explosion and Kunu-ri with us, and then to die in this ugly, desolate, frozen house of the dead.

At the end of the second day, we told Graves Reg guys we'd ride in the truck with the dead from the arty unit, and was told this was not necessary, but we insisted. Joey nodded, and he also refused to ride in the cab. "We'll go with the guys in the back," is what we said.

I'll never get used to any of this.

Once again at the assembly point, we learned that more men had been killed at Hoengsong than at first reported.

We returned twice after the initial trip and found two more artillerymen: Pete de León and Wilburn Rice.

Since the cold continues, the bodies will remain frozen. We found many GIs under trucks; some had been run over by trucks and tanks; others wounded by enemy rifle or arty fire. Some GIs were also found inside trucks.

Charred hulks of burned vehicles stood all over the place; the bodies inside were in bad shape. Medics say the wounded must've died in their sleep.

A disaster. No civilian photographers from what I've seen. This prob due to Army censorship; someone has a lot to answer for here.

Four guys in our detail broke down. They'd been through the Kunu-ri ambush, but they couldn't take this detail and cracked. Got to feel sorry for guys who crack. Os and Old Guys say this: "No reason to chew them out. You pick them up, feed them, give them some rest, and they'll be back to fight. Army doesn't give up on people."

We from Kunu-ri recognize that crossing the Chongchong was worse than this, but as the Old Guys say: the dead stay dead, and they've all got relatives back home.

True enough.

Lt Vitetoe was in charge of our unit's work detail. Hoengsong being called Massacre Valley; that sounds like civilian talk, but it was baptized by the Marines. USMC lost many, many men here.

Still no civilian reporters here on our final trip to Hoengsong; the photogs consist of EM and Os.

Worked on open fields first, then up and down roads. Found dog tags, shoes and boots, socks and rings, etc. Petey Sturmer, the runner from Donora, Pa., worked with us and handled the bags carrying the personal effects.

Said he had seen hundreds of photographs of Gettysburg Battle and no diff from bodies here.

Talked about Penna a while. Says Donora is mostly Polish and German. The Gettysburg Battlesite, though, is near the state capital. I've no idea where any of this is.

Petey asked if Joey and I were cowboys in Texas. Told him no; my brother farms and Joey's dad is a printer and a newspaperman. Petey says his father works in a foundry of some sort.

Passed the time of day talking and I think we all knew we jabbered on to forget what we were doing.

Petey: "As I said, this is no different. As a runner you get to see more war. While this shit is bad, it's bad because these are our own guys. CCFs died too, you know."

So we kept up the work and the chatter. Stopped for a cigarette, and I waited to throw up again, but got through okay.

Petey says runner's job has changed: using jeeps more now. Easier since Gen Ridgway doesn't go all over the map. (We take land, fight, hold and move on, but not at breakneck speed.)

Then Joey said, "Possession for all time."

Petey looked at me when Joey quoted Thucydides again and said: "Catholic school, right? Jesuit?"

"Marist," and we both laughed.

Put out the cigarettes and back to work. In one hour we picked up 80 M-ls and over one-hundred helmets. We then filled more barracks bags with abandoned webbing, ammo clips, etc. Petey said that temptation remains the biggest risk for runners; he also said that dead NK and CCF are usually booby trapped. Asked me if I joined in, said no. Told me I was crazy, and Skinner working with Stang on some helmets and helmet liners, said, "He's not crazy, just dumb."

And we went on like this until time to quit.

As soon as we assembled again, we were broken off into small groups; Lt Fleming talked first and then Hat, and both said the same thing: we'll live with this for a long time. Don't fight it, admit what you've seen and done here, and you'll be done with it in less time.

That, too, is easier said.

In all, we spent three days here. I was glad to get off the detail and back to my binoculars.

After late chow we were rewarded with some beer.

Old Guys took over. Two battles shaping up, according to the Os. Maybe we'll go back to Seoul. Who knows?

Kitchen trucks arrived and the briefing was over. Ordnance guys came in and replaced two blocks, and we checked them out. Frazier scrounged a couple of mess kits for Ordnance guys, and they ate with us.

Mail. Three letters from Aaron, two from Aunt Mati and six from some letter-writing group in Tennessee, of all places. Never been there. They're form letters: "Thinking of all our troops," etc.

Heard of Hollywood actors on USO tours again. In this cold? I would like for them to get a load of the frozen dead at Hoengsong. It's all propaganda, and the shows are so bad not even Skinner would go to them.

Old Guys say they used to corral troops in Europe to watch the shows. I told them I used to see smiling faces on the Paramount News and all.

"Ha!" from Hat. And then, "I don't see you putting in for a trip to go see 'em."

Floodlights went up, and we went to work. Gearing up, taking in more ammo, which arrived after late chow. Rechecked new blocks again (perfect). I got me a new pair of gloves and a pair of mittens to go with them. Cleaned my two scarves by dipping them in hot water barrels, and hung them to dry across our gun. Scarves were getting rank. Froze in a matter of minutes, the steam rising at fifteen degrees F.

Work over, wrote to Aaron, Israel and Aunt Mati. Since it's close to early March, the ground will be turned by now and the cotton seed planted. The last of the oranges were already picked, is what Joey said.

And then, out of nowhere, Joey said, "Orange juice has the same color and consistency as rattler venom."

Sturmer looked at us as if we were mad and said: "Is that true? Really, guys?"

I said it was, but that the smell tied with Korean rice paddies for first place. Sturmer laughed and said that was the runner's motto: "Avoid rice paddies at all costs."

During this, Skinner, of all people, brought me ten books. Haven't read a line in a month. One was another copy of the biography of the actor John Barrymore, plus a biography of a New York lawyer named Fallon. The rest is a mixed bag: Amer Lit from the 20s and 30s. Still, books are books and meant to be read.

Before sacking out, Dumas came up and said, "We'll spend one more day here. The Bn CO says you guys deserve to take a day off after the last three."

We asked if we were going to Wonju, but Dumas said he thought we'd go northwest, to Seoul. To take it back, he said.

Joey brought his arctic bag and a couple of blankets and said he was going to spend the night in our battery area.

Talk got to rumors as always. Part of unit is going to Seoul, but we, this arty Bn will go to Wonju, etc.

We talked a bit about Cloverleaf and Obong-ni and the two stubborn knobs and hills. This is the same site of NK atrocities: burying an O alive and tying up GIs, then shooting and bayonetting them; some were buried alive and suffocated.

Wherever we are to go, we're to meet units we're supporting when we get there. Dug out my next to last USMC cap and read the Marine's name: S. Boers, but pronounced Boris. Some Marines forces are out here again, and maybe I'll run into him, if he's alive. Boers's outfit transferred to Northeast Korea and no idea how fighting went there in Nov and Dec when we got whacked at Kunu-ri.

Cooks came by and said there was plenty of hot chow left over, and out we went. Luxury's lap: two hot meals in one day.

Got sleepy soon after and told to be ready to move out tomorrow at 0530 with early chow from 0430 to 0500.

(I'm scared to talk with the guys about Hoengsong; I'm trying to forget the dead, but it isn't working out. Please, God, don't let me go crazy.)

Rest Area

February 20-22. Sleep, sleep, sleep, and more sleep. We must have been running on empty right after the Chipyong-ni fight. I remember eating and sleeping well during our stay there, but the rest here is different in many ways: no rousting you out of the sack at all hours, you wake up here to the smell of the kitchen truck nearby and, most importantly for us, there's time. Time to do whatever one feels like doing.

I slept most of the first day. I then ate something, visited with Joey at C Battery. We drank some beer, talked some, watched some troops do close order drill, and smoked whenever and wherever we wanted to. I then wrote letters to Aunt Mati, to Israel and to Aaron. After this, I made a new copy of my map and asked Hat to mark Chipyong-ni, Saemal/Hoengsong and Wonju for me.

Reread *All My Sons* by A. Miller; tried but again failed to find interest in the Carson McCullers play. Lt Vitetoe says she's Southern, and that I, as a Texan and a westerner, wouldn't find it interesting.

The Lt is a nice guy and you can talk to him plainly. I said Texas had been a slave-holding state and that we still had a poll tax back home, and that we're not cowboys. Lt Vitetoe said for me to try reading McCullers again, but I made no promises.

While on this, the Lt said he'd heard that Negro units would be joining the regular units, and what did I think of that. During this, Dumas and Hook brought cleaning rods and cloths for our carbines, and the Lt repeated what he'd said about the Negro troops.

Hook said, "They'll fight; some will run away just like some of our guys, but most will stay and fight."

Dumas nodded at this and said he'd known many Negro regulars who'd fight till Hell melted and refroze.

It's something to think about, is what the Lt said.

So I cleaned the carbine bores until there wasn't a speck of dust on them anywhere.

During foot and shoe inspection, I was ordered to turn in the old pair of combat boots for a new pair. Applied some dubbin right away and then walked around a while to break them in. These are for saving until the second pair starts to give out.

Skipped fumigation yesterday. That stuff gets in your lungs, you die here. Finished off the day by reading some more and then asked a Chaplain's assistant (Sal Petrucci, Ormonk, N.Y.), for a Catholic Bible. Told him we'd leave tomorrow or the next day.

At 1300, right after chow, Hatalski requisitioned a weapons carrier and took Dumas, Skinner and me to the ASP (Ammo Supply Point) some seven miles away. We mainly stood around while Hat and Dumas put their orders in for our 105mm and small arms ammo. On the way back, Hat drove off the main road and pulled into another rest area full of British Brigade and Netherlands units—battle weary, like the rest of us. Later Hat said he'd delivered six cartons of cigarettes to the British Old Guys, and then showed us some American beer the British and Dutch had loaded inside the truck.

Sipping on the beer on the way back, we got to talking about Korean place names, but this didn't clear up much. There's a Pyongpyong, a Pyongtaek, a Pyongyang, a Chipyong-ni, and there's an Inchon and an Ichon, and so on.

And, too, although we've seen refugees since the war started, none of us have talked to them. And how could we, anyway?

Dumas then said that it wasn't until the war stopped in Germany that the troops had a chance to talk with the German population, and this wasn't much to speak of since so few Germans spoke any English. From this to their China service, but this was different: it was peacetime and one got to serve in one place for a good while.

We got to the rest area in good shape and to the smell of a kitchen truck.

Hat: "Do what you have to do today; chances are we'll leave tomorrow, the day after at the latest."

Today, Feb 22, is our third and last full day here. The morning started off miserably with a heavy snow fall, and so we fell to the guns and checked them thoroughly. The snow then turned to sleet, but even this finally stopped, and the last three hours of daylight today brought the invariably blue, chilly, Korean sky.

Ordnance gave our guns the once over just one more time, signed them over to Lt Waller, and we were told to be ready to move out early tomorrow morning. (This usually means we're to be up by 0430 or 0500, chow down by the kitchen trucks and be ready to move out by 0630 after we've policed the area and re-checked *all* the gear, assembled, etc.)

To bed at 2100. Petrucci brought the Bible and visited a while. Learned from him that during the Pusan Perimeter, Chaplain's assistants were issued M-1s and fought like everybody else.

Still very cold here in the eastern corridor. Feel good, though. Rested.

Seoul Redux

February 23-March 13. Everyone feels and looks relaxed. Got away at 0620 on the nose. Lt Waller said we were to go north, toward the Han. We of the 219th were to join up with our old friends of the 25th Div and then were to report either to its 24th or 35th Inf Regt. In any event, we were to go north and that was it. I put the journal away and saw to the guns.

When Seoul was lost to the CCF back on January 4, that was part of the CCF's big winter push, which began with our rout in Nov and Dec at Kunu-ri. So now we are to retake Seoul one more time.

Got to the assembly point by early evening, and we could see the Han clearly enough. From where we are, the river curves southward and then to the west of Seoul; some other I Corps units are facing the capital city, but we're down river.

We're only a small part of the artillery power here. We're still in I—Eye—Corps, with the 35th Inf Regt of the good old 25th Div this time.

The outfit's been in Korea almost as long as us. Been told that in arty alone there are ten battalions here, and there's no stopping the crossing of the Han. The way we've been going with Gen Ridgway, we take a little or a lot, but we take it and hold on to it; and, no unit is alone, isolated. This isn't that cowboy drive up north of last Oct-Nov. No sir.

Patrols are said to go out all the time; they bump into each other almost. They and Engineers are looking for places tanks can ford. Bridges will be built, but tanks must get across to provide much protection.

Patrols report a thin crust of ice on the river, but the tanks will take care of that at the first crossing. We're mostly resting here and hiding the build-up from the CCF and NK, according to the Old Guys. Skinner and I rubbed dubbin on boots and talked some about home. Put in some reading time afterward.

February 25. Since we have some new guys in each battery, we're spending most of our time going over some of the pregistered targets, the best way to wheel a gun when one of the guys drops out, how to coordinate fire with the other batteries, etc. Training.

The ground, though, remains frozen as do the roads. Of course, if it rains, then all bets are off—the roads can turn into cold swamps. Winter is still hanging on, so there must be some weeks left before the thaw.

Os and Old Guys say crossing must be done soon, since the thaw may wash out bridges and will flood many sections of the Han. Time, time, time—the Army lives on that too.

The Engineer Old Guys who know our Old Guys tell us the Han is already fordable by tanks in some spots. (I spotted from fifty to sixty tanks in our sector alone—Shermans, mostly.)

As always, the Engineers are here, but in a big way this time. Hat says there are anywhere from four to five battalions of them all along the river front. When the thousands of South Korean laborers are trucked in, and if we're still here, then you'll see what a big job looks like, is what Hat said.

Last night, on the 24th, we watched a good number of units pass to the right and left of us and first got to check out some Greek and then some Turkish volunteers riding on tanks. I counted fourteen of them riding on one of the tanks, all armed and hugging blankets against the cold.

Of the ten arty battalions, four are posted to our sector. So, the concentration will be from this point. We're west of a British arty unit with 25-pounders; we crossed the River Chongchong with these guys last year. Lt Vitetoe says there are three British brigades in Korea: the 27th, the 28th and the 29th made up of English, Canadians, Australians and New Zealanders. (I have no idea what a brigade is.)

Battalion HQ sent another warning: too many GIs abandoning their helmets for their pile caps. Well, I wear a pile, but the pot is always nearby; it's saved my head and face at least three times.

February 26. The training routine is getting old, but without it we'd go crazy. Stayed up for sixteen hours since the day started at 0400. Cold, dark, some wind, but not enough to cause shell deviation if we're called to fire. We're now in preparation for the 27th Infantry Regt; our original regiment, the 35th Infantry, is in reserve. For now, all the arty units in this area remain massed.

After chow, we received more shells, loaded them up to our trucks, and got everything shipshape for firing. No reason to uncrate them since supplies keep coming in daily.

February 27. The 25th Div is strung along the Han; we're near where the Han meets the River Pukhan; the other Infantry Regts of the 25th are to the right and left of us. A change: now the 27th Infantry Regiment is back on reserve. No idea why the US Army moves units in and out all the time.

March 1. The Old Guys all say that we're to cross damned soon. The build up is incredible, and the rumor about our having ten artillery battalions in the area proved to be no rumor.

Lt Fleming: "The count of all artillery, guns and howitzers, is now from one-hundred-forty to one-hundred-fifty pieces of artillery."

We're getting spoiled: eaten hot chow every day, three times a day, too, and we sit and watch patrols cross the river and return, cross the river and return once again. I'm running out of reading material. So, it's been some Bible reading and what not. Skinner (who is Catholic himself) trotted out the old lie about Catholics not being allowed to read the Bible, etc.

Not much to do except train. It's a creepy feeling of not earning your pay or something. But the Army never stands still, even now, because there's much movement going on, what with the constant building up of supplies, the Engineers building their bridges and all kinds of equipment moving in. Something I'd not seen or heard of before: huge, massive searchlights which require the Army's biggest trucks and trailers to lug them around. Half a dozen guys are needed to operate them. The lights have a range of some 30,000 to 40,000 yards is what the guys claim. That's a bunch of miles.

March 2-7. A week of training. Got to see Joey and some of the guys over at C battery. Played cards, shot the shit and picked up some books from Joey. Had my picture taken with some of the C battery gunners. Wrote home.

Much preparation. Engineers working overtime, and I've seen truckload after truckload of South Korean workmen; prob here to rebuild Seoul, but most probably here to work on roads, bridges, wire entanglements, etc.

March 8. Our Div crossed the Han yesterday morning; the 27th Regt had been on reserve, but it was then tapped to cross first, while we were to remain south of the Han. By staying put, we were assigned a firing mission along with the million other guns here. I guess we'll go with the 35th Regiment, to which we are now reattached.

We started yesterday's fire at 0555, sharp. We fired for 15 minutes. Stopped for five minutes and then started again at 0615. I've never heard so much fire, and this goes back to the firing of all the ammo on the ground when we crossed the Chongchong.

This was a big league fire. Was told later that the first fifteen minute fire mission came to seven thousand rounds from the one-hundred-forty-odd guns of the ten arty battalions dug in here. Can't be much left of anything after that. If a shell hits near you, the concussion can pop your eyes out of their sockets, but concussion alone can knock you senseless too; and never mind what happened to those left inside the city of Seoul where most of the shells hit.

The second fire mission (0615) lasted two hours; this was heavier than the first one because there was firing for miles around. To be on the receiving end of ten arty battalions is, as Lt Fleming put it, " ... to stand at the gates of Hell for an eternity."

I can only imagine (although I *can* imagine) what the inside of Seoul looks like after this. It was almost leveled the last time we rumbled through there.

Refugees. The runners and the South Korean agents estimate there are some 100,000 of them waiting by the river to reenter Seoul. The Lord only knows what they'll find once inside the city, and only the Lord knows how many CCF, NK and civilians died as a result of our fire and the air strikes.

There was much troop movement all day long across the bridges today; I guess we won't be going directly into Seoul ourselves, since that honor belongs to another unit, most likely some ROK Div.

We're on another push but different this time: no recklessness.

Korean laborers were again trucked through us early this afternoon; most likely to clear the streets of civilian and enemy dead so the trucks can make good time; the roads are also cleared for psychological reasons. It's bad enough to see uniformed dead without adding refugees and other civilians to the mess out there.

(Right after the fire mission, and just before we crossed the Han, some Os drove through us; they were checking to see if we were wearing our steel pots, which we were. Found out that those Os and enlisted men were from the Provost Marshal with orders to book anyone not wearing the steel pot.)

Stang: "What are they going to do? Pull you out of the line? Hell, no. You'll cross the river, but not before they take your name, rank and serial number, and then, if you come out alive from all this shit, then and *only* then, will they court martial your ass."

We crossed the Han, drove up some seven mi with only small arms fire for opposition (but no mines on road and no roadblocks). We're standing some eight mi north of the Han, some six to seven mi northeast of Seoul. A town called Uijungbo is north of us. Runners and line crossers have been there and say it's a dead town, blasted worse than Seoul. CCF may defend that point, but that's not where we're going.

An easy crossing; but it was the artillery and those deadly air strikes that pushed the 35th Infantry Regt up and across.

Was standing by the kitchen truck waiting for coffee and sandwiches, when a tank patrol brought in some CCF POWs—one O and his enlisted men. Artillerymen; their arty instruments similar to ours. Their O was a forward ob.

Been a long day, and I'm ready for the sack. Will stop here; it's 1900 hrs and looks like another clear, cold night.

Five hours sleep; up at 2400 hrs to hot chow and felt refreshed; heard continuous firing to left and right. Runners eating with us told of a group of Turks. CCF struck along parts of I Corps where the Turks were assigned. The Turks were forced to withdraw, they then reorganized, rallied and recaptured the lost ground. Tough bunch of people.

March 9. Stood and held ground. Told that Seoul was a mess again, but that CCF hasn't given it all up yet. That the war is far from over, etc.

Dumas: "Best prepare your rookies, Rafe. CCF bound to start their push back, and that means roadblocks and ambushes all over again."

True enough, but how does one train rookies to deal with roadblocks? Unless you've been in them, there's no other way to explain them to anyone.

March 10-13. UN troops inside Seoul. Took it on the 12th. The word: ROK and parts of Third Div found some CCF and NK soldiers lying on the streets, unburied and dead due to starvation. But CCF and NK main forces made an orderly (and successful) withdrawl from the city. The conclusion is obvious: CCF is, for the most part, intact.

We're to remain holding here. Waiting for CCF, I guess. All three Infantry Regts of the 25th Div (35th, 27th and 24th) are next to each other, according to Dumas. Supplies continue coming in across the river. No idea how truck drivers bringing stuff to us are holding up; they're working eighteen hrs a day, and unless wounded in combat, all truck drivers in hospital have been released and put to work. It's crazy, but necessary if we are to be supplied with ammunition. As for the trucks, maintenance must be working 24 hours a day to keep them on the road; there's no other way.

(Runners and line crossers bringing in all kind of information, CCF building up, planning a big, big offensive, a counterattack, a-this-and-a-that, it'll come, etc.)

It doesn't much look like Retreat City for I Corps, though; there's been too much preparation for us to bug out. Bug out isn't a term one hears now; it was all the rage a few months back.

Before turning in, I reported to Hat and told him I wasn't feeling well. He pointed to some red spots/welts on and above the eyebrow and nose areas, and said: "Report for sick call tomorrow, and I'll check on other guys to see if they've got whatever that stuff is."

A Spring Break

March 14-17, 1951. Got back from the hospital within three days. There must have been fifty of us who were infected by some sort of rot; penicillin took care of it. The doctor says we have more deaths due to accidents and disease than to combat. He has the figures, I guess, but I'd rather be in a back area anytime.

As usual, when the CCF stops fighting, it stops flat out. They move out of an area and go off to reorganize. They probe some, but mainly they pull back. This is now a usual tactic, and they may be short of food, shoes and other equipment. It doesn't mean they're through fighting.

Still no *official* word on Charlie; he may be a POW, and if so, I hope it's CCF. (It'll be some time before everyone is accounted for, and this is the main reason why Lt Waller didn't write Charlie's family and why he told me to hold off a while back; but I had to write the Villalóns, and I did.)

On the way back from the field hospital, the trucks stopped for refueling and a checking over by maintenance; this gave us a chance to look at a section of Seoul. I'd not noticed just how big a city it was; although now it's mostly leveled (our arty and CCF's). No refugees to impede our crossing this morning, but they'll be back in greater numbers, now that we've crossed the Han and they think it's safe to be back in Seoul.

Intel/Recon guys stopped by our unit and gave us the word: Be very careful in dealing with refugees, there may be NKPA among them. GIs warned to be prepared to shoot. (How can we tell who's who? They gave us some great advice: use your best judgment.)

As we pulled out, we saw more refugees streaming in. A Military Policeman said if we wanted our convoy to get on the road, we better not start handing out C-rations to the refugees. We'd be here forever, he said, so we moved on and had no trouble with the refugees.

The Han is still very, very cold, so the refugees had to be patient, although many chose to cross right away. What a place to come home to. Our Infantry escorts say that the Chosen Hotel is a heap of broken glass and cement and said the same thing about the Bento Hotel.

These refugees are the poorest of the poor. Everything they own is on their backs. Everybody—kids included—carry a load. Their shoes are a mess, and then there's the ice. Jesus.

Much equipment has been moving across, but, as soon as a new bridge goes up, the refugees start using that one too.

News: Gen Ridgway's liaison plane landed not 1500 ft from where we stopped for a 15-minute break. He's still visiting as many units as possible. I think the Gen doesn't care how you look in the field as long as you fight, wear the steel pot, and don't lose equipment.

Most of the guys in the trucks are artillerymen; a group of them says that the reason we got the rot was that the water was bad, that the rations were contaminated, etc. All I know is that the rot is disappearing, and that's as far as I'm going to take it.

Was dropped off at the 219th area and lugged my junk over to my battery.

Hat and Frazier came by: How's the leprosy, and how the hell are you? Was told that Dumas, Stang and Skinner were in a back area for two-three days. On their return, Hat and Frazier will get some days off too. I'm to get two new gun crews to break in, and we'll see after that.

Played cutthroat pinochle with Crazy and Ichabod and then to the sack.

March 15. The Infantry is at work again and the Intel/Recon guys go out early. Those units carry much firepower for a platoon: five jeeps (two with M-guns and three with SCR-300 radios, two tanks, a mobile mortar section, and some Infantry to accompany tanks.

All reports from runners say the same thing: CCF probing seriously and patrolling aggressively to see what we've got, and then our guys go out to see what they've got. The Air Force has a difficult time spotting CCF during the day, so the patrols have to go out; it's been this way most of the war.

Besides, as Al Skinner says, "It's hard to bring prisoners in when you're flying a plane."

CCF are a tough bunch of people. Os say they're far away from their supply bases, but that they are still being supplied. Our Air Force will shoot at anything that moves: trucks, trains, etc, but CCF is still being supplied, because they also use men and animals for transport.

The Air Force is still a danger for us. It's frustratingly difficult to coordinate with ground troops, and so the AF will sometimes fire on our troops by accident. Just last year, the AF shot at British troops by mistake.

This is how it happened. Things got pretty screwed up in the Pass last November, and the ridges were mobbed with US Army and CCF troops, and much firing all around by our Inf and us. The Gloster arty had cleaned off a hill of CCF and then, suddenly, our Air Force came roaring in and caught the Glosters on open ground, high on a ridge. There wasn't a place for the Glosters to run; they were pinned like flies, and they died the same way.

At first, the Glosters must have looked up, prob relaxed their guard at the sight of our Air Force, and then they had no chance to react. Many were hit and killed. No idea how this was resolved.

Acc to runners passing through our area, there are some good-sized patrols on both sides, and they keep running into each other. Lt Brodkey has registered on everything we have up front. We also have good communication with Signal Corps' help, but the CCF creeps in at night and Signal then has to go out to repair/replace the wire each morning.

The listening posts have been set up below the Forward Ob sites. The CCF patrols at night too, but there's no set schedule for them. Our listening posts report movement in the areas where our GIs are not sent, therefore it must be CCF. But, we can't fire, since this can lead to all manner of foul-ups, so there it stands.

News regarding Seoul is that most of our troops have crossed the Han in good order.

Dumas, Stang and Skinner are back, and out went Hook and Hatalski for a few days rest. Dumas talked about the Pass and the Chongchong to the three of us.

Skinner asked about POWs, and Dumas said that in combat it's best to disarm and abandon them. They become too much trouble to feed and lug around, etcetera

And NK? I asked. The Germans and the Japs also murdered GIs, he said. I mentioned the SS's reputation, but Dumas (he was in Belgium for a while) said that regular German army units also shot POWs outright.

But it happens that POWs are in the way of both sides sometimes; this is one reason why American POWs have been released, and why we release CCF POWs at times. Of course, he said, and this may have also happened at the Pass, the same POWs may be recaptured later and held a second time if CCF holds that ground securely. This did happen at the Pass, since we got some ex-POWs in our trucks and moved them to safety.

He then said that the Pass roadblocks were typical. Sometimes there are rivers to cross, and then there's also night fighting, etc.

Dumas: "You guys have just about seen it all."

Dumas then asked if I've taken any pictures so far. Told him I'd forgotten my camera, that it was probably among some of the equipment I left in my old barracks bag. Stang then said that much of that stuff is rotting somewhere in the port of Pusan. That's God's truth.

We went back to POWs for a while, and I said I'd not heard of our side shooting POWs. Dumas said we probably had, but that the US Army is hell on that, and that the guilty would be tried in a flash. That's the way it works, is what he said.

Dumas made it official: I'm to be in charge of my old gun crew again, and Stang and Skinner are to work alongside.

We heard some small arms fire for most of the day, but it was far away and not aimed in our direction.

Joey came by and brought beer. He's worried about Charlie, and I told him of Dumas's talk on POWs. I said Charlie was prob back in some field hospital getting patched up, and that we just had not heard of it. Some time back, the battery clerk had said Charlie was still being carried as missing for now. Then we remembered the Chaplain reading off the name of the casualties during Mass, etc. Joey and I were on this when the mail truck came in with two new replacements. Surprise! A letter from Sonny Ruiz, in Japan.

He'd been in Pusan most of the time and missed the Pass, but was in reserve during Chipyong-ni and on the drive north to here. Typical Ruiz luck: standing by roadblock while on reserve, wounded twice, lightly, on both arms and hip, but perfectly okay now, he says. More like a burn. Shrapnel of course. He was standing behind the 105 and was partially shielded from the blast, but he still caught two finger-nail sized pieces of NK or CCF HE. He was patched up fast, went to a field hosp for two days, and with no infections was released. He waited two more days in back area, made up his mind right then, and found transport back to Japan. He's left the Army on his own, he says.

He'll marry that Japanese schoolteacher. No plans after that other than he'll remain in Japan. Says his Mom's taken care of by Chano's WWII insurance and social security which is still more money than she ever earned working as a maid for the Logans, the Paxtons and the Ripleys. (It was Sonny who had forced those families to take out his Mom's social security deduction; malgre lui, is how Sonny put it.)

He also said Capt Bracken (who is now with us) just came to Korea four months ago. Sonny served with Lt Edwards's replacement and ran a crew for him.

Sonny had also checked on Hiro Watanabe and the money; that Hiro was doing okay and that the money was still in the Nihongo Bank and at the Tokyo whorehouse. Sonny said we needed to give power of attorney to old Yoshiko Ogura in case something happens to us. Good idea.

Got a second letter; from Aaron, who writes that people in Klail are saying I'm going blind. Aaron then said that Brother William was right when he told some of us at Saint Boniface that we'd go blind some day.

Nice lazy day. Got permission from Lt Vitetoe to go to C Battery and ate there. Joey said three guys in C Battery got the rot, too. He too heard from home, and all's well on that front.

The day dragged by, so I asked Dumas if there was something I could do, and he said to go see Lt Brodkey. This got me out of the area, and I took a comic novel with me, *The Zebra Derby*.

Ross, one of Brodkey's crew of runners, said that that type of book is neither serious nor of any use to me. That's an old argument between us, and I usually avoid Ross. If he'd ever gone through rank racial discrimination in Texas, then, I once told him, then, "You could talk to me about brotherhood."

I then asked him if he'd read *Manhattan Transfer,* and he came up with that jargon of his: that Dos Passos still had some "residual ideology" and so on and so on. He said my turning my back on Catholicism wasn't going to save me. I agreed, but I also told him that reading Max Shulman, whom he mistook for some socialist, was good enough for me. As usual, I swore to avoid him in the future, and I'm sure he did the same in my regard. We'll prob all get killed here anyway, for all the good his theories are going to do him. He's smart, though.

Got to the Forward ob holes (which aren't holes or deep ones either.) They usually sit on some hillside with a good view. Lt Brodkey, Crazy and Ichabod are adept at arm and hand signals, and have developed a workable system between them.

This afternoon, during my visit with them, Crazy Brom told me how Lts Bricketto and John died a while back. The two SCR-300s crapped out early during the fight. Two telephone lines were working okay for a while, but since we were wheeling the guns around to fire here and there and back again, and the ranges had to be adjusted and readjusted constantly, both Lts would get up and give arm and hand signals. And then, since each one fell like a stone, Lt Brodkey figured they'd been picked off by sniper sharpshooters. I've no idea when they were brought back to base camp. That had been a long, intense day of fighting with much movement in and around our area; I must have missed their being transported by the trucks carrying the dead.

Told Crazy I was going up to the guns, and I left a book with Ichabod who reads some. Screwed off most of the afternoon and finished off the rest of Fowler's *Great Mouthpiece*.

March 16. USO troupes were landed some 40 mi south of Seoul. That must be a secured area if those people are that close to us. Bracken ordered two truckloads to take in the show. Escaped that, so Skinner and I got together with the Old Guys.

Lt Waller came by and asked about the rookie replacements and their training. Coming along is what the Old Guys said. (Lt Waller looks better; looked terrible in November from that pneumonia he caught right before the Pass.) Still no news on Lt Edwards. Lt Fleming came by to check the shell inventory, and after this, Lt Waller and I then went to see Lt Brodkey.

Got to the hill and Crazy and I waited until Lt Waller left with Brodkey. I dumped some beer cans in Crazy's hole and drank a couple with Ichabod, spelling him on the binocs. Crazy tells the worst jokes in the world, but he's good at his job. Ichabod is a good partner, says Crazy; trouble is Ichabod can go days without saying a word. Crazy says Ichabod is part Trappist; Ichabod had no idea what that meant.

I asked Crazy if he was a Catholic; he said yes. From Catholic schools, catechism, serving at mass, etc to this. He went to a Christian Brothers school. Told him of Marist Bros, but he said the Marists are tame when compared to the Christians. He called them and the Jesuits the Gestapo of the Catholic Church.

This is the first long talk with Bromley; his first name is Billy, not Bill or Wm. He's from Muncie, Indiana; he wants to be an actor, and he wants to be rich.

Walked back to base camp with Lt Waller. He talked about his twin sister; a spastic, he called her. Don't know what that means. She went to a private school in South Carolina. He asked me if I planned to return to college. Sure, if we live through this.

He reported to Capt Bracken, and I then went to the hot water barrel and dropped in two cans of hamburger patties.

We still had two hours of daylight when the gun crews returned from the USO show. We then listened to a lecture by Intel/Recon guys. There's to be increased night precautions, and they take effect tonight, since the CCF is getting bolder.

Asked Joey about the USO shows; except for Al Jolson, a piece of shit, acc to him and to everbody else.

Almost as soon as Hat and Frazier were driven in, that damned Bracken told Hat for me to be issued a regulation fatigue cap, right away, and to stop wearing the Marine cap. Told Joey about it and he said he sided with Bracken."After all, Rafe, your wearing that cap could change the course of the entire war." I then turned to Hat and asked if I'm to pay for the cap, and Hat, smiling, said: "Well, it'll probably be deducted in your next pay period."

One of the bothers with no fighting going on in the area is that Os get chicken shit, since they've little else to do.

Joey put it better: "It's different with Bracken; he's to the manner born, Rafe; he's a Texan."

Surprise order after late chow. Two gun crews (mine and Skinner's) were placed on reserve and trucked to this assembly point. Looks like the fighting will be on us soon. Got me a new pile cap along with the soft fatigue cap, and loaded up with C-rations.

Kept the USMC cap, since I'll be out of Bracken's sight for a while.

Above All, the Waste

March 18. Lt Brodkey up and shot himself today. One of the tank patrols was making its way across a lane with uncharged mines, when their Old Guy (JB Rouse, Frankfort, Ky) spotted Lt Brodkey half in-half out of his forward ob hole. He'd shot himself in the heart.

Given the force of a 45, Sgt Rouse thinks Lt Brodkey shot himself inside the hole, and then the force of the automatic caused him to be thrown out and across, half in-half out. Said the Lt prob used both hands to fire and this and the impact of the 45 pushed him back and across the hole.

According to Sgt Rouse, he found the Lt's helmet, binocs, charts, pencils, two packs of Luckies and a Japanese lighter all in a row. To his right, the Lt had placed the phone, the aiming circle, the range finders, a slide rule and the other surveying equipment also in a row, neatly done.

It's been quiet in our firing zone for two days in a row, and it was earlier this afternoon that the Lt ordered Crazy and Ichabod up the ridge to enjoy a hot meal from one of the kitchen trucks. No need to report back in any hurry, the Lt said. "See you in a couple of hours; just leave me your binocs here, Bromley." And that was it.

We'd been goofing off too; after a check of the guns and the shell inventory, I spent most of the morning and early afternoon reading the Dos Passos book Lt Brodkey had given me for a second time.

No idea why he shot himself. Skinner said the Lt just snapped, but that can't be it; most of us here are half crazy anyway.

The rumors regarding rotation were proved to be the straight dope, but with a big catch: the Army needs experienced junior officers for leadership roles; this, then, meant that in our unit, Lts Billy Waller, Vitetoe, Fleming and Brodkey wouldn't be going home. Lt Merritt came in with Capt Bracken, and he hasn't had enough time here for rotation acc to Hat.

As for the Old Guys, the great losses back in Nov-Dec created a shortage of Old Guys as well. And then when Stang, Skinner and I (along with Joey over at C battery) were made buck sergeants, and put to running and training our own crews, that meant we wouldn't be going home either until "capable replacements could be transferred in," etc.

It could be that Lt Brodkey was counting on going home, was actually pointing to it. As Hat says, "That's always a danger."

But there it is, junior Os and experienced NCOs will remain here. And, it doesn't mean a damned thing that we've been here since Osan/Suwon back in July.

Sat and talked with Dumas and Frazier a while; suicide is normal in this situation, both said. I said that was a crazy thing to say, and they admitted it, but then went on to say that war itself is crazy, so it's a wonder and a miracle most people don't kill themselves. That went for them too, they said.

Talk got around to guys shooting themselves in the foot, some in the hand, etc. Some guys will do anything to get out of combat, but they're stupid if they think a US Army doc won't know how the hell they got wounded.

Skipped chow and went over to the medical tent to see if I could pick up anything on Lt Brodkey, but somehow I missed the last trucks carrying today's dead and wounded. I'd asked if there were any chance Lt Brodkey's body would be sent home, to Philadelphia, and Clayton Sams, the medical orderly, said, "They never tell us anything, Rafe."

Most likely Capt Bracken will write some piss-poor letter to his parents; what he should do is to leave the letter writing to Waller or to one of the other Os. They're the one who knew him, not Bracken.

Beyond the 38th Parallel

March 20-28. Another slow week at the office, although we've been on attack orders since the unit was ordered to the 38th Parallel and beyond. It's the former South and N Korean boundary line, but little else: no high ground, no ridges to fire from, etc.

Hat says that we, as usual, will go for the higher ground just beyond the 38th; nothing new, since the CCF and NK will want that too.

Talked to Hat a while. Told him we'd noticed CCF was up to old tricks of fighting some, delaying some and retreating while we chase. He agreed but then said this is different. With Ridgway in command, there's no unit isolation, thus the CCF will have to figure out another way to trap us this time.

Frazier came by with hot coffee for all. He said another big investigation is under way regarding Hoengsong mess. Parts of artillery, Hat thinks, didn't coordinate with or didn't get the orders in time for, what he called maximum effectiveness. Too many guys killed and many Marines also bought the farm at Hoengsong/Saemal. When this happens, heads roll. He didn't know if we'd be questioned again, but he said an investigation will be done one more time.

Both Hook and Dumas told us of reports of much fighting to the west of us; part of our I Corps units. So far, we haven't had much of that. This is fine with me. Patrols report light engagement, but runners and line crossers say CCF and NKPA are massing troops for another offensive.

Rotation rumors at chow line again, but no evidence of anyone going back to the States.

Jerry Ling (Albion, Michigan), one of the rookie gunners, came over from B Battery with some books for me. Joey found some in C Battery and sent Ling over; he's a reader. I gave him what I had (I was down to three), and he left me half a dozen. One of the books, *Number One,* is also by Dos Passos. (I'd finally finished off *Manhattan Transfer* and was sorry to pass it on, since it was a present from Lt Brodkey to me. Ling seems to be a nice guy.)

Will turn in shortly.

Our situation: Seoul is behind us, and we're just above the 38th and making for higher ground, Line Kansas. We're to defend here, fire like crazy, make an orderly retreat, kill CCF and hold on to the new line. We're to repeat the same tactics until we get to just north of Seoul (Line Golden). The retreating is intended to be nothing more than a slow, planned retreat to kill as many NKPA and CCF as possible.

There's been bitter fighting all around to the north, northeast and more to the northwest, it being hit the hardest of all. The Old Guys say we're all doing our part here by holding. The CCF units ahead of us doing their part too; it's always a matter of time, they say.

How does one explain the following. Right before I sacked out, Stang came by and told me a story: Along with NK and CCF POWs (stragglers, deserters, wounded), three CCF female nurses were also captured and brought back.

They were then stripped (and searched, I imagine), but it was brutal since it was freezing. Stang also said the nurses were photographed buck naked. *That* is a hell of a note.

Temps around 10 degrees F at sack time.

The Baby Sitters

April 3-25. All of a sudden on the last days of March, fifteen of us were pulled out of the line: Hat, Dumas, Frazier, Stang, Skinner, Joey and me plus eight gunners, loaders, etc. We were then flown out of Pusan to Southern Japan. Just like that. Great duty promised. (Anything away from the war is great duty.)

The seven of us are from the original Task Force Smith, and I guess we have some easy time coming, because we've been in this since June, '50. There were some guys with the 7th Division along with us.

April 3. This is the softest duty yet, and it's a form of R & R for us. We're to escort newcomers and take them around southwestern Honshu; we're to be tourist guides, is how Frazier put it.

We're back in the Kwansai district, and it's almost like coming home for us. Joey and I have been receiving post cards from Sonny Ruiz, who's holed up in Kobe with that schoolteacher of his. Our Old Guys know nothing of this, and Joey and I aren't about to give Sonny's game away.

Sonny was wounded lightly both times, but he said the third time could be a charm, and he sure as hell wasn't going to take a chance. He made his way to Japan somehow, and soon after we started receiving postcards from Kobe.

They were in Spanish, and he dribbled bits and pieces of how he made it back to Yamato; Sonny always uses the poetic name for Japan, and he says he's at home here.

Since we've been kept fairly busy with the rookies, taking them all over the area, we haven't had a chance to see Sonny up at Kobe. Our chance will come, though.

April 4-5. This is strange duty. We're now on our second day with this batch, and they'll be on their way to Korea o/a April 6/7 for further training. After that, we get a new batch and show them the sights. A sort of orientation for new State Siders. They have no idea what's going on, but at least they ask questions about Japan and Korea, how things are over there; they haven't been here long enough to start complaining about the Japanese, the food, etc.

158

Joey and I have noticed how much the Kwansai District has changed since June, 1950. Factories have opened up, the Japanese are building ships for the US Army over by the Inland Sea, and we're told that other parts of Japan are serving as warehouses and as manufacturers for the Army.

There's more money now and much movement up and down and from here to there by the civilian population.

No idea what Tokyo looks like, but if it's as active as this part of Honshu, it ought to be buzzing.

We're supposed to be given the day off tomorrow. Joey and I will play it cagey. If anyone tags along with us (Stang, Skinner, etc), we'll just go over to Nara, look up old Kazuo Fujiwara, drink up and spend the night and day with the girls at the Temple of Pleasure.

April 6. No day off today, and it was just as good. It rained from sunrise to sunset. To top it, one of the buses broke down during a trip around the ports, and we limped back to the motor pool. Have been promised the day off tomorrow, if it doesn't rain.

Met a couple of Texans in the new batch. An Anglo (Jimmy Coalson), from Olney, Tex, which he says is near Dallas, and Rudy Hernández from Bascom, down in the Valley.

Hernández is an older guy, his late twenties, who served as a sailor during WWII. An easy going type. Said he knew where Joey and I were from by our last names. He's a Cpl; said he got the rank almost as soon as as he was sworn in. As a WWII vet, he said, he was considered an old timer.

Most of the guys, the first batch and this one, are small town guys like us—and they'd not traveled much until they joined the Army.

Some of these guys say that the folks back in the States talk some about the war, and some are against it, too. But, as Rudy Hernández says, "You'd think there wasn't much of a war going on at all. Things are pretty normal."

Joey asked him how those Valley families who've lost sons out here feel about the war.

"Well," Rudy said, "they sure as hell know there's a war going on. I'll say they do." Rudy says so many guys volunteered for the Air Force (to escape the Army; the Inf, really) that the Air Force recruiters had to close shop. I imagine they'll take them anyway, and then put them in the Army, but this is just a guess on my part.

April 8. Rained again off and on this morning, and we took the guys up and down the Inland Sea, and then the convoy made for Nagoya, where we stopped for the night.

Copies of Stars and Stripes were handed out to us; none of us had read a thing about the war. No interest either. About the only thing we pay attention to is music from AFRS. Other than that, screw it; the last thing any of us wants is to be told about the war.

April 9. Took these troops to a ball game: Yomiuri Giants v the Whales. As much fun as when we saw the Y Giants go against the San Francisco Seals in the Fall of '49. *That* was a ball game.

The Japanese love the game, and they know it, too. Joey and I started quoting statistics, and the few English-speaking Japanese assigned to us are just as nutty about statistics as we are. At least two of them had heard of Robinson, who came down from Montreal to Brooklyn in '47.

Told the State Siders about that game back in '49; a strange affair, but it showed Gen MacA's use of psychology.

The three of us had almost begged on our knees to go see the game, and Lt Waller arranged it: three days off and everything. We were driven there by bus, and all of us had to wear starched, class A uniforms, shoes sparkling, etc. It was a hot September day, miserable. And then the surprise:

We scrambled off the bus, assembled, when a Major, not from our outfit, said we were to stand at attention for our anthem. And then, when the Kimagoyo, the Japanese anthem, came on, we were to come to attention. And then, when the Japanese flag was being run up and the band playing, we were to stand there and salute. Show respect. And we did.

Well, the game couldn't start for some ten minutes, because the Japanese kept bowing and bowing and bowing until the loud speakers came on and told them to sit down.

Then the cheering started by the Japanese, and this held up the game for another quarter of an hour. It was great; they didn't serve beer at the game, but they kept pushing ice sticks at us, and the game almost turned into a picnic.

And it was a great game, too. The San Francisco Seals had Triple A guys on that club, and those guys were either former major leaguers or guys on their way to the majors, etc. A great game.

The State Siders then had all sorts of questions, and this must have broken the ice, because all of a sudden the bus rides became "more relaxed." They asked more questions, and our three days with them turned out to be all right.

After work, we went to a Japanese tailor shop inside the PX to be measured for tailored shirts and for something new: dress cotton belts to replace the regular web. Bought two tailored o'seas caps and asked for and got red piping for artillery.

Finally got to wear our brown, low-quarter shoes, and they feel strange; light as feathers, too. They lack the arch and ankle support of combat boots, but I imagine they'll feel okay after a few days.

April 9-11. Got three days off and went to Nara for a day, and then took the train to Kobe to see Sonny and his girl, Tsuruko.

Sonny is serious as hell about staying here. (Joey and I, each, mailed Sonny's money to his Mom in Klail; all we did was to go to the Red Cross people, and they telegraphed the cash right away.)

He showed us a good time, and it turned out that Tsuruko speaks Spanish; it's part of her job, Sonny says.

Had dinner with them at some noodle place; Sonny wore one of those light beige suits so popular among the Japanese. Got himself a couple of hats, too, and he sported the snappy straw hat with a black band. Pretty sharp.

Joey and I left them at their rooms, and we caught a ride in a weapons carrier full of guys here on a regular R & R. A quiet ride.

April 10. Lts Waller and Vitetoe showed up today. Gave us the poop on what's going on here. A new Army program. The rookies see the sights with us for three days, and then go on to lectures about Japan, Korea and "the Oriental mind," as Lt Waller put it. These are called Army Talks, but not like the regular Army Talks which everybody finds deadly. This is an Army program of indoctrination plus orientation by Os who've been through it; and it's the Army's idea of psychology, etc.

New orders on bulletin board after morning chow. All NCOs, from Cpl on up, are to wear ribbons on our class A uniforms. So, there we went to the PX this noon, and walked out as honest-to-goodness heroes of the Korean War. (Dumas, Hat, and Frazier have three-and-a-half rows of ribbons, plus their Inf combat badge.) One of the Japanese tailors showed us some fatigue tops cut up like Ike jackets. Sharp, but they wouldn't work in combat, I don't think. And they sure as hell wouldn't do during winter.

Something new: Our arty unit was cited for heroism of some sort, and we then had to buy unit citation patches that are to be sewn on our left sleeve some seven to eight inches below the stripes. (It'll be back to the tailors for that little job.)

April 12. The post bulletin board placed a special notice in memory of President Roosevelt's death back in 1945. After morning assembly, we were all awarded our warrants, making our NCO ranks permanent instead of temporary; they were signed by Pres Truman as was the unit citation certificate. (The Old Guys told us to send these home immediately; if we didn't, they said the certificates would get lost or torn or wrinkled. So Stang, Skinner, Joey and I went to the post mail room and sent the stuff home.)

The State Siders were pretty impressed; all this show is prob the Army's way of indoctrinating these guys, instilling pride, etc.

Late this afternoon, all the rookies (some three to four hundred of them) were assembled in the outdoor movie arena. Some Major (Inf 7th Div) lectured on Japan, Korea and "Why We Fight."

The rookies were pretty attentive, and afterward they wanted to know "what combat was really like."

Talked to some of the 7th Div guys; they had landed in Inchon last year along with the Marines, cut across Korea and wound up on the Eastern side of the Peninsula. They had a hell of a time in Nov-Dec, just like we did.

(Combat conditions are the favorite questions of the guys we're running through here. We talked of the CCF entry into the war, Kunu-ri, the cold, etc. These guys did not read a word about Korea when they were back in the States.)

We'll be done with this bunch tomorrow and either get a new batch or the two promised days in Tokyo.

April 13. Tokyo-town. It's still the most exciting city I've ever seen. They're great believers in neon lights. The First Cav MPs with their yellow helmets and raincoats and their yellow jeeps look like men from outer space when they walk around the wild neon-lit streets of Tokyo. When you add the reflections from the wet streets to this combination, the place looks like some crazy carnival midway that's gotten out of hand.

Checked on the money at the Nihongo Bank and called on old Yoshiko Ogura; she too had banked the additional money we've saved for Hiro Watanabe. She fixed me up with one of the girls, and after this I set out for the School for the Blind. It's over in northwest Tokyo, not far from a park and from the Cath cathedral we attended before the war.

Hiro and I passed a quiet, peaceful afternoon with the rest of the blind kids and with the nurse in charge. There were some ten or fifteen of them. Bought them all ice sticks (popsicles) and had a fine time.

The money now comes to $450 plus interest, and Hiro will have something to start his life with when he's returned to his parents. The nurse said Hiro is one of the brighter students there.

Left Tokyo and caught a train to Hayama (Camp McGill) and looked in on some guys from our outfit who are also on this indoctrination trip: Crazy, Ichabod and a new enlisted forward observer who works with them. After this visit, to Nara and then back to duty.

Joey and Dumas went fishing and had themselves a good time; Hat and Frazier went to the Temple and got themselves the usual rubdown/massage, drink and a girl each for the two nights.

April 15-20. We worked with some rookies and some Old Guys (who'd not served in the Orient before) and drove them all over south and southwestern Honshu to Shimonoseki. From there on buses again and ate at Itazuke AFB, the same place where we started out from back in June with TF Smith.

Caught a double feature at the air base; both are at least two years old: *Treasure of Sierra Madre* and a western called *Red River*. Before the movie started, Rudy Hernández told us to look at the actors' faces when they fired the blanks: they'll flinch, all of them, he said. And sure enough. We sat there at the outdoor theater drinking beer, hooting and having a hell of a good time.

As usual, Mexicans got gunned down in both movies, and this is when Joey said, "Between Bogart and John Wayne, they'll get rid of all the Mexicans in Hollywood." This brought on more hooting until some Os (and wives and girlfriends) started asking for "quiet down in front," and all they got for their trouble was a horselaugh and a "blow it out your ass, Sarge." We all knew it was the Os and their women, but by saying "Sarge" softens the blow.

The Old Guys could give a shit about all this.

Afterward, to the PX and beer garden for more drinking with the Air Force guys.

The next day we took the rookies to two lectures. One by an Air Force O who spoke about close ground support for the troops and so on; he wasn't a pilot, though. The naval officer was an officer of the line, and he spoke about the Navy's role in shelling shore installations from their cruisers and other ships on both sides of the Korean Peninsula. (The Old Guys say Navy chow is better than anyone else's.)

After we mounted the bus, Lt Waller then explained that because there is now a Department of Defense, all the services are to work together and cooperate without rivalry. (Our Old Guys say that this will end the minute budget time comes round; then, it's every man for himself.)

April 22. Off day. Sent picture postcards home. Joey and I hitched a ride to Osaka and bought stuff to send home: silk, miniature paintings, etc. We then went back to the base, to the PX, and left some pictures to be developed; pay in advance, please. We gave them our Kwansai address, which the Army PO will use to forward the stuff to us.

Dropped by a house Dumas recommended. We drank, ate and spent the night with two of the girls there. Told the manager we needed to be up by 0600 to be back at the base by 0715. (The girls got us up at 0500, and we went for a dip at the house bath and were served tea and pastry right afterward.) Got dressed, left money for everybody there, and then the manager came over and held the umbrella for us while we waited for transportation.

April 23-25. This was our last batch of rookies. We're to be off on 4/26 for Tokyo, for one more fling and then by ship to Pusan. Which is the long way around.

Hat, Dumas and Frazier got themselves a two-and-a-half ton truck and a driver for the seven us, and we loaded up with beer and some great ham sandwiches and stuff. Hat got the food and drink from an old buddy of his, a Mess Sgt, who went back a long time with Hat and Frazier.

The driver drank now and then, but he took his time driving to Tokyo, and we had a hell of a good time drinking, B-essing and, eventually, talking about going back to Korea.

We were to meet our Os there (and we did) and after we mustered with two other batteries, into the truck again and we boarded an Army APA waiting to take us to Pusan.

The class A uniforms and the low-quarter shoes were put away, and out came the fatigue uniforms, the boots and the webbing.

Back to the war for a while.

And the Rocket's Red Glare

April 27-May 4. Tokyo General. Capt Perlman first started out by saying I should write what I remembered most. He then said I should write what I remember, and to let it go at that.

We've talked some nearly every day; there are thirty guys in this ward alone, so how much time does he have for us and for the rest of the guys in the other wards?

Some guys prefer not to talk at all; some have told me they'll be discharged as 369s or worse: 368s, if they talk to a psychiatrist. They don't want the Army or their folks to think they're unfit or that they're crazy. At chow, others talk about everything except battle action. Me, I find I'm smoking about the same and still craving chocolate candy, but I don't suppose wanting candy means anything. As for smoking, I was already a two-pack man before we left for Korea last year.

Dr. Perlman didn't start by asking me about home, my background, etcetera. He first wanted to know what it was I did, what my duties were as an artilleryman, etc. No idea what he was digging for there; it was most probably a way to get me to talk, to say something. And, we wouldn't have gotten on the subject of books if I hadn't asked when I could start reading again.

I didn't mention my journals at all, and I don't imagine that the hospital staff went over my barracks bag. He said he put two and two together and guessed that, as a reader, I could probably put down some thoughts in writing.

The next afternoon I told him that putting two and two together would make four, as he said, but I also told him that adding two and three together and then subtracting one would also get the same result. It was then he looked up my personnel file.

Told him that working with figures out in the field gave me plenty of time to work on numbers and possibilities. Also told him I read some and that was why I'd asked him if I would lose my left eye.

"What," he asked directly, "would you do if you lost your eye?"

"What *could* I do?"

We both laughed at this, and he dropped that part of the conversation. Then, the next day, he said: "Your eye's okay; it needs a daily cleaning here, and that's what Dr. Chapin does. Do you trust him?"

After I said yes, he said he wanted me to trust him, Perlman, and that he didn't care in what order the writing came, as long as I wrote something down. "I'll read what you write, but you can keep it after you leave, if you want to. Fair enough?"

He left some loose-leaf paper and some pencils the next day, and two days after that I started to write.

When the rocket hit, Dumas was standing between the kitchen truck and the Ordnance weapons carrier—and, although unhurt—the concussion pushed him against the Ordnance Old Guy, and both were then thrown to the ground.

Joey, who had come calling that morning, caught it in the chest and face, and he died instantly, as did Frazier and Hat. At the instant of burst, I was lying on the ground steadying the binocs against a tree stump as I fixed on our Inf patrol making its way up Hill 280, directly to our right.

The blast tore the binocs from my hands, which, along with the left side of my face, were then peppered with dust, gravel and, as the medic at the Aid Station said, "With CCF rocket shit."

I thought I'd gone blind; was told I staggered around until I passed out. At the Receiving Station, I saw that Jacob Mosqueda (who had been returned to us again) was unhurt. Stang said Mosqueda screamed and cried and took off running down the hill until he tripped in the mud and fell against some splintered apple trees.

This time I thought I'd gone blind forever. From the Receiving Station, I must've been taken to the Clearing Station. My face was covered in bandages except for my mouth. According to the medic at the Clearing Station, I had come to earlier, but I don't remember any of this. I do remember waking up to find my canteen cup in my hand; at this point, I asked the medic how long I'd been out. He said I'd been up and talking to some of the guys from my unit.

Most of what I remember clearly, and this happened soon after all of us got back from Southern Honshu, was waking up, looking at my bandaged hand and finding that I was now drinking coffee here, at Tokyo General.

But I do remember that Dumas and Stang came to see me before I was driven out of the Clearing Station; that they said Joey died on the spot; that Hook and Hatalski were thrown against our gun and died right there and then. And, that I'd gotten up, staggered some and then slipped on the binocs some fifteen yards away. Both said I landed on my back in a gun rut full of mud.

That part remains hazy, but I remember quite clearly talking to Dumas about what happened; I feel okay now. I mean that my health is as good as it can be. I've been here at Tokyo General for some time, and Capt Bracken, of all people, has called on me.

I've pretended to be asleep both times. I don't like the man, and I've always suspected he feels the same way about me. One of those things.

Joey. I've tried to think back how the day started that morning. It was a clear, blue-sky day; the first after four days of rain, and Joey had come over from C Battery with a knapsack full of beer.

There'd been the usual reports of sporadic North Korean guerrillas acting up behind our positions again, and the daily patrols going out after them became routine.

I now remember this from the Clearing Station. After the rocket burst, Dumas told me a patrol rounded up four NK who surrendered peacefully; they hadn't eaten in days, they said. They'd had but one rocket, and fired it from some beat up launcher that could just as easily have blown them up in the firing. These must've have been the guys that killed our guys.

A fluke. That's all. Irony, too, and Joey would've laughed at that. And now? Charlie Villalón died sometime in December; Joey this April, and I'm still here.

I don't know how I'll feel months from now. For now I feel angry and sad and tired. Dr. Perlman has asked me if I feel guilty.

"Of what?"

"Of being alive," he said.

What I feel is a sense of loss. Charlie, Joey, we'd all known each other next to forever; we went to school together; we played football the same year; and Joey and I quit the next year when Charlie was kicked off the team, and so on and so on. It's a loss, not guilt.

What about the Villalóns and the Vielmas? What have they been told about their sons' deaths? How was the news given to them? They have no idea what goes on out there, what happens to us, what we see and do. They haven't a single, solitary idea.

Dr. Perlman has always listened attentively and (I guess) sympathetically, but even he doesn't know about us, about home, Texas.

I explained that we were different; that that part of Texas is *home, our* home. We're not like the rest of the guys in our outfit; they can go live anywhere in the United States, and many of them talk about moving to California, wherever. We *can't*, and we don't want to, either. That some of us leave for a while, but that we have to come back. Home. And so on.

I finally said, "Dr Perlman, you're a Jew. You should know this better than anyone."

No reaction from him. Nothing. I've been writing on this journal for him and for me, but I don't trust Dr. Perlman anymore. I will not trust anyone who doesn't react, who doesn't feel happy or sad or rejected or angry. If this is called "being a professional" in the psychiatry business, then psychiatrists miss what living is about: people, people who do or don't do things, who act and react and are not given to mere observation.

I may be wrong about many things here, but, at the least, I've gotten this off my chest. And, I'm the one who *will* make it back. I know this. I'm the one who'll talk to Charlie's sisters and dad. I'm the one who'll talk to the Vielma family. This is what we do.

How will they feel, I once asked Dr Perlman.

His answer, as usual, was too long, too complicated; too clinical, to use his term.

I thank Dr Perlman for his recommendation I be assigned to Pusan duty, "to get you away from the lines." I do not mean to be ungracious, but I think he says this automatically.

He's not a bad man, the doctor. He's got a tough job, and all of us in the ward think we're individually special, and so we take it out on him. He also knows and he understands we're scared to death out there.

Well, we should be. We know what goes on in the field. Still, I've requested to return to the 219th. That's home for now, and home is what I'm looking for.

Dr. Chapin has said my eye is back to normal, and then he added, "It's remarkable." And my head, Doc? That, he said, is Dr. Perlman's department.

Today, I went to see my favorite nurse and turned in my hospital stuff.

Captain Bracken showed up again two days ago. We talked, and I felt I've no resentments about anything, and I doubt I'll ever be angry at anyone anymore.

This last, Dr Perlman, sir, is not an afterthought.

This is the end of my journal for Dr Perlman.

R. Buenrostro, Sergeant, 219th FA.

Will hell around Tokyo first, then to the Kwansai District to see how things are in Kobe and Osaka.

I'll look up old man Kazuo Fujiwara, buy him a beer, and spend the rest of the time in Nara. Too cold to go swimming in the Inland Sea, but it's never too cold for a picnic.

Would like to see Sonny, but he and Tsuruko haven't written in a while, and I don't know how to operate the Japanese phone system for long distance calls.

Will leave for Korea o/a May 1.

The Trade of Kings

May 4. So, goodbye to Tokyo, to Drs Perlman and Chapin, and goodbye and good riddance to anger. If this were a movie, we'd all be talking about "how we're going to get it" or bring up that business about "we'll never make it out of here alive." From what I've seen, every guy here, including me, is sure he'll not get killed in combat. Someone else in the outfit, the guy next to you, but not Number One, no sir. Besides, as the field doctors tell us, there are more deaths and casualties due to noncombat than to combat; accidents and guys who screw up can kill anybody, but that happens to them, to somebody else, etc.

That belief of *living through,* as our Old Guys put it, is what drives you on even during the worst of times. And I'm a believer.

It was a long boat ride; sailed around Pusan and made for the port of Inchon on the western side of Korea. Finally got to see the invasion spots. What a mess.

Dumas and Rudy Hernández met me at the assembly point in Inchon. Dumas says that during our retreat last Nov-Dec, the Army blew up everything, at times unnecessarily so, since the CCF had no ships to speak of. Everything, he said. Floating docks and other port facilities were sunk and the electric plants went up in rubble. A complete job of demolition. And now? Well, they're still working on rebuilding most of the port, but that's a two-year job, says Dumas.

The three of us assembled next to one of the blown-up floating docks here. Dumas said we'd leave tomorrow after a new guy shows up as a replacement. I then reported in, and the three of us went driving around.

Rudy popped a can for me and said it'll be I Corps for us again. No idea how long, though. We're to be sent back, just north of Seoul one more time. No idea what awaits us there, but for now we're to wait in Inchon until tomorrow.

Dumas said Bracken is now back in Japan permanently on some staff or other; and that's all he said. Billy Waller is a Capt now and has taken over the Battery with Vitetoe as Exec. Lt Fleming has replaced Lt Brodkey as Forward O and works with a brand new crew, but all experienced; transferred in from some of the many arty battalions we have here. Dumas summed it up with, " Much fighting; bitter, too."

A warm night. Lightning flashes but no rain. The flashes can't be artillery fire, since we're too far south for that. Probably the first hints of the Monsoon; it'll be here soon enough.

May 5. The replacement came in and complained of fever, etc. So we waited at sick call for him. Turned out he was seasick.

The drive here was okay, no hitches of any kind. When we got to the area, Lt Vitetoe came over, shook my hand, and said I had six new guys to work with, all but one inexperienced. Asked me how I felt. I said I was glad to be back, and that was that.

Dumas laughed about the inexperienced guys: "We figured you'd had too much time off and that you needed the work."

May 6-14. A week of patrolling in our area. Much time on our hands. Ammo in the crates and on the ground, guns at the ready and in working order, but no orders to fire. The Inf guard spends most of its time oiling and cleaning the M-guns; since there's much dust about, these guys are always ready for infiltrators.

Trained some, and got to know the new guys. Nothing special.

Told of some heavy fighting in that blown-up town north of Seoul called Uijungbo. ROK and Amer units engaged, and CCF acting tough and hanging in there. CCF pulls back just enough to make our units want to chase them, but 8th Army isn't falling for that anymore.

As for us, we're told to wait; our time will come, and it's up to CCF to call the shots.

Books. Brought back over a dozen paperbacks. Army p'backs are the best in the world. They look like thick checkbooks only wider and a bit longer, easier to fold too, and they won't crack in the fatigue pockets.

Finished a small book by a Greek soldier, Xenophon, who brought back his army across the Middle East when they got stuck there, and he led them to the sea. The title given in Greek is *Anabasis*, but the title is also given as *The March of the Ten Thousand.* Aside from auguries, omens, oracles and other stuff, it's a hell of a little book. In some ways, much like Cabeza de Vaca's trek through Texas and the Southwest.

Started another Greek classic, *Histories*. Pretty fantastic stuff at times; some entries read like the stories Columbus' men brought over from the New World. Still, it's highly readable.

Got two detective stories, but could find none by Manning Coles, whose stuff I read and liked.

Training. Since we have many new guys in the other batteries again, we spend much time in practice runs, but no firing.

Changes. Gen Ridgway is now (and has been since last March) the Big Boss, the Honcho (does this come from Honshu?). In any case, he now runs the whole shebang here. His successor is Gen Van Fleet now that Gen Ridgway has replaced Gen MacArthur. Gen MacA was replaced about the time we were baby-sitting in Japan. Since this happened before we joined Lts Waller and Fleming in Hayama later on, we paid no attention to it.

Our Old Guys said it didn't much matter. We're still here, and that's what counts.

Dumas is now an SFC and has replaced Hat. I'm to replace Hook, but my rank stays at Buck Sgt, and I get no rocker to go with the three stripes. The other Old Guys are also Depression Era vets—knowledgeable, sure of themselves, and can teach any dumb animal how to fire a 105 in nothing flat.

Dumas's pal here is Andy Thornhill (Nampa, Idaho), and the other two Old Guys are Sid Croft (from Washington state), and Bill Kiser (Havre, Montana; Kiser is Indian and regular Army; doesn't look Indian to me, but he says he was born and raised in the Rocky Boy Reservation, near Havre). I'm to work with Dumas and Thornhill.

Wrote Aunt Mati all about Japan, but did not say a word about my being wounded again. (As for Sonny living in Japan, all it takes is for some jackass back home to spread the word, and bang! Sonny will be hunted down by the MPs. Tsuruko writes to Aunt Mati, who then reads the letters to Sonny's Mom; and, since many people in Klail think old Tina Ruiz is crazy, they don't pay attention to her when she tells them that her David is well and safe.)

May 15. Runners in and out all day. The word is we'll be in the thick of it soon, and as early as tomorrow. Much fighting elsewhere, but not here yet.

We're still east/northeast of Seoul. The blasted town of Uijungbo is still there, and the runners say fighting there is on and off, but bitter. It seems to me, that's been going on for a long time.

We're to be in it, since there's no escaping the fact that our arty remains massive. General Van Fleet believes in artillery, and we'll probably fire a two/three-day shell supply in one day, Billy Waller says. The Supply Points fill up, and we're to get all we want, is the word. But the routine today was a mirror of the preceding days: dull.

May 16-19. The CCF first hit an Inf Company to the right of us, and that started the CCF offensive for our sector. So, for the last seventy-two hours, the CCF pressured the Inf Regt next to us, and we were kept busy with both indirect and concentrated fire.

The forward observers adjusted fire for us all day and night. Crazy and Ichabod put in a long day and night. During the first night, the flares provided the daylight, and we fired. One click down, two up, adjust, fire! Adjust fire, adjust fire! Three clicks. Got that? Fire. Hold it, hold it. Wheel the guns to the right. Range six-hundred yards. Fire! Fire!

It went like that on the 16th and 17th and part of the 18th. We ate on the run, got tired, got our second wind, and there we went again. Adjust fire! Check those pre-registered targets. Fire! Fire! Wheel 'em to the left. There. Range, four-hundred yards. Go get 'em! Fire! Fire!

No idea how Crazy and Ichabod can stand it out there. They and Lt Fleming finally got two new Lts to work with, Jim Nix, a Negro O, and a Minnesotan named Howard Mothershill. Both are ROTC guys with a tour in the Ft Sill ranges.

We pulled back on the 17th amidst heavy fire from all sides. We were losing Inf support on the right, and their own situation was critical. When this word is used, the Army means exactly that.

Much, much night fighting.

Told that two Infantry battalions to our left being pressured too, but runners say that battalions remain intact. We were driven to high ground overlooking a gap which the CCF created by bitter fighting and which it intended to fill with troops. We were to fill it with our fire and so we were placed next to three other 105mm batteries.

We set up, stood by and then began shelling with both direct and indirect fire. We could see CCF running into the captured gap and firing as they ran. We fired right at them, but they kept coming; they wouldn't quit. This lasted at least two hours, and then our Inf units to the right were rolled up despite our fire against the CCF.

The CCF rushed in. There were targets everywhere, so we had to be selective. The Air Force also flew over the place, and we fired for twelve hours straight; we got pretty punchy after all that cordite in the air.

CCF must have lost hundreds out there. We couldn't miss. Some French Inf were trucked here, and down they went to meet the CCF in the gap. But no matter, the CCF kept coming.

Mines. Our engineers had mined the gap heavily, but the CCF must've been told to march right through the mine fields, and there they went. That's a tough army.

The fighting in the gap went on like that, crazy. In one instance, after trying to hold some hill next to the gap, one of our Inf battalions was ordered back, and the CCF ran right up the hill and they took it.

This is when we stepped in. Fire mission! We plastered the hell out of that hill. Our Forward Os watched the CCF, tracked them as they climbed the hill, called us in, and we went to work. Was told the reason we ceased fire for a few minutes was that the French had to be stopped from advancing, otherwise they would have run into our shelling.

This fire lasted two hours straight. We were then ordered to stop, to hitch the guns, and were driven to another position. No panic, rookies pretty solid. They followed our lead. The Old Guys just moved around as they always do, keeping an eye on everything and everybody, not missing a thing of what's going on; no wasted motion there.

We got here in a flash, set up fast and were ordered to start firing in fifteen minutes; once again, the forward observers had everything pre-registered. The crates were reopened, and we fired into the gap again and all around the sides of hills for most of the night. A curtain of fire was what was called for. Few get out of these alive. But CCF fought their hearts out.

During the fight, some CCF wounded were brought in, and G-2 got on them right away: identification of units, the quantity of food rations they had available, etc. Another battery then drove up while we were firing, and they set up almost on top of us.

So much artillery here we got pinched in again. Reminded by Os and Old Guys that we were in no danger, although CCF has made big dents in part of our sector.

Runners: Big, big dents; as much as six miles in some big areas. This is a very big CCF offensive. For one example, two of our battalions were attacked in a coordinated attack from four directions: southeast, east, south and northwest. This is pressure. What happens is that if CCF overruns those positions, they'll run into one of our roadlbocks or into some arty fire. (Six miles must be what CCF offensives call for; almost like a book. This may be due to issue of rations, ammo for their troops.)

Large number of US wounded trucked in. Runners say Inf fought well, but CCF not holding back either.

Runners reported another disaster. Over one-hundred US Army vehicles lost: quarter-ton trucks, three-quarter ton, etc. This means those units also lost their arty and their ammo, their communication equipment, prime movers, kitchen trucks, etc. A disaster. And it wasn't an ROK unit either. (The wounded in the trucks going to the Aid Stations must be from that outfit.)

May 18. Hoengsong! We're here once again, in the Hoengsong area. This means CCF has been driving hard in this sector despite our heavy arty fire. Told that Seoul safe, even if we're fighting south of the Han. From my old map, it looks like a CCF flanking offensive, but you never can tell which direction it's coming from. War is crazy for other reasons than madness. Everyone has a private battle, and since there is no such thing as one front line, everybody has a front. Sometimes the CCF crashes through a unit only to run full-face into another unit or a big roadblock. And so on.

No idea where we were going in the Hoengsong area, but it was some place important, since there were close to ninety-five trucks in our convoy.

Spotted three helicopters ferrying severly wounded guys; a liaison plane was leading them to the Advanced Clearing Station to our rear.

Rumors. Guys inside trucks talking about us going up to Uijungbo, or back to Seoul, etc, etc. (The convoy ride served as a day of rest for us.)

May 19. A long, long day. On the road again. To Wonju, we were told. All of this is still south of Seoul, but Seoul is not lost we were told again. This is just one part of the CCF offensive, and we're catching all kinds of hell.

Runners. The Commanding Officer of an Inf Regt was killed during bitter fighting on the morning of the first day of the offensive; then, by midafternoon, the Exec got killed. Casualties from the same outfit; most of the battalion staff killed plus two company commanders wounded, or evacuated. This hurts.

When Os are evacuated, this usually means they've had the war for a while, just like us, the enlisted men. The Old Guys and First Lts took over the running of the Bn and were joined by 2d Lts as usual.

Just as we got to our area, an Inf battalion began moving out; they'd been in reserve, most likely.

As soon as the battalion left here, we set up a huge roadblock; we were told that a sizeable, if not the main force, of combined NKPA and CCF units was massing just ahead.

Lt Vitetoe told Dumas, and he passed the word to us. Our roadblock is made up of three arty battalions, aside from other ground units; CCF knows we're here, so stand by.

We sat and waited or stood by the guns when those damned CCF/NK mortars started raining in. They were short at first, and then we came into range, but we started our fire too and then, in the middle of the CCF attack and our firing, a rain storm. Cover the ammo, where's the tarp? Get it! Let's go. At the same time, above the intense fire, all of us could hear the CCF whistles and the bugles giving their unit signals during the fight. It was crazy.

The fire mission for the battalion's pull out and for our support fire lasted one hour straight. The roadblock held up the CCF, and we retreated down the road where another of our roadblocks waited for us. We set up right away and waited there for the CCF main force. We waited for an hour, which gave us time to check the guns, go to the latrine, smoke, etc.

First reports said the Inf battalion caught hell. Were also told we caught and will continue to catch hell, but the Inf kept up the fight, and our fire was effective, accurate and deadly.

Our Infantry guard set up their 30 cal M-guns for crossfire and we waited. Two medics came by checking for minor injuries and went on their way to look at other guys in the roadblock.

(Two forward observers of a neighboring arty battalion were killed outright. Prob a direct mortar hit. Their radio communications went out too, so two other Os and three EM ran down their hill and then up a knoll, lugging their SCR-300, some field phones. The Signal Corps guys were right behind, laying wire amid heavy small arms fire. Don't have the names of anyone in that unit.)

After I was relieved by Rudy, I got into this prime mover and started to write. Pretty quiet the rest of the night. We were fed, rested some more, and at 0430 were told to prepare to move out by 0515, and we did.

The other outfits there stayed put and waited for the CCF.

May 19. Told that ROK was pushed around and all over the place. Our unit is not near any ROK outfit.

We were sent to some assembly area; saw wreckage of two light liaison planes (L-5s or AT-6s) that helped us direct fire. Thornhill said they were caught in last night's sudden rainstorm and that that was it for the pilots and the observers with them.

Got here at 0815, and two arty units coming in from the south were sent to a blocking position as soon as we got organized.

Opened up some ration cans and ate whatever was in there. Most likely what the Army calls beef stew, but which always tastes like mutton.

At 1000, we moved out of the assembly area, joined still another arty battalion already set and waiting. We set up in a flash and just as soon as we gave the word, Billy Waller said, "It's to be a short fire, men, but I want an intense, heavy, concentrated fire, and don't spare the horses. Here we go, ten, nine, eight ... "

The CCF never saw us; there were twenty 105s pointed at them in the hills, the surrounding woods, on the road, and we were to fire long, short, etc. And some of us were to give direct, others concentrated, and still others were to fire five-gun salvos.

It was only an eight-minute fire to salvage some remnants of a US Inf main force. But Lt Vitetoe (who looks old and tired) said that we and the other arty battalion fired 2000 rounds in those eight minutes.

Now *that* is a curtain of fire. An armed force of one hundred riflemen advanced on the main road toward what was left of the CCF, and we made preparations to mount up again and leave that area, which we did in double time.

May 20. Got to a new place and told that here, last night and all yesterday afternoon, there was prolonged bitter fighting.

Many US Inf killed, but more wounded and, as usual, the missing are always the highest count. (I think that our old unit, the 2nd Div, leads in the number of combat and noncombat casualties.)

What happens here is that the missing may still be alive, as stragglers, lost out in some field or hill, or they're scared and won't come out no matter who controls the area, or, they may fall as POWs.

Sid Croft: "It can be any number of things, and it can happen to anybody, to us ... "

Sometimes, some missing troops manage to get gangs of guys together, and if there's some leadership among them, they'll fight or make their way back. The figures for the missing are then changed continually.

Dumas: "Yeah, but the artillery creates permanent missing 'cause when we hit somebody or somebodies, there's nothing left."

Croft again: "A natural fact."

Our supporting Infantry unit has been told to hold here, so that means no one moves. Our Forward Os began to pre-register just as soon as we got here, and we spent a good three hours on the phone checking the firing charts. (When the sun went down, we ran down to chat with Crazy and Ichabod while we checked ranges, and ran right up again.)

Right after chow, Capt Waller got the NCOs together and told us that the situation in this spot is critical, vital. "Stand by the guns. We won't move unless God tells us so."

Translation: We're to hold here, and we don't move unless the order comes directly from the I Corps Commanding General himself, and no one else.

Various units were trucked into this sector right after us. Some were driven one hundred plus miles to get here. This is a full-scale CFF offensive, and if I Corps Staff has guessed right, this will be a major fighting point.

Who the hell thought this war was over?

Saw this during the afternoon: Many wounded on jeeps going by; each quarter-ton truck carries from five to six, at times eight, if two lightly wounded guys can ride on the hood. The severely wounded are put one or two to a jeep. (Back in Kunu-ri, a Col was in the back seat of a quarter-ton truck cradling a badly wounded rifleman; the Col himself was bleeding from a head wound.)

There's an Aid Station up ahead but the badly wounded go directly to the Advanced Clearing Station. Counted nine jeeps in all.

May 20 night. With clear weather all morning and half the afternoon, many air sorties. (Have not seen NK or Chinese props or jets in any of our areas for months. Dumas says their air force may be used to protect supply lines.) Air Force, Marines, and Navy air counted for good number of NK and CCF casualties during the day. Then it rained, and the sorties stopped. When night fell, the B-29s came in for another mauling of the ground troops.

When this was over, we watched the Inf patrols assemble around 2000 hours; since it was still light, out they went for a body count of the CCF and NK. Engineers verifed the road and the area as unmined; and that's always a relief.

Woke up around midnight, to latrine, and ran into Inf guys: CCF count of casualties (and they brought back six wounded CCF as POWs) came to two-hundred fifty. This was Officer verified and Old Guy checked.

Also brought back two US POWs; the patrol rescued these guys right after B-29 dispersement of CCF.

Wild story: Those guys had been POWs since Kunu-ri; that's six/seven months of captivity.

An Inf guy, a Negro PFC named Carl Jenkins (Boulder, Colorado), said both GIs in bad shape, but full of information for Intel guys, though.

Still much fighting in our area, but we're not firing; that end of it being taken up by two arty battalions in another part of our sector.

May 21. Driven out of Hoengsong area by 0615; stopped for chow and then found ourselves setting up a CP, the guns put at the ready, and we waited for orders. Around 1400, three US wounded came out of the woods to our left. They were carrying safe-conduct passes. Lucky for them the NK respect CCF safe-conduct passes.

A runner stopped by on his way back from the Command Post; verified by patrols and by South Korean agents that the enemy is massing some seven miles from us. Right after that, we were ordered to rehitch the guns, were assigned new firing position up on some small hills and knolls on both sides of roads, and driven there fast.

Pretty soon, a liaison plane landed on the dirt road, followed by a second one; both were coming from where the enemy were supposed to be assembling.

Since these aircraft fly so low, the pilots and the observers are plainly visible, and sometimes they wave at us.

We marked time, waited, and then one of our Infantry battalions went out with one company to the right, another one to the left and the third one in reserve. Another thirty minutes went by, we waited, but we heard no fire of any kind.

We ate again at 1800, stood by the guns, were brought coffee at 2000, and were then ordered to rest at 2100.

At 2200, HQ requested liaison planes verify their report given earlier that day regarding massive CCF concentration. The report was the same: CCF there as well as some NK units.

We waited, were relieved at 2300, and slept. Woke up at 0530 and started journal before returning to guns at 0700.

Having early chow by the guns when three runners drove in. They said that sometime before dawn, CCF pulled out of our area and moved northward. Their rear guard set up a fireblock on the Hongchong road, seven miles from here.

Liaison planes returned by 0900 and confirmed runners' information. We were told to pack up, and to be prepared to move by 1200.

That's the way it goes sometimes.

May 22. So, from the Hoengsong area to Hongchong. We're now assigned to X Corps. Seoul remains to our left but no CCF action in that front, we were told by runners and agents.

We were joined by another battery, and that made three batteries on a line. We waited for orders and didn't have long to wait.

Then it happened. By 1600 we were given the order for rapid fire.

If I'm not deaf now, I never will be. Ordinarily, if a battery has three 105s and each 105 gets a ration of 50 shells, then, with three batteries, that means 150 shells, and so on. On this fire, each *gun* had 250 shells as its ration. That's two-hundred and fifty shells per gun. The result was much firing, too much at times, and some batteries burned up their barrels. Ordnance must be happy as hell with that.

Some of the runners tell us we have some twenty-one arty battalions against this latest CCF offensive. If each battalion has anywhere from nine to twelve guns per battery, that means that the twenty-one artillery battalions up and down the line fired more than a quarter-of-a-million shells last week. Great God.

On this fire, this afternoon's, we were following the Inf and the tank battalions; they overran some trapped CCF and NK Inf in a pocket, and when the Inf then called us, we began the fire.

This is what happened in this sector today. No idea what went on in the others. But the Os say this is Ridgway's pattern: Kill CCF and NK and forget the real estate. The added twist is Gen Van Fleet, who has given the order we are to fire artillery like never before.

May 23-24. South Korean agents say they saw CCF units moving northward in force for the first time since their offensive started last week. Retreating or reorganizing? The agent didn't know. If the report is true, it's true only for our sector. (Still no idea how fighting is going on elsewhere.)

Went to latrine and ran into Stang: One of the clerks at the Command Post told us of another high officer (a Regt Cmdr) who died of a heart attack. He's not the first; a Major General died the same way sometime ago. There may have been others—these are only the confirmed ones I know of.

I don't think it's combat alone; I think it's part that, part tension, and also the long hours Os put in. I know it only seems they're everywhere, but one can see them going here and there at all times, at all hours. It's a different war for them.

To top it off, the higher ranks are not young guys either. I still remember how Col Warrington and the other field officers looked when they walked out of Taejon in the summer of '50. This condition goes for everybody and that includes the First and Second Johns, and the Company Cmdrs. But, when you add old age to tension and long hours, it's a wonder more of them don't die from heart attacks. Added to this, they're in physical danger too, especially the officers of the line.

For one close example, Capt Waller caught pneumonia last winter; he was sent to a hostpital in Pyongyang. He recovered, and came right back to us with no appreciable rest. Lt Vitetoe looks like a ghost, yet he's all over the place; he doesn't lose his temper, keeps calm and is also a hell of an Exec. Dumas says Vitetoe is also one of the bravest Os he knows. Cut, as Dumas says, from the same fabric as Billy Waller. He says Lt Fleming is a quiet guy, but he's always there, too. We're lucky to have these Os. Except for Brodkey, all three are West Pointers; and, says Dumas, that's a high ratio of West Point graduates for one arty battery.

We're still in the thick of fighting around here, but our unit and the ones to our left and right have been at peace since we stopped our fire yesterday afternoon. I ate at 1100, rested some, and watched Ordnance come in from the Supply Point to replace some of the 105s from A and C batteries.

Our hours are still screwed up when it comes to eating and sleeping. No rain in the last thirty-six hours, and this is a blessing.

Part II

The Last Entries

August 27. It's been two months since I was pulled off the line for good; it's been good here in Supply and away from the noise and fire, the fear, the deaths and, sadly/personally, away from the friends one always leaves behind, both living and dead.

We've had long, hard rains this summer; much like our first days in Korea in June of last year (with a civilian town band egging us on), when we pulled out of Taejon station and on to Osan.

Finally met Capt Fred Macías; he too has been assigned to Supply and runs this Ammo Supply Depot and the one across the way. I made it a point to meet him, since I'd heard of him during the early days and had no idea he was still around. He's a quiet, solid guy, and a fighter.

He too was pulled off the line; in his case, by the battalion commander who knew the Capt did not have enough luck left to survive many more battles. He's a nice guy, too; from Arizona, and he speaks Spanish the way I do. We talked on this point yesterday and found it strange to have New Mexico between us and then for us Texas Mexicans and Arizona Mexicans to speak that identical, slightly nasal but clear, Northern Mexican brand of Spanish.

August 28. It was bound to happen; I lost my journals for June, July and almost all of this month's notes, to the Monsoon.

Small wonder I didn't lose everything, but it's no great loss. Not when one considers the men—on both sides of the line—who've died here, who are dying still.

When, too, one remembers stupid accidents and tanks and trucks sliding off embankments and thereby killing all of the men inside. Other blunders, too, through human carelessness, miscalculation, lack of skill at the job assigned, cowardice, laziness. But there was also abnegation to a high degree; and individual and group courage and bravery.

No. No great loss the journals, not when I think of Charlie and Joey, of Hat and Hook Frazier, Crazy, Ichabod and Lt Brodkey—among others whose names I never knew. Or when I think of those faces I met briefly, perhaps just the once and never again, but whose names I copied down faithfully as if I were some big time reporter instead of who and what I am: a youngster from Texas, from the Rio Grande Valley, who remembers now—as clearly as on that Mass of Septuagint Sunday, 1949—when Chaplain James P Leary, SP, quoted Luke 17:10 to us: "Well, will we then be like the useless servants who did nothing more than that which was commanded of us?"

Charlie was still very much alive then, and he too quoted from Luke that cold Sunday after Mass, only to have Joey finish the quote that made all of us laugh on the way to noon chow.

Charlie: "Old Luke also said, 'Speak evil of no man,' didn't he?"

Joey: "Aye-man, brother, and then he said, 'And be content with thy wages.' Well, screw that, you guys."

This writing is also for Hiro Watanabe, whom I'll never see; which is an irony in itself.

And it's for all the other useless servants, the CCF, who also fought for their masters in a foreign land.

Some promises I made to myself in the lines, I've kept. Others will be met and kept when I return home, home to Texas, that land described by my late father, don Jesús Buenrostro, as "Texas, our Texas, that slice of hell, heaven, purgatory and land of our Fathers."

Vale.

Port of Pusan. September 1, 1951.

Four Letters

I

Dear B'rostro:

I am writing you these few lines to let you know me and the gang are still here. Old Rudy Hernandez is the crew chief of your old gun and has been made a Buck Sgt. How about that?

You wouldn't recognize many of the guys, and pretty soon all the officers, Capt. Waller, Lts. Merritt, Fleming and Vitetoe will be transfered out of here. Rotated is my guess, since they have been here long enough, West Point graduates or no West Point graduates.

This is my last month in Korea, too. I may be transfered to Japan. Or I may be sent state side. With the Army you never know, right?

I am up for Master Sergeant and if a unit needs one in Japan, I will take that job. It doesn't much matter to me.

I got a brother, Carl Dumas, and he has a nice grocery business in Murfreesboro, Tenn. (my home town). He says for me to retire there in Murfreesboro after my Army career, and he will hire me part time to keep my hand in and to keep me of the streets, he says. As a store guard or something like that. He says I should do this when I retire because Murfreesboro is my home and the cite of a Vet's Adm hospital is not far from there, in case I should need help later on.

But I'm going for the Master Sgt stripes. If I happen to get a diamond to go with the six stripes all the bets are off, I told my brother. Being a First Joe in a line outfit is like being God, and I sure want to end my career at the top of the heap.

Well old friend did you go to college after all? I hope so.

Do you remember my old buddies Sid Croft and Billy Kiser? Well they both got killed a while back. They were just like Frank Hatalski and Hook Frazier to me. But it's a different war now. Much more artillery use too. More long range, less maneuvering. You would be bored stiff, I bet.

So this is just a letter to a civilian who knew how to be a soldier and how to be a good friend. You take care of all those Texas women for me and save me a 40 to 45 year old one for your good friend,

John Dumas
S.F.C

II

Dear Rafe:

How you doing, buddy? John Dumas says he got your letter and it was pure luck he got it too since I think he's beeing sent to Camp Carson, Colorado to start up a cadre and from there to Sill.

Dumas says the Army is going to grow and that I should stay in it. I am and I had made up my mind to do that anyway. Did Dumas tell you I made Buck Sgt? Can't keep a Valley boy down is what I say.

Ran into a *tocayo* of yours. You remember a jeep driver from California named Ralph Gonzalez? He's now a cook and he says you and Joey and Charlie Billalón (sp?) were the only Mexicans who spoke Spanish to him in southern Honshu. You may not remember him but he was in the motor pool with Jesse Aldama.

The war has changed guy and you wouldn't recognize it no more. The infantry now sends out strong patrols, 300 guys, and that sounds like a battalion of infantry to me. But it's all artillery now Rafe. Much firing. I think we kill more Chinks now and of course we lose many of our guys too.

Have the States been talking about Peace Talks in a place called Pan-mun-jom? Their suppose to end the war, but the fighting goes on here.

Did I tell you I re-upped? Signed on for 4 more and that's the way I'm going to go from now, four years every time until I hit twenty or more.

I *like* the Army. Remember how you and Pepe Bielma used to laugh and say I found a home in the Army? Well I did. Its a good life and one of the reasons I am also writing you is to please take time off to go see my folks, Mr. and Mrs. Rodolfo and Paula Hernandez. They don't live right in Bascom, but over by your families cementery. Right close to the Pumping Station and that old Church that was burn to the ground before you or me was born. Well its right there where they live. He farms for himself and he rents land from your cousin Rufino F.G. And goes on thirds, fourths, or halves with him. Anyway, everybody knows my Dad and my Mom there, you just ask for them.

Tell them what a good life I will have in the Army. Your family is well known and I am banking on that.

Thanks for the favor your good friend, Rudy.

P.S. Don't forget to drink a couple of beers for me at the Linger Longer Inn in Bascom. Just mention my name Rudy Hernandez to the guys there.

P.P.S. Remember Benjamin Pardue—the Louisiana guy called Rusty? Well, he got a Bronze Star with a V just like yours. He was in B battery and he talked a lot. He remembers you. So he was in B battery, which had been hit hard and this time by infiltrators who sneaked in and killed many loaders, gunners and two Os with small arms fire. Rusty got seven cooks and clerks and got them to operate two 105s to stop a Chink charge in B's area. They held theyre ground and stopped the charge. Cooks and clerks!

III

Dear Friend Rafe:

Thank you very much for looking in on my folks one more time. I know it's hard and that's why I appreciate it. It can't be harder then looking up Pepe Vielma's folks or those of your other friend Charlie Villalón. I rather face Chinks than to go and see folks of guys who got killed here.

Dumas is on his way to Fort Sill; no Colorado for him and went directly to Lawton, Okla. Made Master Sgt before he left. He will run some 105 battery in training camp. Well, to celebrate the stripe and his going away we drank a few. He's a good man and a good soldier. Full of advise in that quiet voice of his. Talked about his old buddies Hatalsky and Frazer and Croft and Kiser. All dead and gone. Said you were a good soldier. Told me he knew from the start you hated the war but that "you saw your duty." That's a big complement coming from John Dumas.

I know I havent been here very long but my name is somewhere in the Rotation List already and that's fine with me. You wouldn't know the 219th. New officers, Capt. Jack Hayes and his Exec. Lt. Patrick Schau. One of the new johns is a Negro called Albert Johnson and he's a Forward Ob. The other Negro officer, Lt. Nix made first and may transfer out as exec to another battery. He's a great guy and has a good sense of humor for an officer.

You would not know the rest of the guys here. Remember Al Skinner? Decided to go Regular Army like me. Got his two stripes back and added a third. I think he's in Monmouth up in Jersey, since he wants to do Signal. Stang got out 3 months after you and I guess he went home where he came from somewhere back East. The rest of the guys you don't know because at 31 I'm allmost an Old Guy now.

Well old Valley friend, many thanks for helping my mother and my father. I still think he's getting to old to farm, but Rudy Jr. isn't going to be the one to tell him to leave the land. As if he would listen to me. Ha, ha.

Dumas told me to tell you to stay in college. From what you said in your letter it sounds like college is something like the Army, since you got to do the same things at the same time and you got a routine and everything.

Remember what Sgt. Hatalsky once said about the Army? You get paid
regular every month you get 3 squares a day and you get free clothes and
then you don't have to worry about what your going to wear the next day.

God willing I'll be leaving here in 2 or 3 month. If so, and I get a delay
enroute and furlough time to the next station, I will take a bus to see you in
Klail City or up in Austin.

Your friend,
Rudy Hernandez, Jr.

IV

Dear Rafe:

One month to go and I'm in supply in the port of Pusan. Most of the
guys here have served on the lines and this duty is to keep us safe until we
get home.

Any news in the Valley about rioting at the offshore POW camps here?
NK POWs raised hell and kidnapped a colonel and held him. Qué huevos,
right? I mean, those are cojones the size of a whale, right? Anyway, a new
general was placed in charge of the camps and he straitened out that shit in
a hurry. A Texan I think. Anyway, his name is General Boatner and he just
sent troops in and some POWs were shot on the spot is what the guys told
me.

They found many guns, knives, clubs, weapons of all kinds, for all the
good it did the NK. It was a bad riot and the MPs were brought in with tanks
(yeah, into the compound) and jeeps with their 30 caliber machine-guns and
they showd up with an M-16 remember those 50 caliber bastards with the
four machine guns pointing at you? Well one of those was placed in a rise
on the road and everybody could see it.

I got this from guys who clerk and cook in the island there. Probably
worser than I am telling you here, but it's over now.

Capt Hayes the Battery C O is a West Point Man. He fought in the 7th
Division on the east coast but is now in our sector. Well he recommended
me for Supply duty and told me he wished me luck in my Army career. With
that two other guys and I were taken by jeep to an assembly point and we
went by truck to Pusan and here I am.

Don't forget I will see you soon and besides the beer if your in Klail City
I want you to come with me so we can visit with my folks and other relatives
of mine.

Your friend,
Rudy

PS. Are you married yet? I have a *prima* and she is good looking and looking good for a husband. Ha. Ha. Just kidding.

Epilogue

The night has been unruly: where we lay
Our chimneys were blown down; and, as we say,
Lamentings heard i' the air; strange screams of death,
And prophesying with accents terrible
Of dire combustion and confus'd events
New-hatch'd to the woeful time. The obscure bird
Clamour'd the live-long night: some say the earth
Was feverous and did shake.

     Macbeth, II, iii

What now avails those dead
By ice, steel, and shot?
And who's in Heaven
And who is not;
Forgotten lie.

        Pvt. John Sims, Inf.
        (1931-1951)
        Chipyong-ni Clearing Station